5 DAYS TO LANDFALL

A NOVEL

Robert Roy Britt

Published by Ink • Spot Books
P.O. Box 74693
Phoenix, Arizona 85087
InkSpotBooks.com
Published in the United States of America
First printing, 2016

Cover by Trent Design

5 DAYS TO LANDFALL/Robert Roy Britt. 1st ed.
ISBN 978-0-9977614-3-6

Praise for 5 DAYS TO LANDFALL

"THRILLING. The perfect storm of drama and suspense. One part natural disaster tale, one part crime thriller, and one part romance make for a fast-paced ride."
— *IndieReader*

"A vigorous tale in which a violent, inescapable storm terrorizes everyone, even the villains. Perspectives from multiple characters are a worthy setup for an exhilarating final act, with a relentless hurricane and a frighteningly high body count."
— *Kirkus Reviews*

"A page-turner ... masterfully blends a fictional thriller with science and history."
— *Bestsellersworld.com*

"A tense thrill ride from start to finish ... a rollicking good story."
— *Self-Publishing Review*

Praise for the author's Eli Quinn Mystery Series

FIRST KILL

"Jam-packed with thrilling fight scenes, witty banter, and well-worn characters, FIRST KILL is an excellent addition to the private detective genre with a likeable hero and a lovable sidekick."
— *IndieReader*

"Methodical, yet fast-paced thriller… FIRST KILL solidifies Quinn as a deeply developed hero with great potential for future installations."
— *Self-Publishing Review*

"Britt offers a sharp, hearty narrative… Another worthy outing for the quick-witted, ever evolving private eye."
— *Kirkus Reviews*

"An exciting thriller … full of intrigue, sex, and even some humor."
— *Bestsellersworld.com*

"A well-plotted story full of twists and turns with a cast of attention-grabbing characters and dialogue that throws sparks all over the place."
— Silvia Villalobos, author of *Stranger or Friend*

DRONE

"A brisk detective novel sequel that packs a punch."
— *Kirkus Reviews*

"Quinn's second case reads as if it were written by a master reaching the height of his craft. With its witty banter, cast of colorful secondary characters, and promising detective agency, DRONE sidles into the genre with aplomb. ... Characterizations are top notch, the plot is believably paced with ratcheting tension, and the prose is highly polished. ... Quinn's personality gives him an everyman feel that makes him easy to connect with. Unlike more intellectual literary detectives, Quinn is relatable and fun to root for."
— *Foreword Clarion Reviews*

"Fast-paced with a few thought-provoking twists, DRONE is reminiscent of a noir detective story with a 21st century flair."
— *IndieReader*

"Britt's writing moves briskly with prose that Dashiell Hammett or Raymond Chandler might have applauded. Clipped, no-nonsense dialogue, fast-paced prose and tough-guy characters recall classics such as *The Maltese Falcon* or *The Long Goodbye*."
— *BlueInk Review*

"Immediately absorbing and thoroughly entertaining."
— *Bestsellersworld.com*

CLOSURE

"Fascinating characters, hard-edged action … Catapults the series off to a great start."
— *Bestsellersworld.com*

"A gritty, hard-boiled detective thriller, with a twist of self-awareness that keeps the read fresh and engaging. The story keeps you on your toes through a murder case that proves to be less than typical. Eli Quinn begins his saga as a private investigator with a bang … Quinn is truly a classic protagonist in the making."
— *Self-Publishing Review*

"Quinn's narrative often sports the hardened cynicism of a seasoned veteran … Solo nearly steals the story; he can intimidate with a single bark and a follow-up growl."
— *Kirkus Reviews*

~ ~ ~

"Many New York City metropolitan area transportation systems are vulnerable to flooding, some possibly with catastrophic consequences... Government officials and citizens alike must understand that New York City will be struck by a catastrophic hurricane sometime in the future and that preparedness is of the utmost importance."

— From the 1994 U.S. Army Corps of Engineers New York State Hurricane Evacuation Study

AUTHOR'S NOTE

Decades and even centuries before the destruction of Hurricane Sandy, tropical storms terrified and crippled the Northeast multiple times. But history is easily forgotten. At the turn of the millennium, the idea of a hurricane striking New York City was unthinkable, except to the scientists who knew their history. Despite advice from the research community, the City had yet to put an evacuation plan into place, and residents and officials alike were dismissive of the risks.

Sandy, a horrific storm, was not the worst nature has to offer. Had Sandy moved as fast as the storm characterized in this book, well, you can read for yourself.

This story is based on real science and the state of technology, politics and preparedness of 1999. Every attempt has been made to achieve accuracy, both in portraying plausible meteorological and hydrological events and the documented effects of historical storms.

~ ~ ~

EXCERPTED FROM
HURRICANES: HISTORY AND DYNAMICS,
BY DR. NICHOLAS K. GRAY,
HUMBOLDT UNIVERSITY PRESS (1998)

In the late summer of 1938 a wave of energy moved off the coast of Africa. Winds were sucked into the atmospheric depression and curved by the earth's spin into a counterclockwise rotation.

The storm churned unnoticed across the open sea, gathering strength from warm tropical waters. On Friday, September 16, a Brazilian freighter reported the storm.

Gordon Dunn and Grady Norton, U.S. Weather Bureau forecasters in Florida, issued a hurricane warning for Miami, expecting the storm to hit Tuesday. Miami residents stockpiled supplies, boarded windows, secured boats. But on Monday evening, the storm turned north and sped up to twenty miles an hour. It followed a typical path of recurvature—resembling a giant C—around the Bermuda High, an area of high atmospheric pressure in the mid-Atlantic that pushes air outward from its center, bouncing hurricanes off its edges like bubbles.

Dunn and Norton lost track of the storm off Cape Hatteras

and assumed it would curve eastward. The national weather map for Wednesday, September 21, showed no hurricane, only a storm moving out to sea. But winds increased to 140 miles an hour. The storm moved north and picked up speed. The Bermuda High had moved to forty-four degrees north latitude—from its normal September position of thirty to thirty-five degrees—blocking the hurricane's path and deflecting it northward. Abnormally warm water fed the storm as its forward speed increased to *sixty* miles an hour. Waves tore up boardwalks in New Jersey. No warnings were issued. It had been 117 years since the last great storm hit New York, on September 23, 1821. History had been forgotten.

By Wednesday afternoon, shingles were flying from roofs on Long Island. The sky grew dark. Trees were uprooted and telephone poles snapped like matchsticks. Three hours before high tide, residents reported a thick bank of gray fog, twenty-five to forty feet above the water, rolling in toward the south-facing coast. Some residents fled to relative safety across the bridge. Many did not. Most of them died as the "fog bank" turned out to be a wall of water known as a storm surge.

Created partly by the vacuum of reduced atmospheric pressure and more so by the wind blowing over the water, the storm surge was highest in an area just east of the eye—the right side of the storm when looked at from above. There, in the right-side eyewall, the counterclockwise winds combined with the storm's forward speed to create gusts exceeding 200 miles per hour.

The eye of the hurricane passed some fifty-files miles *east* of Manhattan, a near miss in meteorological terms. Had it been a few miles *west* of Manhattan, forensic hurricanologists agree it would have devastated the island.

~ ~ ~

SUNDAY, AUGUST 22, 1999

CHAPTER 1

NATIONAL HURRICANE CENTER,
MIAMI, FLORIDA
9:30 A.M.

Amanda Cole had never been to Atlantic City, never put a dollar down on a blackjack table, never pulled the lever of a slot machine. Hurricanes were the only thing she ever bet on, and she usually did so conservatively. Amanda figured she had until the end of the day—the bet had to be down 120 hours before landfall. But she was ready. She launched the email program on the PC in her cubicle, double-clicked on her own name. An email to herself, dated, proof of her bet.

```
To: me
From: acole@nhc.gov
Subject: 5 days to landfall

my pick on harvey: atlantic city, 11
p.m., friday 8/27.
cheers,
me
```

Amanda hit the enter button to send the email, then closed her eyes. If Harvey did what she feared he might—the eye making landfall in Atlantic City—then the worst part of the storm, the right-side eyewall, would slam into the most unprepared city in the East, and she would win dinner at a top Miami restaurant from Frank Delaney. It was a bet she hoped to lose.

Amanda scanned the official bulletin on Harvey, a twenty-four-hour forecast she'd released to the public from the Hurricane Center earlier in the morning:

BULLETIN
HURRICANE HARVEY ADVISORY NUMBER 21
NATIONAL WEATHER SERVICE MIAMI FL
8 AM EDT SUNDAY AUG 22

...HARVEY BECOMES HURRICANE... MOVING TOWARD LEEWARD ISLANDS...

AT 8 AM EDT... 1200Z... THE CENTER OF HURRICANE HARVEY WAS LOCATED NEAR LATITUDE 18.4 NORTH... LONGITUDE 53.2 WEST OR ABOUT 560 MILES... 900KM... EAST NORTHEAST OF ANTIGUA IN THE LEEWARD ISLANDS.

HARVEY IS MOVING TOWARD THE WEST NEAR 12 MPH... 19 KM/HR... A GRADUAL TURN TO THE WEST NORTHWEST IS EXPECTED DURING THE NEXT 24 HOURS.

MAXIMUM SUSTAINED WINDS ARE NEAR 75 MPH... 120 KM/HR. SOME STRENGTHENING IS LIKELY TO OCCUR DURING THE NEXT 24 HOURS.

Likely to occur. The forecaster's language was always guarded. Any forecast beyond twenty-four hours—even for a specialist in the nation's nerve center for hurricane forecasting—stretched weather data, computer models and human understanding to the limits. But a hurricane specialist couldn't resist taking a stab at a five-day forecast for earth's most powerful storms. Amanda Cole and Frank Delaney had been doing it for a decade, making the guess and placing the bet, between friends.

She opened her brown eyes and squinted at the satellite image on the PC. The whorl of clouds had been a fluffy, ill-defined pinwheel all morning. Amanda leaned closer, put her finger on a blurry dark spot at the lower left of the pinwheel.

"I see you," she said.

Hurricane Harvey's wide, fuzzy eye was becoming more distinct.

Amanda leaned back, gathered her straight black hair behind her head into a short ponytail, took a deep breath.

"Gonna get into your mind, Harvey," she said to the satellite image. "Give me a couple days. Then you don't go anywhere without me knowing. Got it?"

From its genesis off Africa seven days ago, the seed that became Harvey developed routinely, winds rushing counterclockwise and inward around the low-pressure center. As Harvey strengthened, he controlled more atmosphere and created erratic winds within a well-defined storm system. Organized instability, Amanda called it.

Harvey was Amanda Cole's responsibility to forecast. But the storm was nearly 2,000 miles out in the Atlantic, a threat to no one for the moment.

She got up from her cubicle, crossed the vast, colorless room, and walked unannounced into the director's office. Frank Delaney sat behind a simple desk, his athletic, six-foot-two frame hunched forward, wise black eyes peering from underneath graying eyebrows and through a lattice of fingers pressed together in thinking mode. *Mr. Rogers plus twenty pounds*, Amanda thought, *and more serious*.

"I don't like what I see on Harvey," Amanda said.

Delaney smiled as though he expected her to say that. "Get in his mind yet?"

"Not completely," Amanda said. "But he's got purpose. I can feel it. He's growing so fast. Couple days he's going to be a monster." She visualized the green line for Harvey, a 72-hour forecast that pointed vaguely toward northern Florida. A red line did the same except for a slightly more northerly inclination. "Bermuda High is strong. But Friday it's going to be sitting up where it was in 1938. The *operational* computer models don't understand that this far in advance. And Harvey could be here Friday morning."

"If he hits the Southeast," Delaney said.

"If he hits the Southeast." Amanda inclined her head.

"But you don't think he's going to."

Amanda smiled tightly. At fifty-six, Frank Delaney was twenty years her senior, and in many ways like a father. He knew her as well as anyone, and right now he would know she had an idea trying to skirt the scientific cautions of her mind and become grist for the what-if mill. He would have also compared the green line of the operational forecast to the red line they were both reluctant to talk about.

"Could be Florida, could be the Carolinas, might go out to sea," Amanda said. "But I think he could reach the coast by Friday morning, which means…"

"…He could be in New York by Friday night or Saturday morning."

"Five days to landfall in the most vulnerable city in the East," Amanda said.

Delaney sighed and put a hand up. "I know. Listen. We've feared it, me more than anyone. But, Christ…" Delaney got up, walked around the desk and closed the door. He returned to his chair. "*Christ*, even a hint of New York gets out of this place and we've got a helluva problem on our hands unless we're right."

"We can't stick our heads in the sand, either. You know how people think hurricanes never make it to the Northeast."

Delaney made a church steeple with his fingers. "You off tomorrow?"

"Yes." *Don't ask me what I'm going to do.*

"What are you going to do?"

Damn. Amanda knew exactly what she planned to do. There was another storm out there, closer, and she had two days off. Hurricane Gert was just 400 miles offshore and barreling toward the Carolinas. Amanda pulled her shoulders back and spoke with a lifted chin: "Chase Gert."

"Oh, Christ, Amanda." Delaney rolled his eyes. "You do good science. Great science. Why do you need this thrill-seeking crap?"

"Off my case, Dad," she said with a blend of affection and anger. Frank Delaney was not her father, but sometimes he acted like it.

"Alright," he said. "What about Sarah?"

Amanda looked away, at the floor, and took a second. "She's going to go spend two weeks with her father. His summer vacation. He picks her up this evening."

"Why don't you just tell him no?"

"I can't. He's got visitation on the weekends, which he hardly ever takes, then he gets two weeks every summer. That's the agreement. I want to just keep her all the time, you know. But sometimes I think I get hyper-maternal and I know I've got to try and relax a little. I guess what it comes down to is I really want her to know her father."

"Must be really hard."

"It'll be hell for me, Frank. She's six. The selfish part of me doesn't want to be away from her for twenty-four hours, let alone two weeks."

"So you go back to chasing hurricanes, your great escape."

It *was* a great escape. At thirty-six, she wondered why she kept at it. The answer was always the same: She was still searching for the passing eye of a hurricane: First, there would be violence. Then, calm. Then violence again. It was a goal she'd come close to several times but had never achieved.

"What else am I going to do? Sit at home and worry about Sarah? At least I'll have something to focus on." *Can we change the subject?*

"I guess I understand," Delaney said. "Listen. Where you

headed tomorrow?"

"Not sure. Start in Charleston, watch Gert, take a guess. Supposed to meet up with that *New York Times* reporter."

Delaney raised an eyebrow. "Jack Corbin?"

"Yep."

"You meet him before?"

"Once, years ago," Amanda said. She squelched the deep breath her chest wanted as she thought of Jack Corbin. "He wants to write a feature on me, my work, my hurricane chasing. I think his real motive is to use me to be in the right spot at landfall."

"That would be Jack Corbin," Delaney said. "He's aggressive. So, he uses you—that's OK. Maybe more people will pay attention to the storms. Listen. If you're careful—I mean really careful—you could plant a bug in his ear about Harvey."

"Good idea. Jack knows the risk, and he knows what a mess the City's evacuation plan is in. He could be a great asset later in the week. Frank? Can we…"

He put his hand up. "I know. What should you do if he asks about the LORAX. Listen. You know more about Harvey than anyone. I trust you to get proper coverage. But under no circumstances can you discuss the LORAX. Christ, word gets out that we're paying attention to a non-operational forecast model and it's both our asses."

"Are we paying attention to it?"

Frank Delaney sighed and slumped deep into his chair. Amanda waited.

"Not officially, no," he finally said.

CHAPTER 2

OUTSIDE SANTO DOMINGO, DOMINICAN REPUBLIC
12:30 P.M.

Maximo never made the calls. His people called him. If they didn't, they died. Maximo had become wealthy by virtue of a lot of simple rules like that. The phone rang. He looked at his watch. The call would be from the United States.

Maximo's soft voice was as gruff as he could make it. "Nombre?"

"Octopus."

"My friend." Maximo let his jovial nature out of the box. His voice was velvety and distinct, a hint of an accent and practiced enunciation, but warm. "How are you?"

"I'm well," the Octopus said. "How is your lovely girlfriend, Maximo?"

"Thank you for asking. Which one?" Maximo's hearty laugh turned into a smoker's hack. He looked around the pool at the three young, curvaceous, bikini-clad women who were keeping him company today. "They keep me happy. We have lovely young women here in the Dominican Republic, my friend. You will have to come see for yourself one day."

"I hope to," the Octopus said.

Maximo's tone became serious. "Did you get the package, then?"

"It arrived. I'm letting it cool down a little."

"Problem?"

Maximo could hear the Octopus shift in his chair. "Nothing we can't handle."

"Very well then. I trust you, my friend, even though you are not Dominican." Maximo laughed again, coughed twice. "Besides, we have more important things to discuss, no?"

The Octopus lowered his voice. "We do."

"Very well. What company?"

"Global Insurance Company, NASDAQ ticker symbol GLIC."

Maximo: "What do you know about this GLIC?"

"Overexposed in North Carolina," the Octopus said. "Looks like Gert is going to hit there. If she does, GLIC is a sure bet. Trading at fifty-six dollars a share today. I think we can wait until tomorrow to make our bet."

"*My* bet. Do not forget that, my friend."

"Of course not," the Octopus said. He cleared his throat. "I'm only thinking of the organization. I think you can wait until tomorrow sometime to sell the shares short. Make sure where Gert is going first. It'll be a couple days, at least, before the market realizes what has happened, and then it won't take long for the shares to lose half their value."

"Let us hope so," Maximo said. "Five million is a lot of money, even for me."

"I have every confidence you'll be able to buy the shares back at a much lower price."

"Very well. I feel so American, you know, profiting from another firm's misfortune."

"Yes," the Octopus said. "That is the American way."

"By the way, I commend you on your research so far, though I fear your methods may have been underhanded?"

"The information is not widely known, and no one knows we have it."

"Ah, just as I feared! Well done," Maximo said. "Of course, if you are wrong…"

"…You will have to kill me."

Maximo laughed again, friendlier this time. He knew the Octopus would squirm around in his chair. The threat was no joke. The Dominicans didn't trust most non-Dominicans as far as they could throw them. The Octopus was a rare exception to Maximo's exclusionary policy, and he'd done well in the organization, but it was critical that he be reminded, now and then, of Maximo's simplest rule: a single slip-up could cost him his life.

Maximo's laugh wound down. The Octopus took the opportunity: "I have two more I'm digging on that might come in handy when Harvey decides where *he's* going. I'll call you as soon as I know more. One of them looks real good if Harvey visits New York."

"You have mentioned New York before, my friend. But, really, when was the last time a hurricane hit New York?"

"1938," the Octopus said. "Long Island. I realize this is a long shot, but the payoff would be huge. And remember, I can affect the outcome."

"I haven't forgotten," Maximo said. "Maximum death and destruction, as you so quaintly put it."

"Harvey would do the heavy lifting, but I can lend a big hand. And the connection you gave me at Goddard may come in handy. We're going to do a brief test tomorrow night just before Gert comes ashore."

"Connections. That's how the world works."

"And connections are the key to our plan," the Octopus said. "The way these companies have spread their risk around combined with the extensive interruptions to business that the storm would cause, well, the financial market will be rocked when we finally get a New York hurricane. I wouldn't be surprised if we see it cascade into a bear market, which would only help your investment."

"You'll have to explain your theory on that to me sometime," Maximo said. "Meanwhile, let's concentrate on this first storm. Perhaps our *next* investment will be a bit more substantial, if your system works and if the wind does as you hope. Trust that you will be duly recognized either way."

Maximo hung up first, as he always did. Terese climbed out of the pool wearing a bikini bottom, no top. The long-legged twenty-eight-year-old blonde was the only American on the Pérez estate, essential now in helping Maximo understand aspects of the culture that sometimes baffled him. She was a good find, and once he got her off the drugs she proved to be better in bed than anyone he'd ever had.

Terese pulled her long wet hair back and returned to the lounge chair next to him. Nobody sat within listening distance when Maximo was on the phone. Not even Terese. It wasn't that Maximo hid much from her. She'd been his primary lover for a year now, and Maximo was prone to confiding in the woman who most frequently shared his bed. But it was a simple unspoken rule around the estate that you didn't eavesdrop on Maximo. If he wanted you to know something, he'd tell you.

"The Octopus says we have a shot at New York," Maximo said. He watched glistening drops of water dribble into the crevice between her copper breasts. Terese didn't look at him. But Maximo detected a stiffening.

"Do you have a problem with me making money from the misfortune of your hometown?"

She lit a cigarette, puffed once, then held it perched above a bent wrist and ignored his question. "Won't that hurt business?"

That's what Maximo loved most about Terese. She could think to the next step, she was willing to challenge him, and she was smart enough to do it in private. Maximo couldn't afford to accept challenges to his power. But so long as Terese kept hers private, and so long as she continued to give him such pleasure in bed, she would be an exception.

Lately, though, her irreverence had seemed to sharpen. Maximo wondered if she had something else, or someone else, on her mind. He made a mental note to keep his eyes open.

For now, she seemed to have relaxed again, so he did too.

"We're going to move the main business to San Francisco soon anyway," Maximo said. "I have been planning to do that for some time now. New York is getting too crowded. It seems every expatriate has set up shop there. It would be nice to go out with a bang."

"Just be careful," Terese said without looking at him.

"I'm always careful."

CHAPTER 3

MIAMI SUBURBS
10:15 P.M.

W earing a plain, oversized gray t-shirt and plaid boxer shorts, Amanda sat in her sparsely furnished study, a few miles from the Hurricane Center. The room was bathed vaguely in dim blue light from her computer monitor. Behind her, the door to a short hallway was open, allowing in a whisper of brightness from a distant floor lamp in the living room. Open windows pulled a light breeze through the house.

On her desktop computer were various tracking and analysis programs for storms. She was normally frugal, but when it came to her job, she allowed herself luxuries. She also had a portable, suitcase-sized satellite setup that worked with her laptop to connect to the Internet from anywhere, without external power and without relying on cellular towers that might come down in a storm.

Sarah's father was late, as usual. Amanda had expected it, put Sarah to bed and then drifted into the study to check the storm. Amanda resolved not to make a big deal out of Joe Springer being three hours late to pick up his daughter for the only two weeks he'd spend with her the whole year. It would only start another fight.

She typed a password into the computer and from over the Internet accessed the non-public section of the Hurricane Center's forecasting database. She pulled up the official forecasted track for Gert. The green line ran straight toward South Carolina, representing the forecast of a computer model developed at the Geophysical Fluid Dynamics Laboratory at Princeton University. The model was known simply as the GFDL. If Amanda had her way, by next season the GFDL model would be replaced by the LORAX, a model she was working on with a small team of researchers, an improved tool that she expected to be ten or twenty percent more accurate.

Amanda typed another command, and the red line appeared over the green one. The northward turn was more pronounced. She pulled up a sea of numbers that explained the path of the red line, studied them. Sarah came in, rubbing her eyes with one fist, dragging a sad-looking stuffed Piglet with the other.

"There's my little girl. C'mere."

Sarah hopped up on her lap, frowning. Piglet fell to the floor. Sarah's hair was like her mother's, dark, hanging straight, but longer. Sarah wouldn't allow her hair to be cut. It hung all the way down her back. She had her mother's olive skin, sharp cheeks, eyes that squinted when she smiled, turned down at the corners. But she had her father's eyebrows, thick and dark. And those eyebrows could frown.

"What are you doing up?" Amanda asked.

"Can't sleep," Sarah frowned. She played with the holes in the feet of her favorite pajamas, the pink ones. Though Amanda kept buying her new ones, Sarah refused to wear any others. "Where's Daddy?"

"He'll be here soon."

"He was supposed to be here at seven."

"I know, honey. Did you read some?"

"Two books already."

"Count sheep?"

Sarah stuck her bottom lip out. "A hundred of them."

"I tell you what," Amanda said. "Why don't you listen to

one of your tapes?"

Sarah brightened. "*The Lorax!*"

The girl had dozens of books on tape. Amanda sometimes worried she was addicted to them, but it was better than television, she decided, and a single mother had to be creative. The Dr. Seuss tape that included *The Lorax* was Sarah's favorite. Amanda's, too. She was never too old for Seuss.

Amanda stuck her chin down to her chest, lowered her voice and recited a line from the book: "'Mister!' he said with a sawdusty sneeze…"

"'I'm the Lorax,'" Sarah chimed in, "'I speak for the trees.'"

"We need to get you some more of those tapes," Amanda said.

"*Winnie the Pooh!*"

"I'll look for it. Now how about you go off to bed. If you don't get a nap in you're going to be extra cranky."

"When's Daddy coming?"

"I don't know, sweetheart."

"What are you working on, Mommy?"

"My forecasting program."

"Is it broken?"

"No, it's just not quite finished yet."

"What's it for?"

"Well, if it works right, it will tell me where the wind will take hurricanes."

"How come there's so many hurricanes all of a sudden?"

Amanda chuckled. The answer to that question—in the long-term sense—had to do with, among other things, the diminishing El Niño, which when it was strong tended to suppress the formation of hurricanes in the Atlantic. When El Niño subsided, the Atlantic tended to fire up hurricane production. Amanda thought it humorous that even the absence of El Niño could be blamed for severe weather. In the short-term sense, there was a simpler answer for her daughter. "There's always more of them in the summer and fall."

"Why?"

"I've told you before. Can you remember?"

Sarah looked up into a corner of her brain. "Um. Because the ocean has to be warm?"

"Good for you."

"Why does that make hurricanes?"

"Well, you remember when I showed you how thunderstorms worked?"

"Yes," said Sarah, the bored look of a too-smart child in her rolling eyes. "The warm air goes up." Her head and arms moved in exaggerated undulations. "It gets cold, makes rain, comes down."

She's going to be just like her mother. God help her. "Let's see. Well, hurricanes are like thunderstorms. Actually, a hurricane is made up of a whole bunch of thunderstorms, all gathered together in one big swirl."

Amanda found a pen and some blank paper, drew a pinwheel with several bands that grew in width as she sketched inward, curving counter-clockwise. In the middle she drew a black dot.

"This is what a hurricane looks like from outer space. Each of those swirls is a band of thunderstorms," Amanda said. "And the wind is rushing to the middle."

"Why?"

"Because the warm, moist air is rising in the middle. Remember what happens?"

Sarah fingered a hole in her pajamas, studied it. Her forehead knotted as she thought. "The other air has to take its place?"

"Yep. So air rushes in from all around. Now, the warm water is the hurricane's fuel."

"Like gasoline?"

"Maybe more like the fire in a hot-air balloon. Like the one we rode in last summer. Remember how the pilot would turn the fire on, and the balloon would go up? In a hurricane, the air gets warmed by the water instead of a fire."

Amanda drew a cross-section of a hurricane, with a tall cylinder in the middle and a series of clouds on either side representing thunderstorm bands. With a red pen she drew arrows pointing upward in each band of clouds. "The air is rising in each of these thunderstorms. The worst ones are near the center, where the air is rising the fastest. So what happens to the wind at the surface there?"

"It blows harder."

Amanda nodded. "So the wind is circling in and going up. The faster it rises, the harder it sucks other air in, and the stronger the wind gets."

Sarah was shifting in her seat. Amanda was about to explain how the rising air condensed, how the condensation produced heat and caused the air to rise even more, how the increasing winds whipped up the ocean's surface, allowing even more water to evaporate into the storm and, ultimately, how the hurricane fed on itself.

Instead, she drew an arrow that curved out from the top of the cylinder in the middle. "The air rises way up into the sky…"

"Higher than the balloon went?"

"Much higher. Higher than most airplanes go."

"That's high!" Sarah's brown eyes were wide and she nodded her head.

"Eight or ten miles. Then the air is pushed out, like smoke from a chimney, making room for more rising air."

Sarah pointed to the cylinder in the middle. "Is that the eyeball?"

"The eye," Amanda said. "Some air sinks back into the center. As it sinks, it gets warmer and it's calm and quiet. There are usually no clouds in the eye."

"Can we go there?"

"To a hurricane?"

"To the eye!" Sarah pointed to some imaginary place over Amanda's shoulder.

Amanda bounced Sarah on her knee. "*I've* never even been there. Yet. And I think it would be a rough ride, sweetie. I don't know if you would like it."

"I'm not afraid," Sarah said.

Amanda believed her. "Maybe someday you can fly a plane

into one yourself," she said. "People fly in and measure the wind. They're called Hurricane Hunters."

"Really?" Sarah's eyes lit up and Amanda saw a reflection of her own young, hopeful and determined eyes. "Can I be a Hurricane Hunter?"

"Why not? You can do anything you want."

"Mommy. Will you read me a book now?"

"Nope. Off you go. It's going to be a long night, and you need sleep."

"I'll sleep on the plane. Daddy said we could go swimming tomorrow."

"You be careful, swimming in the ocean."

"I'm a good swimmer!"

"I know. A real guppy." Sarah had a certificate from summer camp that said so.

"Shark, Mom. I'm a shark now. I passed the test yesterday, remember?"

"OK, Ms. Shark, off to bed or I'll tickle you to death." She played at Sarah's sides with her fingers. Sarah giggled, squirmed off her mother's lap and padded slowly off to her bedroom. Amanda picked up Piglet and took him into the living room, plopped on the couch and held the stuffed animal tight to her.

She imagined for a moment that Piglet was Jack Corbin, the reporter. The thought made her feel better. Amanda had a special place inside her heart where she kept thoughts of Jack Corbin. How different it would have been if she and Jack had tried. She would never have met Joe Springer. *The worst thing that ever happened to her.* Would never have had Sarah. *The best thing that ever happened.* She clutched Piglet so tightly that he would have screamed if he could.

***

Joe Springer showed up just after eleven. Sarah was asleep. Amanda had been dozing, thinking about the night she met Jack Corbin, the night Hurricane Andrew slammed into South Florida. The night she held his hand for a brief instant as the storm shook the building. She set Piglet on the couch and went to the door.

"C'mon in," she said flatly.

"Sorry I'm late," Joe Springer said. "Plane was a little late, then…"

"Never mind, Joe. I'll go get Sarah up."

"She's asleep?"

"Of course she's asleep. It's after eleven."

"I thought she'd be excited…"

"She was excited. Then she got tired. She's six years old, Joe. What do you expect?"

"I know how old our daughter is. Look, if you're going to…"

"Drop it, Joe. I'm tired too. And you know I don't do well when she's not with me. There's her suitcase." Amanda pointed behind the door. "I'll go get her."

Amanda came back a moment later with Sarah snuggled into her, cheek on shoulder, groggy. Joe put the suitcase in the car and walked back through the door.

Amanda shook Sarah lightly until the girl's eyes rolled open.

"Daddy's here, sweetheart."

"Mmm."

Amanda felt tears coming. "Will you call me in the morning?"

"Yes, Mommy."

"I love you."

"I love you, Mommy."

Amanda Cole handed her daughter to Joe Springer.

"Hi, honey," he said.

"Hi Daddy." Then Sarah was out, eyes rolling shut again. A tear spilled down Amanda's cheek. She was glad Sarah was asleep. Amanda wiped the tear with the back of her hand, cleared her throat. "Are you watching Gert?"

"Saw it on the news," Joe said. "Going into the Carolinas tomorrow night, right?"

"Maybe. But it still has a shot to run north." Amanda's first rule: never discount a place as the possible point of landfall until the hurricane is north of that place. "Keep an eye on it, OK?"

"Amanda, look. I get to be with Sarah for a lousy two weeks out of the year. I don't need you watching over us the whole time, OK?"

"Jeez, she's my daughter." She had an edge to her voice now. "It's my job to watch over her."

"But not me. It's not your job to watch over me."

"Just keep an eye out, please." The tears were forming again.

"I will. I will. Goodbye, Amanda."

Amanda watched her ex-husband and Sarah get in the car. The first leg of their journey to the Jersey Shore, just south of Manhattan.

Amanda sighed long. Joe Springer was taking a piece of her. Her best friend. The focus of her life. The little girl who made her laugh, who loved Pooh and Piglet and Seuss and at the same time understood how a hurricane worked.

She turned and closed the door behind her. The click of the lock seemed louder than normal. The house felt empty. Amanda closed her eyes. She held the doorknob to steady herself. Then she did what she always did when Joe Springer took Sarah away: She told herself that it was good for Sarah to be with her father. Amanda couldn't deny her daughter that experience. She repeated the thought, to herself and then out loud: "It's good for her."

She opened her eyes and looked around the room, hoping to see Sarah sitting on the couch. Instead, Piglet sat staring at her, a sad look in his eyes, as though he'd just lost his best friend, too. Amanda's heart shriveled with the sudden loneliness.

She sat on the floor and cried.

~ ~ ~

EXCERPTED FROM
HURRICANES: HISTORY AND DYNAMICS,
BY DR. NICHOLAS K. GRAY,
HUMBOLDT UNIVERSITY PRESS (1998)

E vacuations started early in the morning on September 21, 1989. Hugo was coming. Interstate 26 out of Charleston was bumper to bumper with fleeing residents and beachgoers. Motels booked up quickly, convenience stores ran out of batteries and bottled water. Then news reports said Hugo was turning north, likely to go out to sea.

By early afternoon, most thought the worst was over.

On the six o'clock news, Hugo was reported to still be moving north, and forecasters hedged, saying the storm might go out to sea or that hurricane winds could hit Charleston within three hours. By eight p.m. the massive storm had made a sharp left turn and headed straight for Charleston. An hour later the storm was tearing the town apart. High-voltage lines snapped, dangled and flashed, and transformers atop utility poles blew out, creating blue and white flashes that lit up an otherwise gray-green sky. Gas lines ruptured, causing explosions that were heard miles away. A wall of water pushed over the seawall at the Battery and, together with the wind, damaged eighty percent of the town's buildings.

~ ~ ~

MONDAY, AUGUST 23

CHAPTER 4

CHARLESTON,
SOUTH CAROLINA
8:00 A.M.

Incongruous gusts of wind carried the promise of change through steamy morning streets. Like cotton pulled by an invisible hand from an aspirin bottle, thin curly strands of cirrus clouds bearded half the sky, 40,000 feet up. Over the Atlantic, a fuzzy orange orb gave way to a thickening baffle of cirrostratus clouds.

Juan Rico, Nikon around his neck, stuffed a weathered, workingman arm into a bag of Doritos, rummaging for full-size chips.

"Looks like nothin' ever happened here," Rico said as they drove over cobblestone streets through old city.

"It wasn't as bad as it could have been," Jack Corbin said. "For all the talk, Charleston got off pretty easy."

"Thought it was a Cat 4," Rico said. "Hundred-and-forty-mile winds."

"The eye passed right over Charleston. Worst winds were farther up the coast."

"Right-side eyewall," Rico said. I know. Shit. Like ridin' with a damn scientist."

Jack Corbin smiled. The weather beat reporter's long black hair flew backward in the light breeze as he craned his neck out the window to look at another three-story home surrounded by wrought iron fencing, Jack loved how Charleston oozed history.

"It's like stepping back in time," he said.

"Except for the tourists." Juan Rico pointed at three large, stark white northerners at the corner, sunburns on their forearms and the cameras around their necks.

"Not many around," Jack observed.

"Smart ones left early." Rico fiddled with his Nikon. "Beat the rush. Folks down here know how to evacuate. Not like us stupid New Yorkers, man. We fuckin' drive toward the storm."

"Got to get the story," Jack said.

"Don't worry. You get your story. Amanda put you right in the middle of it. You be wishin' you never asked."

"We need it, pal. There's been so many hurricanes this year the readers are losing track. They've got to be sick of prep stories, and I'm sick of aftermath stories. What's missing is the first-person account *in* the storm. We need that story out of Gert. Bad."

"Speak for yourself, man," Juan Rico said. "I'm not in trouble with *my* editor. Shooter only has to get one good pic now and then, everybody goes *ooh* and *aah* and forgets all the average shots."

That was it, Jack knew. A photographer just needed *the shot*, one click every so often, a 125th of a second, an image that stuck in peoples' minds for months or years. But a reporter was only as good as his last story which, by the afternoon, was invariably sitting in somebody's birdcage being shit on. Editors always seemed thrilled to get just about any picture to go with a story, and they always seemed less than thrilled with most of the stories they got. Jack was overdue for a good one.

Juan Rico had set up the rendezvous with Amanda Cole. He and Amanda had been friends since Rico's days at the *Miami Herald*. The diminutive photographer left a trail of good friends wherever he went. Jack felt lucky to be at the top of that list. Juan Rico had been his best friend for several years now, ever since the two first teamed up. Jack was known around the *Times* newsroom as the guy who tried to get in the path of hurricanes. Rico was the only shooter who would work with him. Jack felt a slight throb of jealousy over the fact that Juan Rico was such good friends with Amanda. But he never let it show, always played his feelings for Amanda close to his vest. *But now she is divorced. I wonder...*

He asked Rico: "Where do we meet her?"

"Myrtle Beach," Rico said. "Couple hours. We gonna eat first?"

Jack ignored the question. Rico was always hungry. "Hope she hurries. We need to get into position soon."

Jack thought some more about Amanda. They'd met in the days before Hurricane Andrew came ashore in 1992, and there had been an instant spark. When Andrew hit, they found themselves next to each other in the crammed sixth-floor offices of the Hurricane Center.

Then there was a loud crash on the roof like a muffled bomb or a dropped car.

"Radar's out!" one of the meteorologists reported.

The building swayed. The center's wind gauge recorded a gust of 164 miles an hour. Then it broke. The room went quiet. Amanda reached out and found Jack's hand. She curled her fingers through his. He didn't resist.

After Andrew devastated Dade County, Jack and Amanda both became burdened with endless sixteen-hour days, he reporting and she analyzing the storm's effects.

Then Jack flew back to New York.

Jack often relied on Amanda as a source. But their careers kept them apart. And then Amanda got married and had a kid.

"What's she like? I mean, it's been years. I talk to her on the phone a few times each season, but..."

"Smart," Rico said. "She smart. Looks smart. Acts smart. Is smart. And don't underestimate her."

"About what?"

"About anything, man" Rico said. "She talk circles around

you about weather, computers, baseball, you name it. Piss her off she probably kick your ass, too."

"I knew about the intelligence. Didn't know she was a brute."

"No brute. Strong beauty. Like a racehorse. Pure. Why you ask?"

"No reason."

"Yeah right."

"I just hope she finds the spot."

"She find it," Rico said. "What you guess?"

"Landfall?"

"Yep. Time to place your bet."

"How much this time?"

"You won twenty-five bucks from me last time," Rico said. "Double or nothin'?"

"OK. But I don't know where the heck it's going. Tell you what." Jack thought about the Hurricane Center's forecast. "I think Gert's going to skirt north on them. I'll pick Topsail Island."

"Wherezat?"

"Barrier Island in North Carolina, up by Cape Fear. It's where Bertha and Fran hit in '96. I count those people unlucky. You?"

"What's the farthest south you figure it can go now?"

"I don't know," Jack said. "Maybe Georgia."

"I pick Savannah," said Rico with a smile. "They haven't had one for awhile."

"Hurricanes aren't like computers, pal. They don't keep track of where the last one went."

"Savannah," Rico said again. "I just like to say the word. Savannah."

***

The cirrostratus clouds moved inland and reached to all horizons as the reporter and photographer drove north. The sun gave up to being no more than a bright area to the east.

The thick dead early morning heat was being carried away by gusty winds.

"You know about the snakes?" Jack asked.

They had crossed the three-mile long bridge spanning the Santee River delta, and drove north to Myrtle Beach. The lowcountry they had driven through was made up of lazy rivers lined with sweet gums, magnolias and cypress, their murky waters filled with alligators and poisonous snakes. Snakes were Rico's one big phobia.

"Snakes?" Rico munched on a pepperoni stick, wiped the grease on his pant leg.

"The ones in the trees after Hugo," Jack said.

"What the fuck?"

"The storm surge picked them up out of the swamps and deposited them in the trees, or at least the trees that were left standing. Or maybe they swam for high ground and climbed into the trees themselves."

"Don't fuck with me."

"I'm not kidding. People saw them in the trees for weeks."

Rico set the pepperoni stick, half finished, on the dashboard. Jack drove on, letting the snakes sneak into Rico's subconscious.

In Myrtle Beach, traffic was heavy. Many cars had beach chairs and bright towels stuffed into the rear windows. The tourists were leaving. Jack checked plates. Several from Ohio, Kentucky, Tennessee.

Some had furniture tied to the top—and South Carolina Plates. The locals were getting out as well. Jack pulled into the parking lot of a convenience store, which was doing a great business.

The shelves were nearly bare. He scanned the store to see what was left, to catalogue it so he could write about it. Two loaves of rye. A decent selection of cookies, but not many crackers. Most of the canned foods were gone. The beer was gone, but there was still plenty of soda. Bottled water gone. Juice depleted. No milk. Choice of frozen dinners getting thin, but plenty of ice cream.

"Gert's fourteen, maybe sixteen hours away," Jack said. "At least the worst of it. If it comes here. And everybody is either gone or has already stocked up."

"Told you, people here know 'bout hurricanes."

Jack gathered up what he could for lunch. Potato chips, two colas, the last hunk of cheese. Rico warmed to the idea and bought a half-dozen long, flat and greasy jerky sticks.

They headed for the car. Far down the road Jack spotted a green line moving toward them, growing larger. At first it appeared fuzzy and wavy through the rising heat from the asphalt. The closer the caravan got, the longer it became, seeming to have no end. Jack knew at once what it was. Emergency officials in South Carolina had learned their lesson with Hugo, and they weren't taking any chances this time.

The lead vehicle was a Humvee. Directly behind it was a flatbed tractor-trailer carrying two bulldozers. Next came another flatbed loaded with portable generators.

The National Guard was moving in.

Rico stared at the green line, set a piece of cheese absentmindedly on the hood of the car and fiddled with his Nikon. He pulled the short, 28mm lens off, grabbed a 300. "Here you go, baby, nice and smooth," he said, screwing the 300mm lens on the digital camera. He pulled the camera up to his eye, buried one elbow into his stomach, "Amanda better hurry. They gonna snap this place shut like a fuckin' crime scene."

Jack looked at his watch. "She's still over an hour away."

Rico took a deep breath.

Click-click-click.

***

Jack and Rico waited. Lower clouds shuttled landward below the thickening cover. The wind, steadier now, lifted Jack's long black hair, made a flag of it.

"Cut that shit off, would you?"

"What? My hair? It's me."

"It's out of style," Rico said.

"I don't follow styles."

"Oh, yeah, right. You make 'em." Rico laughed.

Jack looked down at his plain dark trousers, simple white button-up shirt and conservative tie. "Screw you," he said. "You're still wearing short-sleeved plaid. You look like somebody's dad from the sixties."

A blue Chevy pulled into the parking lot with a screech, curved into the spot next to Juan Rico's open door, stopped too late with a jerk of the brakes and scraped something on the curb. Amanda Cole got out. Her smile was broad, warm.

"Fuckin' nearly killed me," Rico said.

"Missed you by a mile," she said.

"Scraped the car up."

"Rental."

"C'mon, Amanda. Cars are like best friends," Rico said, only half-joking. "Gotta take care of 'em or they go to shit." He stood, walked past her, got down on one knee and stuck his head under the front bumper.

She put a hand on her hip in mock frustration, then folded her arms. "Juan, it's a freaking car. Now give me a hug."

"What if I treated my ol' Dodge that way?" Rico said. "It'd be a junker by now."

"What year is that thing, anyway?"

"Sixty-seven."

"Dinosaur."

"Looks and runs great. 'Cuz I take care of it." Rico mumbled something under the car, then stood. "Looks OK." His voice became warmer. "So do you. And sorry 'bout the language."

Amanda laughed. "Bar of soap for you. Now come here."

Rico kissed her cheek and hugged her, then took her hands and let the smile, which he'd been stifling, spread across his face.

Jack felt himself flush in the morning heat. Amanda was as beautiful—in a sultry kind of way—as he remembered. She was about an inch taller than Rico, maybe five-eight, and had a slender strength that hinted at running and weightlifting, a sculpted valley between shoulder and bicep, warm healthy skin exposed by a sleeveless black cotton shirt. She wore blue jeans. Jack's imagination worked to picture equivalently sculpted legs. She was Jack's age but she looked younger. Her black hair danced across her shoulders in flashes of reflected light. He studied her face: Strong cheeks, thin nose, brown eyes that might seem too big to some people, but not to Jack. Big brown eyes that moved constantly, active, curious. Juan Rico held her hands. Jack was jealous. He tried to fend off his imagination.

"…one fine woman," Rico was saying.

"You always make me feel better," Amanda said.

"How's Sarah?"

Something dark flashed across her eyes—quick, like a fast-moving thunderstorm—disappointment, or maybe fear.

"She left last night to spend two weeks with her father."

"Bastard," Rico said. "Oops. Sorry."

"It's OK. He does what he can," she said.

Jack cleared his throat.

"Oh." Rico pointed with a thumb over his shoulder, across the hood of the car. "There's Jack."

"Hello, Jack." Amanda waved. The darkness seemed to lift.

But—a wave. He'd been dying to see her again all these years. Now here she was and he got a wave. The silence lasted a fraction too long. Jack forced a smile. "Hi Amanda. Nice to see you again." It sounded dumb as it came out.

Her eyes squinted, a near-smile. It might have meant something. Then she looked back at Rico. "Are we going to sit here and talk all day, or do we go find some wind?"

"Let's do it," Rico said.

"Hop in," Jack said. "Rico can sit in the back." *Screw you, pal.* He tried to hold back the grin but a corner of it slipped to his lips.

Amanda got in the front seat. Rico jumped in back and Jack started the car. He forced his way out of the parking lot into heavy traffic.

"So," Jack said. "Where to?"

"Topsail Island," Amanda said.

"No kidding?" Jack grinned at Rico in the rearview mirror.

"Why?" Amanda asked.

"Oh, nothing. Just means Rico's gonna owe me fifty bucks."

Amanda wrestled with her seat belt. She glanced at Jack and grinned like a little girl who'd just broken Daddy's rule by popping a piece of candy in her mouth. She looked quickly back at her seatbelt. "There's a guy there—Bill Leaderman— got hit pretty hard by Fran in '96. Now he's used some new high-tech materials to make his house safer. I want to see this stuff in action. Near as I can tell, he's above the expected surge, so we should be safe. Assuming we get supremely lucky and Gert comes our way."

"Should be safe?" Jack said.

"Well, I mean, you never know exactly how high the surge will be. The Army Corps' SLOSH model..."

"SLOSH model?" asked Rico from the back seat.

"Sea, Lake, and Overland Surge from Hurricanes," Amanda said.

Jack spoke over his shoulder: "It's the model that predicts storm surges up and down the coast for various hurricane intensities, different scenarios."

"Yeah, that's what I thought it was," Rico lied.

Jack laughed at him.

"Anyway," Amanda continued, "the SLOSH takes into account the bathymetry, and wind speed, atmospheric pressure, all that, but it's got a wide enough margin of error to breed plenty of caution. But Hurricane Fran didn't get Leaderman's house, and Gert isn't gonna be any worse. The model says we'll have a couple feet to spare."

"You sure of that?"

"Of course not," Amanda said. "With a hurricane, the only thing we're ever sure of is our last measurements."

Jack looked at Rico in the rearview mirror. "You still want to do this, pal?"

Rico leaned forward, rested his chin on folded arms and

laughed nervously. "I'm livin' on the edge already, man. Left the cap off the toothpaste this morning. No stoppin' me now. Got to get *the shot*, push the envelope."

"Will be a little tough to get *the shot* in the dark," Jack said.

"Let's go home, then."

Amanda laughed, warm and musical and rolling. "You guys are *both* wimps."

Jack punched the gas and cut off a car trying to squeeze into the line of traffic.

***

By midday the sun was gone and the sky had lowered. A National Guardsman at the base of the bridge leading to Topsail Island stopped the car. An orderly river of evacuees flowed over the bridge in the other direction. Jack was surprised: The evacuation was going so well that the inbound lanes were still open.

"Gotta live here to get in," the trooper said politely, bayonet pointed at the sky. Jack flashed his press card. The guardsman flicked his eyebrows. "Good luck," he said, waving them on.

Jack gripped the steering wheel tightly and fought the gusty winds on the bridge. A thought had been on his mind since they'd left Myrtle Beach. "Hey Amanda. How come the official forecast is still Charleston and you're taking us to Topsail Island?"

Jack could feel Amanda staring at him. It seemed she'd been doing it quite a bit all the way up, but now it felt more intense. She took a moment to answer.

"Hunch," she said.

"Hunch? You're a hotshot hurricane specialist and you're picking landfall on a hunch? If Gert is going to hit Topsail Island, wouldn't it be a good idea to let the residents know?"

There was an edge to her voice, as though he'd pushed a button. "Forecasting is complicated," she said. "There's a half-dozen computer models we look at, then we add in our own experience, maybe a little intuition. The models are still saying Charleston, but we always try to make it clear that the place we pick is just the midpoint of a likely range of where the storm might come ashore."

"And so you get these hunches."

"Not strong enough to go public with, you know. The three of us are taking a chance with Topsail Island. See, another meteorologist is forecasting Gert today, and we don't always agree a hundred percent with each other. I see something slightly different in the data, but that's normal. That's why you see hurricane warnings from Savannah to the North Carolina/Virginia border."

"This got anything to do with the LORAX?" Jack asked.

He looked over at Amanda, caught her eyes averting his. A hesitation. Whatever she said next was calculated.

"The LORAX isn't operational," Amanda said. "You know we don't use non-op models for official forecasts."

"But you'll use it to make your own guess," Jack said.

"I didn't say that. Besides, the LORAX is down now."

"Why's that?"

"Non-operational models don't run real-time when there's a hurricane within thirty-six hours of landfall. Saves the computer's processing power for the operational models."

Jack smiled. He would have to find out how much the LORAX figured into Amanda's thinking. And how much it might have figured into the official forecast. If the Hurricane Center was using a new model in their forecasting suite, that was news.

CHAPTER 5

TOPSAIL ISLAND
12:15 P.M.

As they got out of the car in Bill Leaderman's driveway, Amanda looked over at Jack Corbin. The wind lifted his hair and blew it across his face. Amanda took a quick breath. Or, more accurately, Jack took it from her.

Since Joe Springer had deserted her three years ago, Amanda hadn't paid much attention to other men. She noticed them, but seldom did she take a second look. Life was too big, too busy, and the pain of being left was still too fresh. Now she found herself staring at Jack whenever she thought she could get away with it. It felt good. And it frightened her.

Bill Leaderman's house was perched atop a dune that was higher than the ones on either side. Amanda felt better. Though she'd checked the height of his house, she still had a knot in her stomach, as she always did when she chased a storm. But Leaderman's house looked comfortably above the surf, and the knot relaxed slightly.

Leaderman's thin brown hair was parted on the side and receding, so that his forehead seemed to protrude. He was average height, thin but muscular like one who does much physical labor. His manner was lazy, movements deliberate. He was out front loading bags into a minivan. Amanda said hello and introduced Jack and Rico.

"Packing up?" She asked Leaderman.

"Wife and kids." Bill Leaderman spoke slowly, too. "They want to get to the mainland. They remember Fran in '96 and they don't want to see another one."

Leaderman's wife came out the sliding door and walked down the long staircase followed by a boy and a girl both around the age of eleven. A black Labrador passed them on the stairs, made a beeline for Amanda and sniffed her shoes. Rico slipped away, surveying the house for angles to shoot from.

"And you?" Amanda asked Leaderman.

"Staying, like I told you. Gert doesn't sound any worse than Fran, and I've hurricane-proofed the house since then. Want to see how it does."

"When you have a minute, could you show us what you've done?"

"Sure. Just a couple more suitcases first." Amanda helped Leaderman with the bags, met his family in a brief and awkward moment, then waved goodbye.

"Coffee?"

"Yeah, thanks," Amanda said.

She studied the way the house sat atop a mound of sand that rose three feet higher than the other dunes. After Fran, she remembered, the surrounding dunes had been eroded to a vestige of what they were now, but they had been built back up.

Leaderman's dune was left relatively intact. All of the homes were built atop a grid of spindly pilings. Leaderman's first floor sat about four feet above the dune on this side and some ten feet on the beach side, a design meant to allow a surge to pass through the pilings and over the dune.

They walked into the kitchen, which opened directly into a large living room that faced the ocean. Two bedrooms and a bathroom were connected to the living room by a hallway to the left. Another bedroom sat at the end of a short hallway to the right.

Leaderman poured coffee and led them to the living room, through another patio door onto a large deck that, because of the angle of Amanda's view, seemed to hang right over the ocean. None of the windows, nor the large patio door, were boarded up.

The wind was stronger. A stray seagull hovered motionless in slanting spray over froth-covered waves. Brass wind chimes that hung from the eaves of the roof made a slow, unpatterned ting, ting, ting, giving voice to the silent wind. The dog paced the perimeter of the deck, brushing Amanda's legs on each loop, stopping finally along the front rail to bark at the wind.

Jack looked at the dog, puzzled.

"He feels the lowering air pressure," Amanda said. "Maybe smells things that come out of the earth as the reduced pressure opens the surface."

"Hmm," Jack said.

Leaderman was relaxed enough, as though the wind were a summer breeze making a hot day more pleasant. He pushed his limp hair aside, pointed lazily at the chimes. "Got to get those down," he said. "They'll drive me nuts."

"So," Amanda said. "The only damage you suffered from Fran was a few missing roof shingles, a broken window and a little rain damage?"

"And we lost the car to the surge. The water went right under the house, though, just like it's supposed to. In the old days, people walled in the area around the pilings, made garages, basements. Anybody with one of those lost it, and in some cases the force knocked the whole house over."

Amanda took a sip of her coffee, which the wind had already made cold. She stole a quick look at Jack, who was taking notes as Leaderman talked. She looked back to Leaderman. "And you've made some improvements."

"This house is storm proof now," Leaderman said. He stood, put his hands on his hips and looked up at the roof. "We were going to replace the damaged shingles, but the real problem, we found out, was underneath. See that gabled roof?" He pointed with a long, skinny finger up toward the wind chime. "If Fran's wind had been much stronger, it might have pushed on that wall and sucked the whole roof off. We also found out that the roof sheathing was attached to the trusses with short nails, which a good storm might just rip out. So we had a contractor come in and tear the shingles off, put new sheathing on, and fasten the roof trusses to the walls with hurricane straps. They're just metal strips they nail to the truss and to the studs in the walls. Then they squirted this foam stuff all around, a new high-tech adhesive called StormSeal 2000. It's a liquid that works its way into all the joints between the wood in the roof trusses, then expands into a foam that holds everything together. They say it's four times stronger than a roof with nails only. I can show it all to you."

"Good," Jack said. "Juan here will probably want to take some pictures, too." Rico had silently reappeared, was shooting Leaderman with his house in the background. Rico nodded. Jack asked Leaderman: "So you're not going to board up?"

"Don't have to. That's the other thing we did. Installed impact-resistant windows. Can't tell the difference, can you?"

"Look just like any other windows," Jack said.

Flying debris often shattered windows before the wind itself was strong enough to blow them out. Once that happened, the wind pushed against the walls and the roof from the inside. The wind outside lifted the roof, pulled at the rear wall, and then the walls collapsed or the roof lifted off.

"These windows were tested by the Dade County building inspector, where Andrew struck," Leaderman said. "They do a whole bunch of tests, but the one I like is that they throw a piece of two-by-four at the window at thirty-four miles an hour. If it doesn't break, it passes."

Leaderman smiled. He was pleased with the improvements to his home.

"All I really have left to do is put the furniture away. I learned that from Fran. She picked up a lawn chair from the neighbor's house and put it through our bedroom window. Our Hibachi crashed into the house across the street."

Jack stood and Amanda watched the wind kick his hair up.

It had increased in the short time they talked. The sea also was growing, and it moved and boiled like a living being, an angry monster heaving and falling with the cycle of waves.

Leaderman led them back inside.

"You all set with provisions?" Amanda asked.

"Got everything I need to last several days," Leaderman said, "so even if it's real bad, I'll be fine. I've got most of my supplies here." He opened a closet.

Amanda scanned the contents: jugs of water, canned foods, briquettes, hammer, nails, flashlights, batteries, fire extinguisher, dried fruits and nuts, rope, a folding hunting knife, first aid kit, sugar, flour, and rolls and rolls of toilet paper.

Leaderman went through a checklist of preparations as he wandered to the kitchen, pointing. "I've got a generator at the side of the house. Bottled water in the fridge. Cupboards are full of canned beans." He opened a cupboard. "And there's plenty of beer." He swung the fridge door open, revealing two cases of beer and several gallon jugs of water. "I'll turn the fridge way up later on and keep it closed, in case the power goes out."

***

Jack recoiled when the first drop hit his forehead. He stood on a point of land with a good view in both directions, watching a surfer a quarter mile down the beach who defied the evacuation—and common sense—for the ride of his life.

Juan Rico was having his third meal of the day, a late lunch with Bill Leaderman. But Amanda had wanted to be out in the wind, wanted to face the oncoming storm. She asked Jack to go for a walk.

He stood behind her, off her left shoulder. She had changed into khaki shorts and a white Lycra running top. Her legs, as promised, had the same slender muscularity as her arms. Amanda leaned into the wind, spread her arms wide like some antenna trying to communicate with the storm. The wind carried a mix of jasmine and something heavier, sexy, to his nostrils.

"Smell that?" she asked.

"Yeah. How'd you know?"

"Reduced air pressure allows for more rapid evaporation of the fragrance molecules. You're downwind."

"Didn't know," Jack said.

"Well?"

"Well what?"

"Do you like it?"

"Oh. Yeah. I do. Jasmine and…"

"Musk," she added.

"Nice." *That'll woo her, Jack. Way to pour on the charm.* He leaned into the wind, too, to keep his balance. He didn't feel as graceful as Amanda looked.

More drops hit them, large splattering drops. The last of the birds made their straggling retreat from the sea, flying low.

"They're struggling in the reduced buoyancy of lower atmospheric pressure," Amanda said.

Jack wondered if she always answered unasked questions. He thought about the birds. They probably knew which way to fly, where to escape. *They're smarter than I am. I come to face the storm. They fly away from it.*

"Flying to safety," Jack offered, wondering what was on Amanda's mind.

"Smart," she said. "Some of the them won't escape, though. They'll die. A few will end up in the eye, ride the storm out, maybe survive."

Sand was beginning to blow across the beach, a see-through carpet skating and skimming along the surface. The tide was supposed to be low, but there was no strip of dark, hard sand indicating it had gone out. The waves had grown to six or eight feet, and were closer together.

"I always think of the fish," Amanda said.

"What about them?"

"The storm messes with their world, too. Churning water pulls some of the deep-water fish up. They explode. Others that live on the surface get sucked out and become birds for a while. Sometimes they eat rocks to try and sink themselves. Bad swimmers, like shrimp, go wherever the currents decide."

Jack didn't want to think about what was going on underneath the angry surface.

It was starting to rain for real now. Soon the wind would get worse and it would seem like the water came from all sides. Each new sign of the storm took on ominous significance. This was a Category 3 hurricane, capable of destroying homes in a single gust, of producing a storm surge sixteen feet high. Only once before, during Andrew, had Jack been in the middle of a hurricane that strong, and he'd rode that one out in the relative safety of the Hurricane Center.

Jack had filed his story for the day, written about Bill Leaderman, the preparations on Topsail Island and how most residents had left. He would update it with whatever news he could include by deadline. There was nothing to do but wait.

Jack didn't feel ready for the danger they were about to face. Gert might weaken unexpectedly. She might turn and go out to sea. She might pound Charleston and dispatch only remnant puffs of hurricane-force winds this far north. Or she might strengthen unexpectedly and pummel Topsail Island with a vengeance nobody expected. Jack knew anything was possible. He couldn't stand to leave the topic untouched. Nobody was that brave.

"Hope we guessed right," he said.

Amanda squinted in the wind, her eyes watering, the rain streaking her hair flat against her head. She pulled her arms in, still faced the wind. "We're stuck here now. Bridge is closed to all traffic, so it doesn't much matter."

"It's a *fucking* island," Jack said. He was soaked now. Wet clothes clinging. "I hate islands."

Amanda turned and faced Jack. Water ran down her face. She might've just stepped out of a shower. At the lower edge of his vision he could see the Lycra top was not designed to work alone when wet. He was afraid to look down overtly, feeling privy to a look many men would treasure but few probably got.

"It's a *barrier* island," Amanda said.

"Sorry. What's the difference?"

"Barrier doesn't sound so *fucking* crude."

They exchanged a smile. Jack would have to work on his language. Hanging around Juan Rico too much. New York street talk wasn't going to win over Amanda Cole. Though she made it clear she could dish it out, too.

"We'll be OK," Amanda said. "Just a little wind and a little water."

"A little wind," Jack mumbled under his breath. Then he said, "You know, we're an egotistical bunch, us humans. We pave a road and build all these houses and we think we own the island."

"Humans always take risks for beauty," she said. "It's our nature."

"Bill Leaderman thinks he owns this island," Jack said. "Thinks a few hurricane straps and some sticky foam is going to save him."

"Save *us,* you mean."

"What?" The wind made it hard to hear from just a few feet away.

"Save *us,* " she said louder.

"Fuc … Damn *hurricane* straps. What are we doing here, anyway?"

"You wanted to come here, Jack. You wanted to see nature at its most beautiful. You're scared. It's OK. That's a healthy emotion right now."

Jack felt pulled in two directions. He *had* wanted to come here, but now he wished he wasn't here. For the first time all day, Amanda's brown eyes—usually flitting and curious—settled, and they settled on Jack. It calmed him.

"Damn right I'm scared," he admitted. "Barrier fucking island. Hurricane straps. What if the sea just decides to swallow us tonight? What good are those straps then?"

"The sea owns this island," Amanda said calmly. "She can claim it whenever she wants. Doesn't think about you or me.

Never has cared that humans dared to live on her island. She goes where she wants to, when she needs to. That's part of the beauty. But this isn't the storm that's going to take the island."

"But you admit that it's a helluva risk," Jack said. He let his eyes drift down. The Lycra top was soaked, clung to her breasts and hid little. He looked too long, and she noticed.

She smiled, no anger in the eyes that still stared into his. She moved a step forward, touched his elbow. Jack remembered 1992, wished she would curl her fingers into his again. She lowered her voice: "Humans always take risks for beauty."

Her smile caused her to squint, narrow lines racing back from the corners of her eyes. It was a smile he recognized from long ago. For a moment, Jack forgot about the storm. She moved her hand slowly from his elbow, down his arm to his hand, squeezed lightly and let go. She nodded her head toward Bill Leaderman's house, ran off like a little girl heading to a picnic. Amanda Cole had other things on her mind.

Jack turned to watch the surfer, trying to draw some courage from him. He scanned the waves and saw nothing but dark water and brown and white froth, wondered if the sea had swallowed the surfer. Just as he was about to turn away, he saw him, pushing forward on his board atop a towering wave, seeming—from this distance—to have no fear. Jack mucked through the sand toward the house. Amanda still ran, fighting the wind and proving she was in as good a shape as she looked.

***

In the waning hours of daylight, the sea became a raging animal, throwing wave upon growing wave against the shore and rising almost visibly by the moment, as if pushed up from underneath. Amanda, Jack and Juan Rico sat with Bill Leaderman in his living room flipping back and forth between CNN and the Weather Channel. Both gave near-continuous coverage of the storm and had just reported the latest information from the Hurricane Center. The dog had grown progressively more nervous and was barking at the gusts of wind that shook the house. The wind chimes clanged together rapidly, making an insanely frantic ting-ting-ting.

"Forgot to take them down," Leaderman said.

The center of the storm was a hundred miles offshore, but Amanda didn't need the CNN reporter to tell her Gert was heading this way. She needed only peer through the impact-resistant window at the darkening sky and the violent sea to know that hurricane-force winds had arrived. The storm had turned north, veering away from Charleston and bearing down on Topsail Island. Just as Amanda had expected. But what she hadn't expected was for Gert to gain strength and pick up speed.

Amanda fired up her laptop, downloaded the latest readings.

"Central pressure at 948," she said. "Eye is still shrinking—she's organizing herself even more, like an army preparing for an offensive. Sustained winds of 115, same as Fran at landfall."

Amanda typed a command to access the current GFDL forecast, the Hurricane Center's primary forecasting tool. The message that appeared on her screen stunned her.

```
Document contains no data.
```

"Holy—"

"What?" Jack asked.

Amanda ignored him. Something was wrong. She went back to the data page, then tried again to access the forecast and got the same message. Never in her ten years as a hurricane specialist had she seen that message. It was not a message served up by her computer. It would have to have been delivered by the main computer where the GFDL program ran, and it was delivered because the computer could not find the crunched data it was looking for to return a graphic representation of the current forecast. It meant the GFDL program was down. She didn't want to think of the consequences, nor did she want to mention the problem to a reporter.

She returned to the data page and continued discussing the storm. "Gert's moving north-northwest at twenty. That's fast for this latitude. We're kinda screwed, guys."

"Same strength as Fran," Leaderman said. "Nothing this house can't handle."

"Fran's forward speed was sixteen miles an hour," Amanda said. "Gert's blazing along at twenty. That makes the winds on the right side another four miles an hour stronger. And it's obvious the models missed this strengthening." She looked at Jack. "*All* the models. Thing is, it's still over warm water, could get even stronger."

Amanda looked back at her computer screen. One more time she tried to pull up the GFDL forecast. This time her request returned the document, and the green line was pointing right at them.

What the hell was that blip? Amanda couldn't answer that question from where she sat. She'd ask Frank Delaney about it in the morning. For now, the GFDL was running and the Hurricane Center would know where the storm was going. She let out a small sigh of tension and sat back in her chair.

The dog was restless, yipping at intervals. Rico sat quiet in a chair, fiddling with his camera. Amanda watched Jack pace the room and run the fingers of one hand through his hair. She loved the hair.

She loved a lot about Jack Corbin. She'd caught herself staring at him several times already. She loved that he was a tough reporter, passionate about hurricanes and fiery in his desire to tell a story, but he still maintained an awkward politeness, a respect for others. A respect for Amanda and her abilities as a scientist. Maybe that was part of the attraction. And, unlike a lot of men, Jack didn't try to hide his fear. She liked that, too. Amanda imagined running her own fingers through his hair. She closed her eyes and took a deep breath.

The sounds outside snapped her mind back to the problem at hand. She looked across the living room and out the window, her arms folded as though she were cold. "It's not the wind I'm worried about. It's that ocean right there." She pointed with her head. "If Gert gets any stronger and we get hit by the right-side eyewall, the surge is going to be like nothing you've ever seen. Like nothing you want to see."

The four of them wandered over to the large window facing east to take a last look at the waves before darkness enveloped them. A steady rain pounded the glass at an angle. The sun would be just setting, but Amanda could see her reflection in the window, undulating with the wind and looking like a funhouse mirror. She refocused her eyes on the tall waves, which were rushed and unfocused—*like Sarah when she's full of energy*—wasting no time or power on grace, crashing straight down with a force that drove them into the sand, carving away at the beach and pulling it out to sea. They were ugly waves.

"Not exactly like *Hawaii Five-0,* is it?" Rico said.

A strong gust buffeted the house. Amanda's ears popped. The dog barked. The sky lit up as though with a thousand stadium lights and the outlines of the clouds were illuminated and a wave appeared to hang frozen at its apex. The light was gone, replaced by a dull gray. The wave thundered into the sand.

"Let's hope she doesn't want the whole island tonight," Amanda said.

She glanced at Jack. She was angry with herself for getting him into this mess. She was feeling like a love-struck teenager again and she wanted to tell him so right now. He was looking at her, too. Time seemed to hang in the air like the wave that had been frozen by the flash of lightning.

Jack spoke first: "You're scared, too."

"Damn right I'm scared," Amanda said.

"It's OK," Jack said. "That's a healthy emotion right now."

***

At a quarter past ten the first wave crawled up and tickled the pilings under Bill Leaderman's house. Amanda knew what it was because the vibration was different, more subtle and steady than that produced by the wind. They were sitting at a table in a corner of living room, near the kitchen. Rico and Leaderman were playing a game of gin rummy. Jack had just filed a few descriptive paragraphs to add to his story. It was past deadline now, he'd said, except for the metro editions, and there wasn't much left for him to do.

"Fuckin' things always have to hit at night," Rico said. He'd finally given up taking pictures. His Nikon, which had hung around his neck since early morning, was on the counter between the kitchen and living room.

"When's high tide?" Amanda asked.

"Pretty soon..." Leaderman said.

"I know. But exactly when?"

Leaderman got a tide book from a drawer in the kitchen and studied it. "11:25," he said.

Amanda shook her head. "The worst of Gert gets here between eleven and midnight. Jeez."

Another wave hit the pilings, this time with more of a crash. The house shook. "This is how it felt during Fran," Leaderman said. "The house shakes because the pilings are so tall. They actually absorb the waves' energy."

"Oh, that makes me feel better," Rico said.

Amanda and Jack said nothing. Even Leaderman was looking less sure. They sat in near-silence for twenty minutes as the waves rushed under the house with increasing frequency and pockets of lightning came and went in violent spurts.

Another thunderstorm was upon them, appearing suddenly out of the darkness. The flashes were close and frequent, the squall coming and ending quickly, followed moments later by another charged cell carried landward on the flailing octopus arms of the rotating storm.

She walked cautiously to the window, wanting to take advantage of the light to gauge the height of the sea, just beyond Bill Leaderman's deck. A white bolt zagged into the waves. The clap of thunder was instant and piercing, base drums and cymbals and a thousand creepy, out-of-harmony violins. Amanda jumped reflexively from the window. But in the instant of that flash she saw it, just offshore, heading dead toward them. The long thin straw that danced from the mouth of the clouds was unmistakable.

"Jesus fuck," said Rico. "Tornado?"

"Water spout," Amanda said.

"What's the difference?" Jack asked.

"Not much if it hits us," She said. "Except that instead of pelting us with bricks and other debris like a tornado, we'll probably be slapped with fish. Either way the wind can rip the roof off a place."

The four of them stood and stared, like deer in the headlights as back-to-back lightning acted as floodlights. The funnel danced and pulsed and jerked like a lithe and wriggling woman in a long thin dress, her hidden feet sliding smoothly left and right, the tapered dress sinuously keeping an unexpected beat at the hips, a mushrooming torso with a curvaceous, roiling bust anchoring her to the clouds. She was full of water, Amanda knew, drawing it from the sea and feeding it into her mother storm.

It was an intoxicating dance that coaxed the surface of the sea upward.

The sky glowed a phosphorescent green. The wind picked up in advance of the waterspout, blew from every direction, even from underneath the groaning house. Rainwater ran upward on the window, then made a 90-degree turn and skidded sideways. Amanda shifted her focus from the raindrops back to the waterspout, stood motionless as if under the spell of the dance.

The dog's bark had turned to a hoarse yip and was steady and rhythmic. It was Rico that broke the trance with the simple but obvious question. "Whatta we do?"

Amanda blinked. She'd forgotten to look at the sea itself. The tops of the waves appeared nearly level with the deck. They weren't supposed to be this high. But that was not the immediate problem.

"Away from the window." She said it calmly. There was

beauty in the power of the storm, a power that exceeded her ability to comprehend, a power that was pure and raw, that painted the sky green, controlled the movements of the sea, danced with it. The beauty awed her, transported her emotions beyond the mere fight-or-flight sensation and somehow settled raw nerves.

"There's no window in the bathroom," Leaderman said, running the words together in a barely intelligible jumble and seeming to question, for the first time, the sturdiness of his home's construction.

The lights went out. "Go," Amanda shouted, guiding the other three with her hands toward the bathroom.

"The dog!" Leaderman said. She was running in circles, whining, jumping into the air and making half turns, bark-bark-bark, but she would not follow them into the bathroom.

"Screw the dog!" Amanda said, shoving the three men through the hallway.

"Jesus fuck," Rico said. "My Nikon." He turned back toward the living room. "No!" shouted Amanda. She lunged for him and her fingers brushed the back of his shirt. Juan Rico was around the corner and into the living room. Amanda, knowing she had only seconds, herded Bill Leaderman and Jack Corbin into the bathroom. "The bathtub!"

Leaderman pulled a flashlight from his pocket, pointed it at the tub "It's sturdy, in case the roof falls in," Amanda cried. "Now!"

A roar approached. She couldn't go after Rico now. She closed the bathroom door. Leaderman climbed into the tub. Jack and Amanda curled up on the floor next to it.

Jack lay behind Amanda, put an arm over her shoulder. She allowed the shiver of delight to run through her for an instant, then lost the sensation to the increasing hiss of the approaching waterspout. She rested her hot cheek on the cool tile, curled one arm over her head, and closed her eyes. She saw the image of the waterspout in her mind, then she saw her fingers reaching for Juan Rico. Damn him. Damn damn damn.

Then Amanda pulled images of Sarah into her mind and

could see nothing else. There was nothing she could do now, and a different kind of shiver, a frigid fear, swept through her. Ear pressed to the floor, Amanda could hear the waves underneath as they slashed against the pilings.

"Over the sea," she said out loud. "Over water. Middle of the storm. Water. Tornado is coming. Over the sea. Over the sea. I'm not as scared as I should be." She smiled in the darkness at the rhyme, and began repeating it, held the image of Sarah's face. She imagined herself telling Sarah about this night, about the rhyme and how calming it was, how peaceful.

It might as well have been a tin roof. Amanda heard the ripping shingles, the splintering of wood, the giant *whumpf* as roof and air and God knows what else was sucked upward. The sounds came together as, with one horrendous motion, the waterspout ignored the StormSeal 2000 and the hurricane straps, and lifted shingles, plywood sheathing, trusses, beams and struts into the clouds.

Amanda couldn't hear her own screams. She rolled over on her back and looked in the total darkness toward the door. In an instant it flashed through her mind that if she could not see the destruction … then the portion of the roof directly above her had remained intact. She heard the rain pounding down now on the carpet just outside the bathroom.

A second later the bathroom door was sucked off its hinges and out into the living room and up into the sky. Amanda was pulled across the tile floor. In the constant flashes she could see into the living room and out into the whirling curtain of water and debris.

Her feet hit the doorjambs and the wind pulled her upright. She grabbed the molding across the top of the opening, a stretch, and braced herself with all her strength. Something crashed into her from behind, forcing her chest out into the hallway. She could see Juan Rico's face in her mind's eye, superimposed on the wall of the tornado, then it whirled quickly into a disappearing blur. "No!" she screamed at Gert. "N*ooooo!*"

As quickly as it came the vacuum let up and she relaxed and

looked behind her to see Jack and Leaderman fall to the floor.

"Fuck," she heard Jack say faintly, though she assumed it was a yell. Jack was OK.

She thought again of Rico. She ran into the open living room and was nearly swept off her feet by the weaker but still dangerous vacuum created by the hurricane's winds as they raked over the open house. Down the short hallway on the other side, a portion of the roof remained. Near-constant lightning lit the night like a disco strobe. She looked for Rico. Couldn't see him. She dropped to the floor and crawled to the counter. The Nikon was gone. She glanced around. No sign of the dog. She pulled her body down flat against the floor, rolled onto her back and, covering her face, peeked up between fingers at where the roof used to be. The sky was an open faucet, the wind visible for all the small debris, shreds of seaweed and small fish it carried through the sky. Large raindrops pelted her bare hands and face like rocks, so she rolled back over and crawled again.

Amanda made her way back to the bathroom. Jack was huddled in the far corner next to the toilet, his arms clutching his knees to his chest, rocking back and forth and saying "fuck fuck fuck" nonstop. Leaderman lay unconscious on the tile.

Amanda couldn't know the track of the storm now. It might have veered one way or another, in which case they may have just seen the worst of it. Or the eyewall might still be bearing down on them. Amanda didn't want any more surprises, decided to assume the worst was yet to come. She tried to check Leaderman's neck for a pulse, but could not feel such a delicate motion amidst the ambient vibrations and thuds and gusts, so she put her hand on the man's chest. It rose and fell.

"Hang on," Amanda shouted to the unconscious man. "Just hang on! There's not a thing I can do for you. Don't freaking die, OK?"

She crawled over and leaned into Jack and held him.

"...fuck fuck fuck."

"She doesn't want the island tonight, Jack. Not tonight."

They rocked back and forth together. "C'mon, you've got a story to write."

"...fuck fuck fuck."

CHAPTER 6

NEAR THE CANAL STREET
SUBWAY STATION,
MANHATTAN
10:55 P.M.

Sweat poured from the large man's forehead as he made his way along the abandoned tunnel, his six-year-old son in tow. His left eye twitched, reminding him of the scar that ran from the corner of his eye, across his cheek. A reminder of the night he killed the intruder. The injury made his left eye droop as if it were not quite awake. The underground population—the mole people as they were known—had come to call the large man Sleepy, a name he didn't mind. He had never been proud of his given name anyway.

Sleepy and his son walked along the abandoned tunnel and crawled into the main, active tunnel through the small hole. A vague shadow crossed his path; he shuffled his foot and sent the cockroach scurrying into the darkness.

Sleepy's stomach grumbled. They were off in search of food. He looked down at his son with a mixture of pride and sadness. Jonathan had his mother's brown hair, short and erratic. He was stringy and agile, curious and polite.

Sleepy wanted to give his boy a better life, but to do that he needed to live above ground. He dreamed of finding a way out, of going to college, becoming a social worker, and returning to help other people underground.

A loud scream echoed through the tunnel. Among the untold hundreds who lived underground, there was plenty of crime and trouble. This close to the place they called home it might be someone he knew. A train would be coming from the south soon. He hesitated, then grabbed Jonathan's hand and turned to investigate.

The tunnel was dimly lit by evenly spaced bare white bulbs, the light absorbed into dull, dirty walls and glinting sharply off the polished tops of the rails. The tunnel was squat and dreary, dripping water from the ceiling.

Shouts echoed from around a bend. Sleepy crouched and moved against the wall, pulled Jonathan into the shadow behind him. His left eye began to twitch.

The tunnel straightened out. Two men faced one another twenty yards away.

Sleepy backed into the shadows. He motioned to Jonathan to stay quiet.

The smaller person, a hunched-over old man Sleepy recognized as a local loner and occasional drug dealer, had his back against the wall. The taller one had the nervous stance of a cat out of doors. The taller man shifted his weight, looked around at intervals and kept pointing his finger into the small man's chest. From his belt hung a large framing hammer.

Though Sleepy had never seen the tall one, he was certain he was Hammer, the only man Sleepy both hated and feared. He hated Hammer because he was a drug dealer who'd ruined the lives of hundreds of people, probably including Jonathan's mother. He feared Hammer because the man was ruthless and power hungry, a dangerous combination in a lawless world. Hammer controlled a large group of men who pushed drugs for him. Word was out that Hammer was expanding his territory, looking for new underground outposts and enlisting anyone he could find to deal for him. This was the closest

Hammer had ever been to Sleepy's own underground home.

Hammer's shoulder-length hair was erratic and dirty. He had broad shoulders but did not look particularly strong. Behind him stood two ragged men.

"...cut your goddamn foot off if you don't tell me where the fuck it is!"

"I told you," the small old man pleaded, shrinking against the wall, "they took it."

"Who the fuck took it?" Hammer boomed in a nasal voice. "Who?"

"I didn't know them. They jumped me and they took it. There were three kids."

Hammer closed in. "You had a grand of heroin, old man. It was mine. It's gone, and I want the money."

"But they took it," the man whimpered.

Hammer backed up, raised an arm and snapped his fingers. Sleepy stared in horror as one of the other men moved forward and hefted an ax into the air. The old man groaned pitifully.

"It'll be only your foot, old man, if you cooperate. Squirm and you might lose your leg."

"No!" cried the old man.

Sleepy got a view of Hammer. His eyes locked on the grotesque face, deeply pitted with acne scars and set in a permanent scowl. His eyes were too close together. His fat nose had been broken and squashed against his face like a mushroom, making his eyes appear more crowded. Thin lips accentuated the fat nose.

The man with the ax moved forward. The other one wrestled the old man to the ground. Sleepy heard the rush of wind and the rumble and screech of steel on steel as a train pulled into the station behind them.

"Put your foot on the track," Hammer ordered.

The man continued to resist, but he was losing strength. He coughed, then began to cry, a pitiful wail that echoed in the stillness before the train started again. He kicked his legs as the man with the ax moved into position, straddling the track.

Sometimes it was too much for Sleepy to believe the things that went on down here. The outside world had no idea. The police worked hard to deny the extent of the problem. Social workers refused to enter the dark world. But here it was, life at its worst, right in front of him. The doors of the subway cars closed.

"It will be your whole leg, maybe both of them," Hammer said calmly, "if you don't put your foot on the rail."

The man resisted.

"Now!" Hammer's towering voice echoed through the tunnel.

Sleepy could see the man deflate, his energy depleted. The crying turned to a whimper. Slowly the old man pushed his left leg out and rested his foot on the rail, pulled his head into his shoulders, stuffed his fists into his eyes.

Sleepy wanted to plug his own ears, but he still held his hands over Jonathan's.

His mind flicked to the violence of his own childhood.

***

Sleepy might have endured the occasional beatings from his father, but the fact that his older brother joined in made a difficult childhood unbearable. His brother was heavier and got laughed at in school. He took his resentment out on Sleepy. Once he broke Sleepy's arm. Several times he bloodied his nose. Sleepy's hate for his brother grew until he was sixteen, when he became taller and more muscular. He never hit back, but the beatings stopped. Sleepy left the house for good and hit the streets. Before he left, he cornered his brother, pinned him against a wall and held a forearm to his throat. Sleepy swore that one day he would find him and ruin him. He waited until he was certain he saw cold fear in his brother's eyes, then he released his hold and walked out the door.

***

The ax crashed down with a crunch and a clink. The sound made Sleepy's ears ring. The man screeched with pain, and he heard that too. He hummed to himself to try and drown out the man's screams and to calm his nerves. But he could not tear his eyes from the four men. Blood spurted from the leg, severed at the ankle. The foot, wearing a dirty, frazzled sneaker, lay between the tracks. Sleepy's knees were rubbery and his mouth dry. He still held Jonathan's ears.

One of the men picked up the victim by the armpits and laid him across the tracks.

Hammer and the others laughed, then disappeared into an adjoining tunnel.

Sleepy couldn't help him. The train was too close and would kill them both. He wished he had not witnessed the nightmare at all. But it would have happened whether he was here or not, he realized, and a new feeling came over him: This new view of his enemy would fuel his actions if push came to shove. He had witnessed evil. He could not understand it, but he could fight it. One thing he'd learned underground: You couldn't run. There was another Hammer around every turn. The only thing to do was fight. Another thing he understood was that he was outnumbered, living with just Jonathan and one other friend. He would need a plan, soon.

The train was nearly upon them. Sleepy turned quietly and pulled Jonathan into a small recess in the wall, knowing he would do anything to protect his son.

CHAPTER 7

TOPSAIL ISLAND
11:50 P.M.

Time was no longer relevant. Forecasts meant nothing. The National Hurricane Center had missed this one. Even the LORAX hadn't called the last-minute strengthening. Living was all Amanda Cole could focus on. She, Jack Corbin and Bill Leaderman had spent what seemed an eternity in the bathroom of a nearly destroyed house that was now sitting *in* the Atlantic Ocean while things had gotten worse. She didn't know where Juan Rico was. The lightning had stopped for now, but the wind was stronger and the sea would be rising. Rain ignored the small portion of roof over the bathroom, slanted in through the doorway. The walls around them were groaning as each wave hit the pilings. They were soaked, cold and shivering.

It felt good to hold Jack. At first she did it for his comfort. As he calmed down, Amanda removed her arm from around Jack's shoulder, but now Jack had his arm around her. He was the first man to hold her in what seemed like ages. They leaned against the wall between the toilet and sink, the unconscious Bill Leaderman between their feet and the tub. She could barely make him out in the darkness.

But the more she did nothing the more Amanda became

terrified of the storm, felt desperation setting in. She clutched Jack's waist.

The roar made talking almost impossible, but Amanda felt she was holding the last person she might ever hold, and a question had been in the back of her mind all day that she suddenly wanted an answer to.

She shouted in his ear: "You have anybody?"

Jack frowned, puzzled. Then understood. Shook his head no. "You?"

"Sarah, my daughter. With her father right now."

"Your husband?"

"Ex. Joe Springer."

Jack nodded: "Springer. Cole."

"Never changed it."

"Good for you," he said. His hand squeezed her shoulder.

Amanda held tighter. She wanted Jack Corbin to meet Sarah. But she couldn't arrange that right now, and she needed to do something, chase the fear instead of letting it chase her. "Take a look around?"

Jack nodded yes.

"Wait here."

Jack ignored her and followed as she crawled into the hall and opened the closet, found a coil of rope and the large, folding hunting knife. They crawled back to the bathroom. She cut one short length and tied it to the plumbing under the sink, then gave the other end to Jack.

"Around Leaderman's waist," Amanda shouted. "I don't want him going anywhere." She tied the longer piece to the plumbing, dropped the coil at her feet and tied the other end around her own waist, leaving about eight feet. That she gave to Jack, who wrapped it around himself and tied it off. Amanda put the knife in the pocket of her shorts.

Bound together, they crawled onto the soaked carpet, through the living room.

She wanted to check the bedroom down the other hall, across the living room, where a portion of roof remained, but the rope wasn't long enough. They crawled to the kitchen. The

63

sliding door was jammed. It had rainwater on both sides, and Amanda couldn't see through it in the pitch-black night.

"Bust it out?" Jack said.

Amanda wanted to break something. She wanted to throw things at the storm, fight back, bust the window and throw pieces of glass at Gert and tell her that she hated her. "Not broken yet," she said. "We're not going to be able to break it. Hold onto me."

She stood up carefully in the driving wind. Jack stayed on his knees and put his arms around Amanda's waist. On the third try she forced the door open wide enough to slide through. Jack pulled to keep her from flying through the door. Amanda lowered herself and crawled through. Jack followed.

Out on the deck there was just enough light to see a few feet. Amanda looked down the remaining stairs that led not into the front drive but into the ocean. There were three stairs, then six, then nine, then three. The dune was an island one second, an underwater berm the next as waves topped it with rapid succession.

They were surrounded by water.

The wind had worked itself into a fever pitch. Shrimp and seaweed rained down on them. Amanda pointed back to the house, and they slipped through the door. The rain was the same on the inside. A dead bird slapped against Amanda's forehead. They crawled into the living room. A flash of lightning lit the sky and Amanda saw the wall of water through the living room window. Without thinking, she grabbed Jack and pulled him into the bathroom just as the wave thudded into the side of the house.

There was that cacophonous mix of thundering water and splintering wood, that instantaneous moment when Amanda's mind recognized what was happening, and then all went dark as the wave pounded through Bill Leaderman's house, knocked the front wall down, lifted the floor from the foundation and shoved it toward the street.

When Amanda finally floated to the surface she gasped for breath, then was sucked immediately downward, banged every which way by walls and pieces of lumber. The sea was ice cold. She felt the rope wrapped around her leg, grabbed it and pulled. She bumped into a body, assumed it was Jack. She was running out of air, trying to think. The rope tugged against her, then it went slack and unwrapped itself from around her leg. Something solid and heavy slammed into her cheek.

Amanda felt the rope go tight around her waist, pulling her down. She fished into her pocket and found the knife. With her left hand she found both sections of the rope. One was taut, which would pull her downward to her death, the other end loose. She did not know which piece led to Jack. Instinct told her to slice the taut rope. It took two passes, and the rope was cut. So was her leg, she thought, though it was hard to tell in the cold and she did not care anyway. She floated up. Then the other rope went tight. She was out of oxygen. "Hate you," she said underwater as another vital bubble of air left her lungs and slipped out of her mouth.

Nothing flashed before Amanda's eyes, open eyes that felt the burning seawater in the darkness. A flash of lightning illuminated the world above and through the agitated froth she saw a dark, geometric shadow. Her hand broke the surface, grabbed the object. She pulled on it and her head rose into the rain next to a floating, tattered section of wall. She took two deep breaths and pulled on the rope that was still trying to drag her down. A second later Jack appeared and breathed desperately. A wave overwashed them both and Amanda gripped the wall with one hand, Jack with the other and they struggled to breathe again.

Amanda climbed onto the section of wall, which pitched in the waves, and she tried to pull Jack up. The wind knocked her over, would have blown her off if she weren't anchored to Jack, partially submerged. She braced her feet and pulled until Jack was out of the water. They were still moving, surfing in a darkness that would not allow them to see the edges of the slab. They lay spread eagle, the wind whipping their backs, showering them with debris, driving splinters of wood into their sides and threatening to cast them into the sea again.

The rain came in a vast curtain that splashed off the wall and made breathing difficult. What might have been a chair crashed down next to Amanda, then splashed into the darkness. A fish slapped alongside her head and was gone. Her hands were bloodied, her cheek throbbed, and she hadn't even looked at her leg yet.

"You OK?" Amanda shouted. Jack nodded once, weakly.

The wall stopped suddenly and threw them into the water. She clung to the edge. Her legs dangled into the water. She felt Jack's arms around her neck. The chilly sea seeped into her bones. She knew she could not hold on for long.

The eye. The eye. I went through this and I don't even get to see the damned eye.

Amanda didn't need any numbers, or any graphics out of a computer, to tell her that she was smack in the middle of the powerful right-side eyewall. If they could just hang on until it passed, the wind would drop by an amount equivalent to the storm's forward speed. She held Jack. The waves thrashed them for several minutes. It seemed longer.

Suddenly Amanda felt sand under her feet, but she was pulled away again. Again she felt the sand. The surge was dropping. Soon the water would be rushing the other direction, back out to sea. Amanda could see that they had been swept across the street and were tangled in the pilings of another destroyed house.

In the distance, emerging from the water and resting atop submerged pilings, was a six-foot by twelve-foot section of floor, all that remained of Bill Leaderman's hurricane-proof home. There was no sign of Leaderman or Rico.

The place they crashed into was no more than a few wall sections piled atop one another. Between the two former homes was the road, several feet down. Amanda raised her head and shouted into the eye of the storm, "Damn you, Gert! You can't take us! We beat you! Ha!"

She knew it was a lie. Gert had taken Juan Rico and Bill Leaderman. The wind had lessened only slightly and would be around for hours. The waves were still dangerous. Fear, anger and sadness overwhelmed her and her head slumped into the cold water.

I won't drown.

She labored onto a ruined section of floor. "C'mon. We've got to get out of the water." She pulled Jack up and tied the loose end of the rope off to a wall stud that protruded from the floor.

Jack lay on his chest, sprawled like a crime-scene chalk figure, conscious but quiet in the noisy night, deep breaths noted by a rising back. She put a hand between his shoulder blades, rubbed gently.

Amanda scanned into the darkness for any sign of Rico. Nothing. Wooden furniture and other floatable household items crashed in the waves, pausing and searching for a direction as the surge rested before its soon-to-come retreat. Sections of wall. A dark shape, round. Moving across her field of vision in what had been the street.

"Juan!" she shouted. The shape disappeared.

Nothing. Reappeared. Still moving. A splash amid a thousand splashes, then another.

"Juan!"

The shape turned, a scant-light reflection. A face. Began moving toward her.

Juan Rico stuck a tired hand out through the froth, Amanda pulled on it. Rico wasn't much help, his other arm hanging limp. She finally got him up on the small piece of floor. The Nikon hung around his neck.

"Other bedroom," Rico shouted. "Jesus fuck."

Amanda pulled Rico into her and made a pile of three terrified humans with their backs to the storm.

"Arm's broken," Rico shouted through chattering teeth. "It almost over?"

"No," Amanda said.

"Jeeee-sus fuck."

~ ~ ~

EXCERPTED FROM
HURRICANES: HISTORY AND DYNAMICS,
BY DR. NICHOLAS K. GRAY,
HUMBOLDT UNIVERSITY PRESS (1998)

In 1941, George R. Stewart published the novel *Storm,* about a tremendous low-pressure system that moved in off the Pacific and did significant damage in the United States. A character in the book, a San Francisco meteorologist, deduced it was easier to name such a storm than to refer to it as a low-pressure system. He also reasoned that a storm so powerful and destructive *deserved* a name, something that up until then only happened after the fact. So the forecaster in Stewart's book called the storm *Maria.* The book was popular among meteorologists, and the idea took hold with military weather forecasters during WWII, when storms began to get women's names.

In 1950 the World Meteorological Organization agreed to an alphabetical naming system, using the military's radio code. The first named Atlantic hurricane was Able in 1950. That year, there were twelve tropical storms, three of which developed into full-blown hurricanes. The last earned the ironic name of Hurricane Love.

Soon officials realized the naming convention would cause problems in the history books if more than one powerful Hurricane Able made landfall. So, in 1953 the organization adopted a rotating series of women's names, planning to retire names of significant storms. Feminists urged the WMO to add men's names, which was done in 1979. The boy-girl-boy-girl naming convention evolved to include French and Spanish names, reflecting the languages of the nations affected by Caribbean hurricanes. Twenty-one names are reserved each year (the letters q, u, x, y and z are not used, a residual consequence of the days when only English names were used). The names are recycled every six years, minus those retired. There will never be another Andrew, or another Hugo.

~ ~ ~

TUESDAY, AUGUST 24

CHAPTER 8

POINT PLEASANT BEACH, NEW JERSEY 12:20 P.M.

"**D**on't bump your head."

Sarah giggled and ducked as Joe Springer bent his knees and slipped through the sliding glass door onto the deck.

With Sarah on his shoulders, Joe stepped carefully down the short flight of wooden stairs onto the narrow sand pathway between his house and the next. He doubled back and walked immediately up a slightly shorter set of stairs onto the boardwalk that stretched for hundreds of yards in either direction. A warm breeze blew out to sea, slapping the tops off large waves that rolled in from thousands of miles away. Against a pale blue sky, thin fuzzy clouds meandered harmlessly, far-flung signatures of yet another hurricane that didn't come this way.

Joe Springer bounced his daughter atop his shoulders. "Where to, kiddo?"

"To the beach," Sarah shouted, pointing at the waves with one hand, using the other to slap the shoulder of her horse.

"OK, but I told you we can't swim today."

"Can we at least put our feet in?"

"We'll see. But you'll have to walk, OK?"

"No," Sarah said firmly.

"I can't carry you all that way."

"But *Daddy.*"

She's got her father's stubbornness, he thought. *I hope she has her mother's brains.* He might have made her walk, but Joe Springer had so little time with his daughter anymore that it was unbearable to disappoint her. He looked at the 200-foot stretch of creamy sand between the boardwalk and the waves, took a deep breath, and trudged off.

Instead of a steep slope, the beach was fairly flat until a sharp dive into the surf. All but the tops of the waves were hidden from view until they neared the drop-off. The recent high tide had topped the crest, leaving a pool of ankle-deep warm water behind it. They splashed through it, then Joe bent forward to let Sarah slide off her horse onto warm, wet sand.

Sarah tugged at her bathing suit, stretching it as much as she could. They'd bought it last evening on the boardwalk, and though her father said it was too small for her, Sarah had insisted on buying the only two-piece pink swimsuit they could find in the tiny shop. Now she was pulling at it, pretending that it fit.

Joe looked at the steep drop-off. The large waves spawned by Gert had carved into the embankment, making it even more pronounced. Another wave rolled in, hesitated, then thundered into the bank and carried more sand out to sea.

"Can we go in Daddy?" She tugged at his shirt.

"No way, kiddo. It'd suck you right out. You see how big those waves are?" Joe pointed. Sarah frowned. She looked down at her feet, wriggled them into the sand. "Will you bury me?"

"Sure."

Sarah's frown disappeared, and she lay down and started piling wet sand around her thin, bony body. Joe Springer scooped sand and piled it around her, too. Sarah giggled again.

"I wish Mommy was here," she blurted out.

Joe didn't flinch. He was used to that sentiment. In fact, he shared it. "Me too, kiddo."

"How come you don't invite her?"

He wasn't quite as prepared for that one. "Well, I guess I would, except I don't think Mommy would come."

"I know, I know," Sarah said with rolling eyes. "You guys would start talking, and then you would start arguing, then you would yell and Mommy would cry."

Joe bunched his lips together. "Guess you got it all figured out, don't you?"

"How come you and Mommy can't get along?"

He didn't want to answer this one at all. At least not truthfully. But he knew that it was mostly his fault. He was the one who had caused most of the fights, coming home late after too many beers. And he was the one who left, who had given up on things too soon. Who knows, maybe it never would have worked out. Maybe it wasn't meant to work in the first place. But maybe...

"I think I just made Mommy angry too many times," he said. "Sometimes when you do that, it's hard for the other person to forgive you."

Another wave slammed into the beach and rolled nearly to the crest of the drop- off. They both watched it to make sure it wouldn't get them. Joe Springer looked back at his daughter. She looked away and piled sand onto herself again.

"Honey, don't be sad about Mommy and..."

"Last summer there weren't any waves," Sarah butted in. "How come they're so big this year?"

Joe Springer sighed. "The hurricane sent them."

"Is it coming here?"

"No. Just the waves."

"How come?"

"I don't know. Hurricanes never come here."

"Never?"

"Well, almost never."

"What if it did? What if the hurricane came here?"

"Then I guess we'd have to leave."

"Why?"

"Because the wind would blow real hard, and the waves might get even bigger."

"You're chicken, Daddy."

"What?"

"You're chicken. Mommy wouldn't leave. She's brave. She's always chasing hurricanes anyway. If it was coming this way, she'd stay and watch it."

Joe Springer smiled at his daughter, let a handful of soggy sand go plop on her belly. "Maybe Mommy's a little *too* brave sometimes," he said.

"More sand, Daddy. More, more."

CHAPTER 9

MANHATTAN
1:20 P.M.

*H*arvey. Amanda thought it might be hard for people to fear a storm named Harvey. She'd been worried about it since the storm first became a hurricane, two days ago. It was easier to fear a name like Hugo. Or Gert.

But Harvey sounded so benign or… happy.

And after looking at the latest information on the storm, she didn't want anyone to think Harvey was happy. Gert had been a deadly reminder of what hurricanes could do, of how they could surprise. And Gert had hit an area that was prepared, a coastline where people were used to evacuating. Still, CNN was reporting a list of twenty-seven dead. One of them was Bill Leaderman.

At least three more names had nearly made that list.

The Coast Guard chopper had picked them up just after dawn today in a routine rescue and flown them to Wilmington. Amanda would never forget the pilot. Lieutenant Meg Evans was a small, thin, attractive burst of energy in her late twenties with a surprisingly bullying attitude and, it turned out, a reputation for being one of the best chopper pilots in the East. So good, in fact, that the Coast Guard shuttled her from station to station ahead of hurricanes, so she'd always be on scene.

"What the hell were you doing out there?" Meg Evans had asked.

It sounded like a childhood admonishment from Amanda's mother. Amanda explained the thin scientific merits of their mission. Lieutenant Evans had scoffed. "I got enough people in trouble without the forecasters looking for it! Holy cow!"

By the time they'd landed, though, the two women had found some common ground and developed a mutual respect. In their own ways, they each threw themselves wholly into protecting other people from bad weather.

"Just stay the heck out of the water next time," Meg Evans had requested.

The doctors in Wilmington said the break in Juan Rico's arm was clean and would heal fine. Amanda had some sprained fingers taped. Her cheek was badly bruised but the cheekbone not broken. The cut on her leg took stitches, and those on her face were taped. One just above her eye took three stitches. Jack Corbin was exhausted, but OK. Frank Delaney pulled in some favors and got them on a military plane for a quick flight to New York.

Jack went straight to the newsroom, mumbling something about an editor having his ass if he didn't file.

Amanda wanted to go visit Sarah. No, to go *get* Sarah. Only a two-hour drive separated them. The near-death experience had stirred a biological need to envelop her child. But even if it were OK with Joe Springer—which Amanda was sure it wouldn't be—Sarah would be frightened by the tape on her mother's fingers, the bruise on her cheek and the small cuts all over her face. Being apart from Sarah was harder on Amanda than anything. A dull ache of loneliness had set in while she stared at unfamiliar walls waiting for Rico, who'd given her a spare key to his apartment before he went to see his doctor.

Amanda let her mind run, daydreaming, as odd thoughts, images, and statistics rattled through her head. It was her version of Zen, to let seldom-used knowledge drift to the surface; it was also a way of retaining those odd, disparate pieces of information, valuable or not, that she might need one day.

A storm like Harvey, the catalogues of her mind told her, released the power of three Hiroshima-sized atomic bombs every sixty seconds. A single large hurricane could serve the country's electric needs for half a year, if it could be harnessed.

Amanda loved having such trivia in her head. Handy whenever she was trying to convince someone of the force of these great storms. She knew more. Really trivial stuff, like where the name came from. The Carib Indians of the West Indies used the word *huracan*, which may be traceable to Huracan, a Central American god of evil. But what Amanda knew most about was the danger of wind. She knew that a seventy-five mile an hour wind pushed on a wall with 450 pounds per square foot of pressure, while a 125-mile-an-hour wind packed a walloping 1,250 pounds per square foot.

Waves as tall as a ten-story building can be spawned in the open ocean during a major hurricane. And, her favorite statistic of all: The highest gust of wind ever recorded, which was 236 miles per hour in Typhoon Paka back in 1997. The low barometric pressure from that storm sent nine pregnant women on Guam into labor.

Some 1,000 miles southeast of her, just a few hundred miles north of Puerto Rico, Hurricane Harvey grew. The island would feel no more than a tickle from the Category 3 hurricane, as tropical storm-force winds brushed its northern beaches. The clockwise-rotating winds around the Bermuda High whisked Harvey along at a brisk pace: twelve miles an hour. Amanda expected this speed to increase. By tomorrow morning, the storm would pass north of the Bahamas—within two days of Florida. But none of the computer models showed the storm hitting Florida.

She studied Harvey from Juan Rico's desktop computer, which had the requisite Internet connection. Her laptop was somewhere in the Atlantic. She would replace it before Harvey hit.

The computer glitch she'd seen last night—the blip in the

GFDL forecast—crowded into her thoughts. She worried about it. In the final crucial hours and moments before a storm made landfall, there was no room for that kind of error. Things in the forecasting room were hectic enough.

Amanda imagined the momentary fits Frank Delaney and the other forecasters must have had last night. And Delaney would be cursing now. It had been a busy season. He was tired. He didn't need Harvey so close on the heels of Gert. And now he'd be having to figure Harvey out without Amanda's help.

Delaney would take the advice Amanda had given him long ago: He would talk to Harvey, try to get to know him, put his arm around him.

Like Jimmy Stewart with his invisible friend Harvey, the tall one with the long ears. Was it a giant rabbit? Is that where the name for this storm came from? Talk to him long enough, Frank, and you'll hear something. Something that was inside your head already that you just weren't listening to.

Delaney would try to sweet talk Harvey into giving away a secret or two, some shred of data that would be the clue to where he planned to go. Would the storm move now, quickly ahead of the developing high and slam into the coast? Wait a day and slide north, ride the wind out to sea?

Get inside the mind of the storm. Harvey's going to break, one direction or another. Sometime.

"Catch Harvey leaning," she whispered.

Amanda felt out of the game. She'd been away from the Hurricane Center for just one day, and already she was antsy to go back.

The phone rang, startling Amanda. She picked it up without thinking that it wasn't her phone.

"You hungry?"

"Juan, hi. What'd the doctor say?"

"Said I was fine, to quit complaining. Want to meet me at Chez Henri?"

"Is food all you think about?"

"Half."

"Don't you want to come home first?"

"I'm tired," Rico said. "I come home I fall asleep. Need a good meal first. Go get a table, OK? Meet you there in twenty."

***

Juan Rico emerged from the Canal Street subway station, left arm in a cast and bent at the elbow, half-drugged and worn out. He headed toward the Hudson River.

Rico paused to absorb a slight breeze at the angled intersection of Varick and Canal, into which the Holland Plaza Building wedged itself like a piece of pie. He looked up at the simple brick building, which had dozens of aged factory windows—each with fifty small panes of glass surrounded by rusted steel—on every floor.

Behind the building was the entrance to the Holland Tunnel, swallowing into its depths the rush of slow-moving cars headed back to New Jersey.

He angled off toward the Hudson and soon he was at the entrance to Chez Henri, the corner restaurant in the old factory building next to where he lived. Juan Rico loved the ornate six-story building. It was constructed of beautiful almond-colored brick, with red brick trimming and arching over the windows. Gothic gables adorned the west side and green patinated copper numbers attested to the durability of the structure, built in 1891.

A developer had recently put up a sixteen-floor apartment complex next to Chez Henri, and Juan Rico was first on the list of buyers. He moved in even before the building was completely finished—the construction elevator was still attached to the north wall, towering over Chez Henri.

Meanwhile, an even taller building was going up next to Rico's, across the street to the south. Planned to be twenty-four stories, the building was so far no more than twenty-two stark slabs of concrete and a wooden platform on top that awaited another batch of concrete. Every single apartment in the unfinished building was already sold.

Tribeca, like much of New York, was booming.

He went into the restaurant, into the tall, dark room whose luxurious wood-paneled walls made the place feel like you'd been there before, made you want to curl up and spend the afternoon. He found Amanda at a table by the window.

"Eat with a cripple?"

Amanda looked up, smiled, and shook her head yes. "You look half dead."

"Thanks a heap," Rico said. He sat down and looked around the room.

Most of the sturdy wood tables were occupied, a few of them with older men Rico recognized. Rico saw the old drunk with the incorrigible white hair, red cheeks, purple nose, sitting in his usual spot at the bar, smoking his pipe. Nobody ever listened to the old drunk, who had a penchant for stating the obvious. "Well, looks like it's Tuesday again," he would say. Or, "I see you're having a martini." It was hard to know what to say to him, but he was a fixture in the place and on the rare day that he was not in his seat, Rico felt that Chez Henri was a different place altogether.

"Keep this shit up and I'll be like that old guy someday," Rico said to Amanda, pointing with his head.

"Oh, c'mon. You're not a drunk."

"Got no wife, no kids, nobody to take care of me when I'm old. I'll *become* one."

"I'll take care of you," Amanda said playfully.

Rico half wished she were serious. Though Amanda was too good a friend to consider getting romantic with, she was the only woman he knew who could fill the giant hole in his life. His mind withdrew to a place where he kept gauzy memories of the woman he had loved, the woman he had thought he would spend his life with. It had been two years now since she left him; it still hurt like it was yesterday. He wanted to talk to Amanda about her, but he couldn't. He couldn't even say her name. The pain was too great.

Henri Mouchet himself, who always greeted Rico, came to the table.

"How is my favorite customer today?" Henri's graying hair was pulled back into a ponytail, revealing a full, dark, creased face and a warm, perpetual smile. He saw Rico's cast. "Ooh, not so good, I see."

Rico's mind returned to the present, and he half-smiled. Henri Mouchet was the other thing Rico loved about the neighborhood. "Why you always so damn happy?" Rico asked.

"Friendly people like you," Henri said. "What happened?"

"Got in a fight with a woman," Rico said.

"Not this beautiful Mademoiselle, I trust."

"Nope. Lady named Gert. Real bitch."

"You should learn to defend yourself," Henri said.

Rico rolled his eyes and pretended to ignore Henri, who smiled and drifted politely to another table. A waiter appeared, Rico and Amanda ordered, and the waiter disappeared. A bus boy brought water.

"How's your arm feel?" Amanda asked.

"Fuckin' hurts. Sorry." Rico dropped his eyes. He hated talking like that to Amanda. "But I guess I'm lucky." He thought for a second. "Amanda, no offense, but we messed up last night."

"I know."

"And I didn't get *the shot*. I'm gonna quit this shit."

"No you won't. You'll keep trying to get the shot until it kills you."

"Yeah, I'm probably that stupid. But last night, well, it was a bust."

"I'm sorry."

"I know. It's not your fault, though. I chose to be there. I got to quit listenin' to Jack Corbin, is the thing."

It was exhilarating, but it also scared the shit out of me, Rico thought. He wondered how fine the line was between those two sensations. *I almost died. That's the line.*

Rico changed the subject: "Where's Jack?"

"Went to the newsroom."

"Oh yeah, has to file. Is all he thinks about. He gonna make time for you today?"

Amanda almost spit her water out. "What?"

"You know what I'm talking about. You two were practically falling over each other all day yesterday, walks on the beach together, you savin' his life just so you can look good and shit. C'mon, Amanda, don't play dumb with me. You like him."

Amanda pressed her fingers to her temples, as though he'd just given her a headache. "I do like him," she said. "I just don't have the time or the energy right now. With my father in the nursing home and Sarah at her father's and..."

"Screw Sarah's father. Find time. Take it from me. I messed up and lost the woman I should be with."

"I'm sorry, Juan."

Rico shook his head to get rid of the thought. "Jack's a good guy. You two need each other. You know, you're the first woman I've seen him go gaga over in a long time. He gave me the same shit, talked about being too busy. Load a crap."

"You guys were talking about me?"

"Course. He been wanting to see you again since Andrew. He think I don't know that. Hah. Anyway, his knees go all Jell-O when he sees you. So, my question? He make time for you today?"

"He asked me if we could meet here this evening and talk about Harvey."

"Talk about Harvey." Rico intoned his disbelief. "Hmph."

"Join us, if you like. Around six."

Rico looked at his watch. "Four hours. Guess I could get hungry again."

Rico worked on a thick T-bone. He thought about Amanda and Sarah, of Jack maybe joining them to make a family again. It bothered him sometimes, that he had no family. He was used to it, but he wondered what it might be like to stuff stockings for kids at Christmas, or teach them how to ride bikes, or go to ballet class. Unless *she* came back—and he knew he would always take her back—there would be no family.

He pulled his vacant stare in from the window and looked at Amanda. Her eyes were closed as she savored a bite of her quail, which sat on a bed of leaf lettuce and rice, surrounded by fresh fruits and sautéed vegetables.

"Question for you," he said. "I been thinking. What if one like Gert *did* come here? What if Harvey does?"

"Lots of places will be underwater," Amanda said. "World Trade Center entrance, tunnel entrances…"

"Which ones?"

"Battery, Lincoln and Holland. Most of them."

"The Holland Tunnel. Now *that's* the shot." Rico looked out the window, east toward the tunnel entrance, just three blocks away. "What else?"

"The South Ferry Subway station entrance."

Rico raised his eyebrows. "Subways would flood too?"

"Lots of them. In some cases, the water would come in through the street vents. Fourteenth Street, Lexington Avenue. Other places it would come right down the stairs."

Rico frowned. He thought of the people he had photographed down there. He saw some of them now and then, the ones who were still alive. It wasn't easy to stay alive when you lived in a dank, eternal darkness among rats, cockroaches and construction dust. Now they had another enemy. "You know 'bout the moles?"

"The what?"

"Mole people," Rico said. "Folks who live under the City."

"Like the homeless people and the musicians?"

"No. The mole people make homes down there in abandoned tunnels, shafts, crawl spaces, wherever they can be left alone. You don't usually see them. Pretty nice places, some of 'em. You know, considering. Furniture, shelves made of scrap wood, even paintings on the walls."

"Oh God." Amanda winced.

He wasn't surprised by Amanda's concern. He knew that most people didn't give a rat's ass about the mole people, whom they considered dangerous, a perception that was sometimes true, sometimes false. Outcasts, they were labeled. They *want* to live down there, so why should we care? But Amanda wasn't like that. Somebody was in trouble, Amanda cared, tried to do something about it.

"They in danger?" Rico asked.

Amanda had pushed her unfinished quail away. She wiped her mouth, then dropped the red cloth napkin on her plate and slumped in her chair. "When one vent floods, we don't even really know what the effect will be. Most of the subways are thirty to fifty feet below the surface. Some are more than a hundred feet down. The whole system is interconnected, so depending on how much water gets in, it can flow through the network to God knows where. We know water would fill Grand Central, Penn Station, the PATH system and the subway system from down at the Battery *at least* back to 14th Street. And that's just Manhattan. We haven't even studied the effects on some of the other boroughs. Thing is, I've been worrying about people from *above ground* taking refuge in a subway station during a hurricane. I didn't know there were people *living* down there. How many are we talking about?"

"Back in the eighties there were, like, five thousand of 'em. Train cops kicked 'em out. Jack and I did a story on them a couple years ago. He reported that there's about a thousand now, but nobody really knows."

Amanda stared over his shoulder, lost in thought. "Can you take me down there?" she asked.

Rico rocked forward nervously. It wasn't that simple. These people were not used to visitors. But he knew she would go, with or without him.

"I know one place we might be able to get into, but I gotta check it out first."

"Get me in, Juan. Today. I fly back to Miami tonight."

CHAPTER 10

OUTSIDE SANTO DOMINGO, DOMINICAL REPUBLIC 2:05 P.M.

A warm breeze fanned the leaves of the palms around the pool and kept the day from becoming unbearable. Even so, Maximo was sweating. He considered the tens of millions of dollars he had stashed in various banks around the world. The $5 million he'd wagered on a hurricane was no drop in the bucket, but neither could it break him if he lost it. Still, Maximo always sweated about money.

The stock of Global Insurance Company had been drifting lower since the opening bell in a lackluster day on Wall Street. By noon it had dropped from fifty-six dollars a share to less than fifty-five.

Maximo had expected a steeper drop. He was in a sour mood when Terese emerged from his sprawling hacienda. He'd sent everyone else inside for the time being. He watched Terese's sensuous body dictate the swishes of a long silk robe as she walked purposefully toward the pool and handed Maximo his laptop computer. She set two cordless phones and

86

a glass of rum down on the small table next to him, then turned to go. Maximo grabbed her robe, pulled her back.

"Stay," he said. "I may need your advice."

Terese nodded. Maximo fired up his computer and connected to the Internet via satellite. He typed GLIC, the company's NASDAQ ticker symbol, into the quote server of his online brokerage account. Trading volume was 200,000 shares. The last trade was at less than fifty-four. Maximo's short sell was looking good, though far from what he'd hoped.

"It's a strange custom," he said. "You sell a stock you do not even own, banking on the price going down, and then you buy it back at a lower price." Maximo had never done any short selling himself. One of his brothers played front man on schemes like this. Maximo just made the decisions and provided the funds.

"Who sells them to you?" Terese asked.

"The broker. And we do it all via a company in Bermuda. I tell you, you Americans have devised a complicated financial system. Too complicated. I think no one person understands how it all works."

"Then it is a good system for people who are not so honest," she said.

"Yes." Maximo chuckled, amazed again how Terese could change his mood, and how much she understood about the world.

The phone rang, right on time. Terese handed him one of the phones. She reclined on the lounge chair next to his. Maximo answered in his stern voice: "Nombre?"

"Octopus."

"It does not look so good yet," Maximo said. He nodded at Teresa and she picked up the other phone.

"It's perfect," the Octopus said. "Price is sliding, volume is only slightly ahead of normal. That's good. Means the market hasn't figured this out yet. Probably just some insiders selling right now."

"Why is that good?"

"Because we have bigger fish to fry." The Octopus

sounded awfully confident.

"Oh?"

"Harvey has become a delicious monster since we spoke yesterday. Official forecast is still Charleston, but the odds for New York are up."

"I don't think I see the point. I have a rather large short position in GLIC right now. I don't give a damn about Harvey."

"Don't worry about GLIC. It will fall. Somebody is going to find out what you already know, and they're going to find out soon. When they do, the game will be up. Everybody will start bailing out of insurance companies that have heavy hurricane exposure. The exodus will ruin your chances to place a bet on Harvey, so I hope it doesn't start for a few days."

"What makes you so sure I will make another investment before my first one pays off?"

"I think you believe the scheme will work. And I know you're greedy."

Maximo laughed deeply. "Perhaps you are right on the first point. You flatter me with the second. What do you have for me?"

"I have two more insurance companies. I'll fax the details over after we talk."

"Give me the—how do you say it?—upshot."

"Clarion Mutual is overexposed from South Carolina through Florida," the Octopus said. "If Harvey heads there, you could turn a tidy profit."

"And the other company?"

"My favorite. PrimeCo Insurance. They don't do much south of Delaware, but their overexposure in Jersey and New York is a glaring oversight. Mostly commercial properties, shipping and trucking, things like that. Lots of vulnerable multi-story buildings along the water in Brooklyn, too. PrimeCo's reinsurance program is poor, and they have staunchly refused to issue catastrophe bonds."

"Catastrophe bonds?"

"Basically the equivalent of reinsurance. An insurance

company sells its risk to other investors by issuing catastrophe bonds. If a hurricane hits the East Coast within the specified life of the bond, the company doesn't have to pay the investors back."

"A risky holding for the investor."

"High risk, high reward. The payoff is large for the investor if the catastrophe doesn't happen. But I'll tell you, the Northeast is overdue for a big one. The shoreline has really been built up in the past couple of decades. If Harvey hits New York, the damage could exceed a *hundred billion*. The effect on the insurance industry would be devastating. I think it could ripple through the whole financial market. For starters, the storm itself would grind business to a halt for days—weeks or more for the shipping ports. And it could be months before the tunnels are reopened. No trains, no cargo. Gridlock. And lots of large companies—not just insurance companies—have been snapping up these catastrophe bonds for the high rate of return. They'll feel the pinch."

"A lot of ifs," Maximo said.

"The only if is if it hits. Just think of all the lawsuits. The more deaths, the better. And I can make sure there are more deaths."

"I know what *you* can do. But we're talking about a lot of *my* money. I want to be assured the situation at Goddard is under control. How did our little test go?"

"Splendidly. We're ready there."

Maximo liked what he'd heard. Before committing, though, he wanted to know what Terese had to say. He covered the phone. She did the same, looked out beyond the pool and into the dense vegetation that tumbled into a lush valley. After some time she spoke with her characteristic American irreverence, and without looking at him.

"Are you sure you know what you're doing, dealing with these insurance companies, and that pig of a man?"

"I'm confident in the scheme, yes. The pig you speak of is devoted to me."

"What about the illegality of it?"

Maximo bristled. "It is business as usual," he said. "So long as I control the local officials I can do *anything*. Santino is in my pocket. He would not arrest me if I raped and killed his own daughter."

Terese wasn't convinced. "But this isn't some underfunded foreign drug agency that would come after you. This is Wall Street. Big money, big power."

"And I would fight with big money, big power."

Terese turned her head toward him, pulled her sleek sunglasses down her thin nose and gave a businesslike stare with cunning eyes as blue as the pool.

"Be careful, darling," she said. "This is new territory, and you sound awfully confident. We don't want you getting caught, now." Her eyes turned playful. "I couldn't bear having to *work* for a living."

"I'll be careful," Maximo said. "Perhaps I'll take out a little insurance of my own against the Octopus."

Terese nodded, satisfied. She set the phone down, stood up and untied her robe. Maximo watched the robe fall to the deck. His heart quickened as she walked naked to the edge of the pool and dove in.

He had to shake his head to regain interest in the conversation with the Octopus. He was still curious about how a hurricane could affect the financial markets—and benefit him. "Now, then," he said. "Tell me more about the financial impact on this PrimeCo."

"Everybody and their brother will be suing somebody. I can also make sure a lot of trucks and ships and trains don't get out of the storm's path. PrimeCo insures many of them. All in all, Harvey could easily trigger a bear market, and nobody is thinking about it. That's why my idea is so brilliant."

"Brilliant, yes," Maximo said dryly. "We shall see. Either way, I do not plan to place a bet on the whole market. My interest would be in this PrimeCo. So then, the company is overexposed for hurricane risk in the Northeast and has not sold catastrophe bonds. What does that mean for them?"

"If they take a big hit—especially in New York City—they

won't be able to make the payoffs on their policies. They'll fold. You'll be rich."

"I'm already rich."

"You'll be richer."

"Now you have given me a good reason." Maximo laughed long, coughed.

CHAPTER 11

CANAL STREET SUBWAY STATION, MANHATTAN
2:50 P.M.

Amanda took Rico's right hand—the one not in a cast—nervously as they approached the end of the subway platform. They did not want to be seen prowling their way off the platform. They waited until just after a train pulled out to start down the tracks.

"We walk along the edge here," Rico said as he jumped down to the tracks. He helped Amanda down. "Stay away from that rail." He pointed.

Rico answered her question before she asked it.

"It's the one with the juice," he said. "You touch it, you fry."

Amanda watched the two red lights of the departing train shrink, then curve out of sight around a corner, taking with them a receding rumble. The air was warm, stickier than outside. Rico, holding the flashlight, took Amanda's hand and led the way down the track. On the right was a crawl space leading out of the tunnel.

"Told you you get dirty," he said. "C'mon. And hold your breath. Might want to pull your shirt up over your nose."

Again, before she could ask, Amanda had her answer, this time in the form of a stench as she stepped through the crawl hole. The smell of urine was sharp, the way a shrill whistle pierces the ear. She pulled her t-shirt up over her nose. They were in another tunnel much like the one they had left, but smaller and in bad repair. It was almost completely dark. A few shafts of muted light sifted through a street vent somewhere in the distance. She heard something that sounded like the flutter of pigeon wings.

"Rats," Rico said.

She thought about that. *I'm not afraid of spiders. I'm not afraid of snakes. I'm not afraid of darkness. But rats?* "How many?"

"Don't ask me," Rico said. "Not exactly an expert, you know."

"Dangerous?"

"Only if they attack."

"Juan."

"Well, I don't know. I don't think they too dangerous. Maybe in the dead of winter when there's less food. Or if you dead. Eat you in half a day if you dead."

"Oh, thanks," she said. Rico shined the flashlight around. The tunnel walls and floor were covered with a layer of dust and grime that absorbed the beam. A few large and weather-beaten timbers lay strewn about. Wires hung from above, and most of the pipes that had run along the ceiling had been torn out, leaving a few loose sections. "Why the smell?"

"Mole people gotta piss somewhere. Lots of them almost never go topside. They eat, sleep, piss and shit here. Sorry."

Amanda rolled her eyes. She was used to his mouth and it didn't bother her. "How do they live with this smell?"

"Get used to it, I guess. You got to remember, lot of 'em have mental problems, and a lot do drugs. Not all, but a lot. The place I'm takin' you is clean. They call it the Block House. Good people, smart people, just can't cope with life above ground or haven't been able to land a decent job."

They headed north through the tunnel for what seemed like four or five city blocks when Rico guided her down into the old tracks and up to a narrow platform on the other side. He shined his light on a piece of plywood, then pulled it back to reveal another crawl space, this one carved crudely into the tunnel wall.

"Wait here," he said.

"You're crazy!"

"I'm not goin' anywhere. Just have to announce us. Wait here."

Rico crawled through the tight space and knocked on the metal plate on the floor. A moment later Amanda followed him down a steel ladder into a twenty-foot-square room with a single light bulb dangling from the ceiling, barely illuminating the dingy cinder-block walls. A boy with unruly brown hair smiled broadly at Juan Rico. Amanda saw the man with the pale gray face and the large, jagged scar across his left cheek. There was something familiar about him, but she couldn't place it. In one corner of the room she saw a hole in the dirt floor, and a small pile of dirt. Rico spotted it too.

""What you diggin', Sleepy?"

"Way out," the man with the scar said. He pointed at the hole in the ceiling. "Things are getting nasty around here. That ladder is our only exit. I don't like it."

"Maybe you should just leave," Rico said.

"Nowhere to go. Same problems anywhere else. I smell a fight coming, and if we've got to fight, we'll fight. But I want to know I can get out quick if I need to."

"Good luck," Rico said. "I hope you don't need it." He turned to the boy and grinned.

The boy spoke first. "Hello, Mr. Rico."

"Hey, Jonathan."

Amanda thought about the strange surroundings, the rats, the man with the scarred ashen face, the scraggly boy with the good manners, the hole in the floor. It looked like there wasn't going to be an introduction, so she extended a hand to the man and introduced herself.

"Rico tells me you're a scientist," Sleepy said in a bored tone.

"Yes, that's right," Amanda said. "I study hurricanes."

"What's that got to do with us?"

Rico said Sleepy was one of the more hospitable mole people, that he was known for being helpful and generous, and that he was perceived among the underground community as a leader. She wondered if she had gotten off on the wrong foot with him. She wanted to accomplish two things. She hoped to learn more about the number of people down here, their lifestyles, the ways they communicated, all in an effort to determine whether or not there would be anything she could do to warn them if a hurricane was coming. And she wanted to warn Sleepy of the danger. If he was the type of leader Rico said he was, that might be the best help she could give.

"There's a hurricane out there that may come this way," Amanda said firmly, "and if it does, this room could fill with water."

Sleepy didn't say anything right away. He chewed his lip and his left eye twitched. His eyes drifted from Amanda's and he studied her, slowly, all the way to the floor and then back up again.

"No hurricane has ever come here before," Sleepy said.

"1821," Amanda said. He was skeptical. She was used to that. "And 1938."

"Long time ago."

"There's been several close calls since, but the storms have veered out to sea. Sooner or later one will hit here, and the storm surge, which is—"

"I know about storm surge. Comes up the river. I'm not stupid, lady. Living down here doesn't make me stupid."

"Then you probably know that the surge moves in quickly, leaving little time for escape. And you'll want to protect your family, of course."

"We've got lots of problems down here, lady. Lots of concerns. I don't think yours rates way up there on the list. Hell, the City doesn't even have an evacuation plan." He paused, momentarily troubled. "But I'll remember what you've said."

Amanda was surprised at his knowledge. Clearly he had worked to educate himself on the topic. Maybe he read the papers, or simply had gotten a good education before he ended up down here. Either way, she could tell by the sharp tone of his voice that the matter was closed, the conversation over.

Amanda wanted to ask more questions, but she already felt like she was invading his privacy.

"I'm sorry we came down here," Amanda said. "I only wanted to warn you."

Sleepy nodded.

"Let's go, Juan."

She turned to climb up the ladder and caught Sleepy's eye. It had softened. His body relaxed. His face looked defeated, as though he was facing an impossible situation and she had just made it worse. But he also looked as if maybe he understood, maybe he believed her. Perhaps she had gotten through to him after all. And if he was the leader Rico said he was, maybe he would tell others.

CHAPTER 12

CONEY ISLAND
4:30 P.M.

Hurricane Harvey, like all low-pressure storms, was a cyclone in meteorological terms. Coney Island had a Cyclone of its own. When it was built in 1927, it was the tallest and most feared roller coaster in the world.

Amanda Cole had never been to Coney Island, and the Cyclone disappointed her.

She thought it would be bigger. It seemed tame compared to modern-day roller coasters. Towering over the roller coaster was the Wonder Wheel, an even older structure, a 150-foot-tall Ferris wheel that looked as rickety as the Cyclone.

The two rides formed a focal point of an otherwise dismal skyline notable by the number of vacant lots that testified to the area's economic woes like missing teeth in a neglected mouth. Bland apartment buildings from the fifties rose modestly around the carnival area, spread behind the boardwalk and into the heart of Brooklyn.

A stiff breeze from the south struck Coney Island's yellow-sand beach at right angles. The sand took flight, made the air brown and hazy, peppered Amanda's face and insinuated itself into her eyes as she strolled west on the boardwalk. A smattering of beachgoers braved the sandblasting, and a few dotted the boardwalk.

She stopped several blocks west. Still within view of the Cyclone and the Wonder Wheel, an unremarkable building stood alone, desolate, behind the broad boardwalk. Wooden letters proclaimed the six-story building to be Seaside Nursing Home. Five years ago it had been the Brooklyn Nursing Home, located a mile inland. But with Coney Island real estate so cheap the business had been moved, renamed, and Ed Cole had moved with it. The building had a rectangular footprint, the broader front facing the ocean, due south. Eight bronzed aluminum windows on each floor indicated the same number of rooms. It was as no-nonsense as a college dormitory.

There were no pilings under which a storm surge might flow.

Amanda made calipers out of her thumb and forefinger, held them to her eye and estimated the distance from the ground to the top of the first floor. Nine feet.

From the Army Corps of Engineers' New York Hurricane Evacuation Study reports, Amanda knew the storm surge from a Cat 3 hurricane would be fifteen feet above ground level for this building. Fifteen minus nine: The water would be six feet deep as it rushed through the *second* floor of the Seaside Nursing Home.

The first floor opened into a lobby, its front a wall of windows floor to ceiling, fake indoor plants placed here and there. The woman behind the desk was younger than Amanda, short, compact, perpetual smile, bleach-blond hair, leathery face from too much sun. A plastic tag over her left lapel revealed her to be Kim, Assistant Manager.

"Welcome to Seaside Nursing Home," Kim said in a bubbly voice. She frowned, obviously scanning Amanda's injuries. "Can I help you?"

"My father lives here. Edward Cole. I was hoping I could see him."

Kim pulled a book from an invisible shelf under the

counter, flipped through it.

Amanda spotted a vintage rotary-dial phone on the counter and toyed with it. It seemed to have no cord and it sat unused.

"Things of the past," Kim said, glancing up. "Helps our residents remember fonder days."

Amanda nodded. Kim put her head back in the book. "Yes, you must be..."

"Amanda Cole."

"Of course. Ed's on the second floor. Can I walk you up there?"

"Thanks," Amanda said.

Kim put the book away, led Amanda behind the desk and down a hallway. The walls were all pastels, the left one robin's egg blue, the right one Easter green. At the back of the building, another hall branched perpendicularly in both directions, running the length of the building's rear. On the back wall were the two colors again, blue to the left, green to the right. Amanda stared curiously at the vertical joint where the two colors met.

"Color-coding," Kim said. "It helps our residents find the elevator or the stairs without making too big a deal out of it. Every room, every facility, is a different color. It's a soft reminder. Most of them hate being told 'elevator' fifteen times with arrows and all that. Reminds them of their disease, agitates them." Kim turned right, pushed the button for the elevator and waited.

"How's my father doing?"

Kim paused, made a brief frown that she wiped away professionally. "You know, Ed's mind isn't as bad as a lot of our residents. But he's kind of ornery. I don't mean to pry..."

"It's his nature," Amanda said. She didn't want Kim to pry, either.

"Well, it keeps him at arm's length from a lot of people. He mostly keeps to himself. Except for one woman, Betty Dinsmore. They're very fond of each other. I think having another visitor will do him good. Will you stay long?"

"No. I have a flight to catch tonight."

The elevator opened, and they stepped in and rode to the second floor in silence.

The doors opened and Kim led Amanda to the right, down the wide hallway at the back of the building.

On the wall were two pictures, one of a woman Amanda didn't recognize, the other of the Brooklyn Bridge at sunset, its spider-web cables glistening. Amanda recognized the photo of the bridge; it was her father's favorite. She looked closer.

"Visual clues again," Kim said. "Each resident chooses something for the wall leading to their room."

Amanda nodded. They walked down the hall. A wad of nerves rose from her stomach, into her chest, constricted her throat. They passed the first door. Kim knocked on the second.

A gruff voice from inside responded, "Already been cleaned."

"Ed, it's me, Kim. Your daughter Amanda is here to see you."

A moment passed. Door opened partway, revealing a fit, barrel-chested man in dark trousers and a sleeveless white t-shirt, frown etched deep into his forehead, hair no more than a wayward tuft.

"Hi, Dad."

"Should have called."

"I didn't know I was coming," Amanda said. "Can I come in?"

The door opened wider. Amanda stepped in, Kim slipped away, and Ed Cole closed the door.

Amanda walked past her father, past a bathroom door, toward the window facing the ocean. Under the window was a well-made single bed. A simple desk sat against the left wall with a smaller window above it, a dresser against the right wall. It reminded her again of her college dorm, only slightly larger.

"Five years, seven months," Ed Cole scowled.

His mind seems fine. How can he—?

"Christmas. It was Christmas. You brought that little baby with you."

"Sarah. My daughter."

"And that prick, what's-his-name." Voice softer, hurt: "Haven't seen you since."

"Dad, do you remember why?"

"I remember fine."

"You called Joe a prick, to his face. You said I was wasting my life, told us to get the hell out."

He might have been right, Amanda thought later, but she always wondered how much her father's lack of respect for Joe Springer encouraged her husband to drift away. It was one in a string of Ed Cole's meddlings that irritated Amanda.

Somewhere under all the hurt, though, Amanda forgave her father. He'd returned from Vietnam in 1975 after missing two years of her adolescence, and they never regained the closeness she remembered from her early childhood. A big wall had gone up. Amanda learned to rely on her mother for everything: love, affection, advice, and early parole from restrictions her father often imposed. Amanda left their Brooklyn home, paid her own way through college. Years went by, and she returned home only for a few days each Christmas.

Then Ed Cole started to forget things. When Amanda would visit, he would tell her she couldn't go out with a boy that she hadn't even known since ninth grade. Or he would ask her if she wanted a teddy bear for her birthday.

One day, he left his security job at Kennedy Airport early, unannounced. He took the subway, as usual, but got disoriented when he got off, became lost, and was found by Amanda's mother in a park near home late that night, confused and angry. He lost his job, and Amanda's mother was forced to put him in the nursing home so that she could keep her job.

When her mother got cancer, Amanda took a leave, stayed with her for three months. When she died, Amanda felt a huge hole. Joe Springer helped fill it, but only slightly. When Sarah was born, the pain faded greatly but the loss remained. Sarah would never know her grandmother. But maybe she could get to know her grandfather. Amanda tried to patch things up with Ed, but he was stubborn.

She hoped it would go better today. She still wanted Sarah to have a grandfather. Ed Cole frowned, looked at the door. "Is your mother here?"

"Dad, she's been dead for eight years, remember."

"Saw her on the boardwalk yesterday. Said she was going to come by today. We're supposed to have lunch."

Ed Cole looked suddenly confused.

"I do love you, Amanda," he said. "Thanks for coming to visit."

Amanda was taken aback. It was the first time he'd said it since she was a little girl. She grabbed the arm of a chair and eased into it. Looked at him.

"I love you too, Dad."

"What happened to your face?"

"Just a little accident," Amanda said. "But I'm fine."

He nodded and looked away, out the window. Wrinkles on his forehead curled into a knot of confusion. Amanda sighed. "C'mon, I'll have lunch with you."

He frowned again, nodded, and walked out the door and down the hall. Amanda closed the door and caught up to him at the elevator. Her father had always hated elevators.

"Don't you want to take the stairs, Dad?"

"Jungle is hell on the knees. Worn out."

They rode the elevator back down to the lobby. Her father was nervous and fidgety. He relaxed as he exited the elevator, turned right, ambled down the hallway toward the dining area. Along the wall was a low, wide shelf. A silver-haired woman ahead of them used it as a railing. Amanda decided that's what it was, a railing in disguise.

As they passed her, Ed Cole put his hand through the woman's arm. "Hello, Betty," he cooed. "Join us for lunch?"

"There you are Ed Cole, you devil. Who's the young thing?"

"My wife," Ed said, a bit of humor that surprised Amanda. Or at least she assumed it was humor. "But you can still join us."

Ed Cole got three boxed lunches, returned and sat down.

"Dad, you remember what I do?"

"Of course I remember. Studying meteorology."

Close enough. Only fifteen years off. "Good. So you'll believe me when I tell you there's a hurricane that might come this way."

"If you say so."

"If it does, you're room isn't safe. Can you remember that?"

"Stop asking me if I can remember everything. Do I look stupid?"

"No, Dad, of course not. But this is important. Your room's not safe in a hurricane. You need to get out of this building, or go to a higher floor and take cover in the hallway at the back of the building. OK?"

"Got a nice view of the roller coaster from my room. Damn place used to be a jewel. All weirdoes and druggies now. I hate the place anyway. Everybody's always pretending to have so much fun. I don't have time for that. Where's your mother? She should be here by now."

"Out of the building or a higher floor, OK?"

"Sure, sure. Out of the building or a higher floor. Where's Sarah, anyway? She in danger?"

"No, Dad. Sarah's fine."

"Have to bring her around again." His eyes seemed to clear for a moment. He grinned. "I'll be nicer next time."

"I'll do that," Amanda said. *I promise.*

Ed Cole frowned, put his sandwich down. Then he put it back in the box, took Betty Dinsmore's arm and the two left without a word.

Amanda let them go. In the back of her mind, she sensed that she might be coming back after him, but she would only do that if she was certain Harvey was headed this way. Otherwise, she could see that taking care of Ed Cole was more than she could handle right now. She put her head on the table and cried.

***

When the tears were gone she returned to the front desk, found Kim.

"Mind if I ask you a couple of questions?"

"Go ahead," Kim said.

"Do you folks have an evacuation plan?"

"For what?"

"Hurricanes."

"Not sure." Kim frowned. "I'd have to look in our manual. Why?"

Amanda ignored her. "Who would be in charge of an emergency evacuation?"

"That would be me right now. I'm the assistant manager on duty."

"What's your last name, Kim?"

"Butler."

"Do you know where the nearest evacuation shelter is, Kim Butler?"

Kim shifted her weight, uncomfortable now. "Not offhand, but I could…"

"Find out," Amanda said. "And find out today. I'm going to call you tomorrow to make sure you know. And I want you to tell me how you would get the residents there. Bus, ambulance, taxi, whatever. Understand?"

"Just a minute. Who the heck…"

"Look," Amanda said, her voice stronger, arms tight. "I'm a forecaster at the National Hurricane Center. There's a big hurricane out there. His name is Harvey. I can't say that he's coming this way, but he might. If he does, the ocean will be *in* my father's room. And there won't be a window left in this place. Now, do you want to deal with the lawsuits, or do you want to look into that evacuation plan for me?"

Kim looked confused. "Seems like a remote chance." Then she gave up. "But I guess it wouldn't hurt to know what to do."

"Thank you, Kim." Amanda smiled in the way she would to indicate approval to a child.

CHAPTER 13

CHEZ HENRI, TRIBECA
6:15 P.M.

Rico had broken his arm. Amanda was bruised and cut. Bill Leaderman was dead. But Jack Corbin was fine, and that made him feel guilty.

The beer was helping. Henri Mouchet brought another, and Jack let it sit and sweat in the evening heat while he waited for Amanda. He'd picked a spot by the window. The table was big enough for four.

He spotted Amanda on the other side of the street, heading toward the restaurant. Her simple, ankle-length black tank dress exposed strong shoulders, hugged her waist, flared against her hips, and moved in lyrical swishes with her legs as she crossed the street. She looked good in black. She looked good in simple. Jack tried to imagine something she wouldn't look good in. He failed. He could see the bruise on her cheek as she got closer, and it only gave a tough look to her sharp-featured beauty. She looked like a street cop in a Hollywood thriller. Jack suddenly wished he'd picked a more intimate table.

He stood when she came to the table, didn't know what he should do. Amanda took care of that for him. She closed in on him, put a hand gently behind his neck, reached up with her lips and touched his, softly. Her eyes were closed. Jack's were open. He could smell the faint mix of musk and jasmine that she must have just put on. He reached with one hand for a chair, table, anything to hold onto. Nothing. As he was about to lose his balance, Amanda pulled her lips away, as slowly as she'd approached.

Jack wanted to say something, ask something, but he didn't know where to start.

He reached up with one hand, put his fingers on his raised eyebrow and thumb on chin, flabbergasted.

Amanda rescued him from the silence: "Juan said you wouldn't mind. I sure hope to hell he was right."

"Mind? Me? Yes. I mean, yes, it's OK. No, I don't mind."

"Good. Jeez, I would have been a fool otherwise, huh?"

"Man. Talk about out of the blue." Jack had the fingers of both hands to his eyebrows now.

"I've been on my own for three years, Jack. Haven't dated a soul. I don't remember how to do it, and I didn't want to waste the time trying to figure it out."

"Wow." Jack wished he could find some real words.

"Well, there it is, then," Amanda said. "The hard part's done."

"You do that all the time?" Jack finally put his hands down, found his chair and eased into it. Amanda sat, too. She took a drink from his beer.

"Never," she said. "Thing is, I've known you for a long time."

"Mostly on the phone."

"Well, we get along, don't we?"

"I'll say."

"And we held hands once," she said. "That counts for something."

Jack smiled.

"Anyway, we almost died last night," Amanda said, hints of pain and exhaustion registering on her face. "Maybe…"

"I almost died, you mean. You saved my life. I didn't know what to do. I feel sort of… can we not talk about it right now?"

"OK. But don't get too wrapped up in it," Amanda said. "It happened, we reacted, we survived. Maybe that made me brave today, or maybe it made me realize how quickly good things can slip away. I just figured that the worst that could happen if I kissed you is you'd tell me to stop. But you didn't."

"No, don't. Stop, that is."

Amanda smiled. Jack felt like a dope, hadn't said anything smart or sensible yet. He'd been thinking about Amanda non-stop for two straight days now, wondering if she could possibly fall for a workaholic reporter who wasn't in very good shape anymore. It took a moment to digest the fact that she was already falling.

"Not going to be easy," he said. "I hear long-distance relationships are pretty tough."

"I hear *all* relationships are tough."

"Touché."

Jack let Amanda stare at him while he studied her curious brown eyes. The silence became uncomfortable—he wasn't ready for that yet. They both spoke at once.

"Where's Rico?"

"You see Juan today?"

Amanda laughed, pleasant lilting music again. "I talked with him earlier. Doc says he'll be fine. He might drop by here tonight."

"You invited Rico on our first date?"

"I didn't know it was a date, Jack Corbin. You said you wanted to talk about Harvey."

"You always wear a slinky black dress to talk about hurricanes?"

"It was a last-minute decision. When I invited Juan, I thought it was just business. Slinky?"

"Wrong word?"

"How about sexy?"

"Sexy it is, then."

Jack put a hand out, palm up on the table. Amanda reached for it. Juan Rico walked in: "Aw, shit, isn't that sweet."

Jack slowly pulled his hand back.

"Amanda, I thought *we* had a date," Rico said.

"Sorry, Juan. Jack kissed me first."

"What? You? Jack Corbin, star weather beat reporter for *The New York Times*, Hurricane Chaser, twenty-five-hour-a-day Jack? You took two seconds out for a woman?"

"*She* kissed *me*. And it was at least three seconds. I still haven't decided if I'm going to kiss her back." Jack looked at Amanda and grinned. "But humans always take risks for beauty."

***

Dinner took an hour. Henri Mouchet doted over them like they were the only customers. Jack got to know more about Amanda's personal life, and picked her brain about Harvey. Rico did a decent job of keeping his mouth shut. He was busy eating, anyway.

Jack looked at his watch. "I hate to do this, but I have to file tonight."

"It's OK," Amanda said. "I have to catch a plane in a couple hours."

"Back to Miami?"

"Duty calls."

"Amanda, I'm not very good at…"

She put a hand up. "Don't think about it. We'll talk after Harvey does his thing. Gert kind of beat us, you know? I've got a score to settle now. 'Til then, business as usual."

"You could drive a guy nuts, you know that?"

"I guess I'm a little messed up after what we went through last night, like I'm not completely in control of things. Looks like it might get worse before it gets better."

"Like one of those Play-Doh machines," Jack said. "Somebody pushes the lever and you get squeezed through the little hole."

"Somebody or *something*," she said. "Looks like Harvey's going to do the squeezing."

Amanda stood and gave Rico a hug. Then Jack. He didn't hold too tightly, didn't want to be presumptuous, but she held him, pressed her muscles and curves against him. She whispered in his ear, "See you on the other side, Jack Corbin."

"Let's go," Rico said. "I need to run some film. You two can do this on your own time."

Jack pulled out his wallet. Amanda grabbed his wrist.

"I'm going to have another drink," she said. "I'll get the bill."

"But…"

She grabbed the check and smiled. "Do you argue all the time, Jack Corbin? That could get to be really irritating."

Jack shook his head. Then he and Rico left, headed up Watts toward the Canal Street subway station.

Jack's cell phone rang. He pulled it from his jacket pocket. "Jack Corbin."

"Jack? Bob Drucker here."

Jack knew Bob Drucker, the *Times'* Business Editor, but the two rarely worked on stories together.

"What's up, Bob?"

"Been trying to find you," Drucker said.

"I had a little run-in with Gert last night. Been a little busy."

"I heard. That's what I want to talk to you about. I got a call from an old college buddy of mine this afternoon, VP of LateNet, an after-hours trading firm. They handle large trades after the market closes, big chunks from people who've got lots of dough. Last night, just a couple hours before you went swimming, somebody took a big short position on an insurance outfit called Global Insurance Company. It wouldn't have hit the guy's radar, except that he noticed it was an awfully large position on a stock that doesn't trade that heavily. Then today he sees the stock slide all day, calls me."

"Why'd he call you?"

"Likes to feed me a tip now and then," Drucker said. "We did a lot of drinking together at Harvard." It sounded like an apology. "Anyway, he wondered if I knew anything about this GLIC. I didn't. But I do now. They hold big policies in the

Carolinas, lots of expensive homes along the barrier islands."

"Somebody made a pretty timely trade."

"Exactly. But that's about all I've been able to find out. Wondering if you know anything more."

"No, but I'll phone around. Who made the buy?"

"Guy named René Perez. He's Dominican. I don't know anything about him. Anyway, any help would be appreciated. It might not lead anywhere. Maybe it's just a coincidence."

Jack said goodbye, then relayed the story to Rico.

"Perez is a big drug family," Rico said. I got a cousin down there, banker, says René is the front man in the family, keeps his nose clean, does all the legit stuff they need done. You know who else is down there."

Jack knew who Rico was talking about. "You hear anything from her?"

"No." Rico looked at the pavement.

"I'm sorry, pal. Maybe she'll grow up a little, get the spunk out of her, come back."

"Yeah. Shit. Maybe. So, I'll see what else I can find on Perez."

"Might be a wild goose chase," Jack said. "But if somebody's betting on hurricanes, it'd make a helluva good story."

CHAPTER 14

ALONG THE HUDSON RIVER
7:00 P.M.

To a casual observer, the blue and white trawler might conjure images of an old, traditional fishing boat without the protruding rigging. The thirty-two foot trawler was steady and sturdy, with a wide beam, a deep keel and a raised, pointed bow that plowed smoothly through rough water. A teak deck surrounded a cabin with a pullout couch, kitchenette, cramped bathroom, and a closet. A trawler on the water was to Walter Beasley what his Volkswagen Beetle had been in the sixties.

With a bag from the deli in one hand and a bottle of red wine in the other, Beasley walked carefully down the ramp, crossed over to the B-dock and walked to the end. He pushed his thick glasses up his nose with the top of the wine bottle, bent his head down to look at where he stepped as he ventured onto the swim platform off the stern.

He smiled at the boat's name, *Slow Times,* painted in large red script across the back. Beasley was a deputy metro editor at *The New York Times,* and the boat was his great escape from the hectic routine of daily deadlines. He grumbled to himself at being stuck late in the newsroom but felt better now that he was at the *Slow Times.*

He climbed in on the starboard side.

"Port and starboard," Beasley muttered aloud as he stepped over the stern and onto the rear deck. He was still getting used to the terms. He noticed the stern line was loose. *Fix that later.*

Beasley slid his thin frame through the partly open cabin doorway and flicked on the National Weather Service station on his marine radio, where the monotone voice was still saying that Hurricane Harvey was headed toward Charleston. Beasley was unconcerned. Hurricanes rarely came this far north. Still, he felt a vague nervousness over the *Slow Times,* the new love of his life and the only true love he'd ever had.

The honeymoon had lasted a month so far. He had yet to sail it beyond sight of the marina, but he slept on the *Slow Times* nearly every evening.

Beasley was relieved that hurricane Gert hadn't come north. Jack Corbin had made the right call: Topsail Island. It was about time the cocky reporter got himself in position to get a good story.

Beasley turned the radio off and put in a Miles Davis tape, *Sketches of Spain.* He opened the bottle of red wine and filled a glass from the small cupboard, then he arranged three kinds of olives, various cheeses, marinated artichoke hearts, and some crackers on a plate and returned to the rear deck. A remote tinge of loneliness surfaced but evaporated quickly into the warm evening. Beasley liked being alone.

He would spend tonight on the *Slow Times.* No one would come visit for two hours. Then the girl from the agency was supposed to show. An escort for the evening, compliments of a good friend who'd guaranteed him a stellar night.

It had been a long time since Walter Beasley had spent the evening with a woman. He was nervous, but excited too. The angel on his right shoulder told him it was all a little too good to be true, morally beneath him. He'd considered asking more questions of his friend, even considered refusing the offer. In the end, though, the devil of loneliness spoke from his left shoulder and won out. Some company would be nice. He hadn't done anything illegal, and whatever happened later would be up to the woman. What was wrong with that?

The lights of Manhattan were beginning to take over from the sun, which reflected off the western clouds and turned the glass skyline a deep orange. *Those clouds are not from Harvey. I'm safe here.*

He noticed again the loose stern line, frowned at it. *She'll move around a bit more tonight, but that's all. Hell with it, I like the motion.*

Walter Beasley settled into his favorite chair, put his feet on the stern rail, looked up at the blurry lights of the City. The air was warm and still. Sirens echoing from the distance were someone else's problem. Water clapped gently at the side of the boat.

He ate an olive, spat the pit into the Hudson, then drank deeply. He was in heaven.

CHAPTER 15

IN THE BLOCK HOUSE,
NEAR THE CANAL STREET
SUBWAY STATION
9:15 P.M.

Father had been thoughtful all evening. *Probably what that scientist woman said about hurricanes.* Jonathan hadn't completely understood the conversation, but he could tell that it meant danger. Jonathan wasn't frightened. Father would protect him.

In the darkness, he waited for Father to tell a story. He decided he better say something so Father would know that he was awake, waiting.

"What's a storm surge, Father?"

"It's like a giant wave that comes up the river during a hurricane."

"And it would flood the Block House?"

"Maybe."

"What would we do?"

Jonathan listened to PJ's snoring across the room. PJ was the only other person who lived with them. He was a funny looking man, small and round with a body like a barrel and fingers like sausages and blond hair that stood straight up on top of his head. But he was nice to Jonathan, and he was Father's friend.

"I suppose we should have a plan," Father finally said. "A plan for getting out."

"Is that what the hole is for?" Father and PJ had been digging all day. "To escape the storm surge?"

"Hadn't thought of that," he said.

"Well, you'll save us somehow," Jonathan said. "Father?"

"Yes."

"Will you tell me a story tonight?"

Father was silent for a long time, making up a story. Jonathan pulled the tattered blankets under his chin, snuggled into the warmth of two bodies pressed together, and waited with all the patience a six-year-old could muster.

"Once upon a time," Father began finally, "there was a young prince—"

"Jonathan, right? His name was Prince Jonathan?"

"One upon a time, there was a young prince named Jonathan whose father was the King of York—"

"Sleepy, King of York," Jonathan butted in.

"I don't know about that," Father said. "Anyway, York was a beautiful place with green valleys and plenty of stone for building and a magnificent castle. The king was sick, and he called young Prince Jonathan, who was only six years old, to his bed."

Jonathan worked hard not to butt in any more as father told another fantastic tale about a faraway place. Father always told of magical places where Jonathan wanted to go. Or maybe they were places where Father wanted to go. He was always talking about *getting out*. About living in a house like normal people. That was more than Jonathan could imagine.

He listened in the darkness with his eyes open. At first, the story was sad. The King of York died. But the young prince kept the vow he'd made to the king on his deathbed, took the throne and made York an even better place. "Father, do we live in a castle?" the real Jonathan asked afterward.

"Sure we do."

"The Castle of York!" Jonathan decided.

"Prince Jonathan!" Father said. "Prince Jonathan Hart of York."

"King Sleepy!" Jonathan said. "King Sleepy of York. Father, what's your last name?"

"Not important."

"Why do I have Mother's last name?"

"Because she did good things in this world. I've never done good. My family has never done good, and I'm not proud of the name, stopped using it long ago. Hart is a good name, anyway. Regal. Makes you sound like the prince you are."

"Did you do bad things?"

"Never mind."

"Father? How come you never talk about the intruder?"

"Go to sleep, young prince."

"King Sleepy?"

"What."

"You're not going to die soon, are you?"

"No. I'm not going to die soon. Now go to sleep."

Jonathan snuggled happily into the warm place and did just as Father asked.

CHAPTER 16

KEESLER AFB,
BILOXI, MISSISSIPPI
10:45 P.M.

The media wasn't paying much attention to Tropical Storm Irene wandering around in the Gulf of Mexico. Irene's winds were at sixty miles an hour, paltry compared to Harvey. She was drifting vaguely toward Texas, her outer edges flinging thunderstorms into southern Louisiana and Mississippi.

Captain Glen Barnes *was* paying attention to Irene. He had a rendezvous scheduled with Hurricane Harvey that he wasn't keen to miss, and now one of Irene's thunderstorms was threatening to delay takeoff of the specially equipped, high-winged, four-engine WC-130 Hurricane Hunter plane that sat on the tarmac, fueled and ready to go. Captain Barnes climbed hastily up the ladder to the flight deck.

Gusty winds swooped under the high wings and shook the plane.

Barnes strapped himself in, said hello to his copilot and put a stick of Doublemint chewing gum in his mouth. He expected to chew on it for about ten hours. The flavor would be gone in less than one.

The crew of six included a navigator, flight engineer, weather officer and dropsonde systems operator. Strapped into the back of the plane were four journalists.

"How's Hugo?" Barnes asked his copilot, a tall, lanky southerner named Duggan.

"Wings haven't fallen off yet," Duggan said.

Barnes knew that Duggan meant the exterior pre-flight inspection had checked out OK. Barnes and Duggan had been flying Hugo into storms together since 1989, when the plane got its nickname. Mission control had told the crew that the hurricane churning across the Atlantic was a Category 1. Barnes flew in at 1,500 feet, far too low for what turned out to be a Category 5 storm. The plane pitched violently in the severe updrafts of the intense storm. Several objects were tossed dangerously about inside. The media people—and even the flight engineer—had thrown up.

Then an engine had died.

It was the closest the 53rd Weather Reconnaissance Squadron had ever come to losing a plane. It wasn't Barnes' fault, but it was a turning point. Until that flight, he'd been just another Air Force pilot, sure of his ability and eager to push the envelope. But Hurricane Hugo had made him white in the face. In the zero visibility, he wondered if his plane could survive, wondered what the hell he was doing up there.

The plane limped back on three engines to the air base, none of the crew saying anything outside of what was necessary to fly the plane. Duggan had pissed his pants. "Glad the wings didn't fall off," he said as they landed.

Next morning, Barnes painted "Hugo" in crude black letters on the silver plane. To the "o" he added two curved wings to make the pinwheel-shaped hurricane icon used by meteorologists.

Now Hugo was the oldest WC-130 in the fleet. A relic, in many ways, made more so by the 53rd's introduction of a Gulfstream-IV in 1997. The high-altitude jet was the new princess of the squadron: Meteorologists said the information it collected—environmental data from high in the atmosphere around and ahead of the storm—helped improve forecasting accuracy by 20 percent.

The Gulfstream-IV was up there tonight, somewhere six miles above the Atlantic.

Barnes had no desire to fly into a hurricane at 40,000 feet anyway. He and his crew were proud of Hugo's rugged, low-altitude history. The name had stuck. So had the joke of the wings remaining affixed to the fuselage.

"Waiting for you to let the clutch out," Duggan said. "Tower says we better roll out soon or we're going to have to spend the night here with Irene. Not a one-night-stand I'm interested in. Wind is gusting to thirty-five knots and picking up."

"Extra attention to preflight," Barnes said to the crew, letting an ultra-thin smile cross his lips as he glanced briefly at Duggan. "Everybody is tired, so let's double check the double checks."

Barnes and his crew had flown into Gert three days straight. Ten hours of flying each day. Today they were bound for Harvey. Assuming the takeoff and first hundred miles through the leading edges of Irene were uneventful—and Barnes wasn't assuming any such thing—a relatively boring four hours awaited them before they penetrated the eye of Harvey.

The team ran quickly but methodically through the preflight checklist.

The dropsonde operator stood outside in the driving rain and watched for flame, smoke or leaking fluid as Barnes started all four engines, each a four-thousand horsepower Allison turboprop.

The dropsonde operator climbed aboard, removed his raingear and strapped in.

"Are the newsies tied down?" Barnes asked.

"Like prisoners," said the dropsonde operator.

The four journalists were tense, clutching at the arm rests as if an extra grip might aid the shoulder harnesses in keeping them safe. Hugo, like each of the WC-130s, had seats for up to six media people. When a slot opened, it was the journalist's responsibility to get to the base on short notice. On board were a reporter and photographer each from the *Miami Herald* and the *Mobile Register*.

"Radar shows big flashbulbs to the southeast," Duggan said. "Moving this way. Better get it up."

A deep voice from the control tower came over the radio: "Teal One Niner, Keesler Tower. Cleared to taxi to runway two-one."

Barnes didn't want to face lightning yet. There would be enough of it around the eye of Harvey. He took the controls himself and taxied quickly to runway two-one.

"Teal One Niner, Keesler Tower. Cleared for takeoff runway two-one. Climb and maintain two thousand, runway heading."

Hugo rumbled down the rain-soaked runway until the ground speed was 100 miles an hour. As the plane rotated for liftoff, Barnes had to fly at an angle into wind, which gusted to forty-five knots just 200 feet above the surface. Crabbing, they called it. Hugo flew more or less sideways for four minutes, bumping and jerking in the erratic gusts, then banked into the storm and out over the Gulf of Mexico, heading for the Bahamas to refuel before penetrating Harvey.

~ ~ ~

EXCERPTED FROM
HURRICANES: HISTORY AND DYNAMICS,
BY DR. NICHOLAS K. GRAY,
HUMBOLDT UNIVERSITY PRESS (1998)

A large winged box floats above the earth, keeping watch over the Atlantic.

Rectangular solar panels stretch behind the box, creating an awkward metallic bird that appears to be diving toward the planet. But the GOES East satellite isn't diving, isn't even moving in relation to the earth. It is, however, whizzing along at about a thousand miles an hour, maintaining a geosynchronous orbit that matches the planet's rotation and keeps the satellite always at a fixed perch relative to the surface.

The Geostationary Operational Environmental Satellite is equipped with an imager and a sounder to profile several horizontal slices of the atmosphere, providing information about temperature, wind movements and cloud heights. The data are transmitted to a command center at the National Oceanic and Atmospheric Administration, which processes the raw data, then transmits the information back through the satellite to the National Hurricane Center.

The GOES dataset is but one element in a vast array of

statistical and imaging data that goes into making a hurricane forecast. Computer models take into account global weather patterns, large pressure differences and wind movements, moisture levels and sea-surface temperatures. Forecasters use data from nearly fifty-thousand daily wind readings from jetliners, some four-thousand land stations worldwide, thousands of ships and fixed buoys that measure ocean temperatures, and perishable balloons released twice daily around the world to sample the upper atmosphere.

In a message to Congress in May 1961, President Kennedy proposed putting a man on the moon by the end of the decade. The same message also requested $53 million to develop and deploy a system of weather satellites to monitor the atmosphere around the globe. The first geostationary satellite began snapping half-globe pictures in 1966.

But nothing did more to allow forecasters to improve their accuracy than the increase in computer capabilities. Before any forecast is made, incoming data is processed by a half-dozen computer models, each using a different method to forecast a storm's movement and strength.

The premier program since 1995 has been the Geophysical Fluid Dynamics Laboratory model, developed over two decades and tested for three years. The GFDL creates a grid of data points showing wind speed and direction, temperature, and humidity. By measuring thermodynamic activity at various locations—how the air is warmed, cooled and condensed—the program predicts rainfall by projecting the grid forward. Heavy rainfall and a warming core indicate strengthening.

The GFDL also looks at the steering winds around the storm. It understands that less intense hurricanes tend to be influenced more by these bullying winds, which push the storm around as if it were a weak child on a playground. Stronger hurricanes, in turn, fight back harder and tend to be more determined about where they want to go. The GFDL uses complex mathematical formulas to incorporate these broader elements of atmospheric physics and the interaction of the storm with the ocean.

But predicting any storm's exact track is like trying to estimate the precise path of a leaf as it floats down a river. Each shift in the current of the river changes the course of the leaf. And while the atmosphere's rivers of air behave like rivers of water, they change constantly as they interact with other rivers, as global pressure differences—created by differences in heating of the equator and the poles by the sun—are created and equalized.

Even if forecasters could measure all these major forces, there are still the butterflies.

In 1961, MIT meteorologist Edward Lorenz was running a theoretical computer model for weather prediction. He had stopped the program mid-stream and, to save paper, printed the status out to only three decimal places—plenty significant, he thought, to maintain accuracy.

When he restarted the program, Lorenz typed in .506 instead of .506127, the more accurate number the program would have retained. The miniscule difference, which Lorenz likened to the effect of a butterfly flapping its wings, changed the outcome of the program dramatically over time. Lorenz deduced that it would never be possible to predict the weather accurately with such a dynamic set of initial conditions, the ever-changing atmosphere. His work laid the foundation for the development of the theory of chaos.

This chaotic nature of the atmosphere causes the GFDL and other models to sometimes make wildly varying predictions, especially in forecast periods beyond twenty-four hours.

The trick to forecasting is in predicting the steering winds around the storm. To understand the steering winds, of course, one has to measure them, and there aren't a whole lot of measuring stations in the middle of the Atlantic.

That is the GFDL's biggest shortcoming. In the center of a modeled storm, the data points are about eleven miles apart. This high density of data is provided largely by the frequent passes through the storm's center by the Hurricane Hunters. Further from the center (and ahead of the storm) the data points become more sparse, relying on buoys, ships, and land-based measuring systems, so the GFDL model is focused intensely on where the storm is. It's a model with a splendid brain, but its head is down and it isn't paying sufficient attention to where it is going. The model's myopia is a shortcoming forecasters hope to correct with a model now undergoing testing, the LOng RAnge eXtrapolation Hurricane Model, known simply as the LORAX.

The GOES satellite provides the data needed to look ahead. Invisible to the naked eye, water vapor in the air moves with the wind. Time-sequenced satellite images reveal wind speed and direction. In the original GFDL model, nobody had figured out how to interpret the altitude associated with the water vapor images. Even if the data had been available to the GFDL, the old Cray C-90 computer would have been incapable of handling the data load. Now both problems have been solved. The nested grid of data points has been expanded hundreds of miles in front of the storm, forming a long-range view of the storm's movement and intensity. Though it is not yet operational, the LORAX is "looking up."

~ ~ ~

WEDNESDAY, AUGUST 25

CHAPTER 17

MIAMI SUBURBS
8:05 A.M.

Amanda had hoped to sleep in. She needed it. Instead, she dreamt of Sarah being swept away by Gert, of Rico trying to save her, of Jack giving her a warm kiss and of not having the will to stop and help her own daughter.

She woke in her small home at five with that feeling of having been awake most of the night.

Once she sorted the dream out, she realized how much she wanted Jack Corbin, his long dark hair, his honesty, his passion. She wondered if it could ever work, if either of them could ever slow down long enough to let a relationship develop. Sarah came first, that was certain. And Amanda couldn't imagine giving up her job—her life, her independence—for anyone, not even Jack Corbin. She wanted him.

But...

Her mind had been stuck in that circle for three hours as the earth rotated the sun into view out her bedroom window.

Finally, she gave up and showered, let thoughts of Harvey take her mind off the intractable puzzle of mixing love with motherhood. She downloaded the latest:

BULLETIN
HURRICANE HARVEY ADVISORY NUMBER 46
NATIONAL WEATHER SERVICE MIAMI FL
8 AM EDT WED AUG 25

... HURRICANE HARVEY THREATENS THE BAHAMAS ...

A HURRICANE WARNING IS IN EFFECT FOR THE NORTHWESTERN BAHAMAS. A HURRICANE WATCH AND A TROPICAL STORM WARNING ARE IN EFFECT FOR THE CENTRAL BAHAMAS... FROM ACKLINS ISLAND TO CAT ISLAND.

A HURRICANE WATCH IS IN EFFECT FROM NORTH OF MATANZAS INLET FLORIDA TO CAPE FEAR NORTH CAROLINA.

AT 8 AM EDT... 1200Z... THE CENTER OF HURRICANE HARVEY WAS LOCATED NEAR LATITUDE 23.2 NORTH... LONGITUDE 70.1 WEST OR ABOUT 470 MILES... 750 KM... EAST-SOUTHEAST OF NASSAU.

HARVEY IS MOVING TOWARD THE NORTHWEST NEAR 14 MPH... 23 KM/HR. THIS MOTION IS EXPECTED TO CONTINUE OVER THE NEXT 12 TO 24 HOURS.

MAXIMUM SUSTAINED WINDS ARE NEAR 130 MPH... 210 KM/HR. HARVEY IS A DANGEROUS CATEGORY THREE HURRICANE ON THE SAFFIR/SIMPSON HURRICANE SCALE. SOME FURTHER INCREASE IN STRENGTH IS LIKELY DURING THE NEXT 24 HOURS.

HURRICANE FORCE WINDS EXTEND OUTWARD UP

TO 85 MILES... 140 KM... FROM THE CENTER... AND TROPICAL STORM FORCE WINDS EXTEND OUTWARD UP TO 290 MILES... 465 KM. ESTIMATED MINIMUM CENTRAL PRESSURE IS 945 MB... 27.90 INCHES. A RECONNAISSANCE PLANE WILL BE IN THE AREA SHORTLY.

TIDES OF 6 TO 8 FEET ABOVE NORMAL... LOCALLY HIGHER IN BAYS... CAN BE EXPECTED OVER PORTIONS OF THE NORTHWEST BAHAMAS.

CHEN

Greg Chen, who'd pulled the overnight shift at the Hurricane Center, was one of the most accurate forecasters the Hurricane Center had ever seen. As a person, he was unpredictable, shifty and slippery, an anomaly among the hurricane specialists for the way he exhibited a disturbing pleasure as storms came ashore. Amanda and the others always felt a sense of defeat and inadequacy. There was no high-fiving in the forecast room. Just drawn faces and knitted brows. But Greg Chen seemed to revel in the moment. Amanda attributed it to misdirected enthusiasm, for one *did* have to be wildly enthusiastic about hurricanes to make them a lifelong study. Still, one always got the feeling that Greg Chen had another motive for the things he did. Amanda respected his ability as a forecaster, but disliked him as a person.

She wasn't pleased with the bulletin Chen had written. She wished he had added a phrase at the top warning of the possible threat to the United States coastline. Greg Chen generally wrote more conservative bulletins than Amanda. Almost as though he delighted in the idea of residents being surprised by a massive storm. *Almost.*

CHAPTER 18

GODDARD SPACE FLIGHT CENTER, GREENBELT, MARYLAND
8:25 A.M.

In Building 28, a technician oversaw the operation of a newly installed, massively parallel supercomputer, which contained hundreds of processors joined together. The new machine, five times as fast as the old Cray C-90 it replaced, ran vast quantities of data through complex mathematical models that produced the information used as the basis for all routine weather forecasts, public and private, in the United States, including the summer hurricane forecasts.

The Class VIII system was part of the National Weather Service's Modernization and Associated Restructuring program, aimed at improving forecasting by maximizing state-of-the-art machines. Scientists had run up against a computational wall with increasingly complicated models.

It was like trying to run modern word-processing software on a small-minded Mac Classic, the technician once said, though the problem existed on a much more complicated and more economically critical plane. More and more people—from farmers to stockbrokers—were coming to rely on the National Weather Service for information about what the weather would do tomorrow, next week, next summer.

The computer was running smoothly. The technician at Building 28 had little to do. But he had his eye on Harvey, the hurricane churning out in the Atlantic. When Harvey got within thirty-six hours of landfall, the technician would enter a series of commands to shut down the LORAX, which was only in the test phase and tied up a huge chunk of processor power. Policy dictated that all the supercomputer's resources be devoted to operational models whenever a hurricane was within thirty-six hours of landfall.

Shutting down the LORAX would be a simple procedure. The technician had other, more abstract and problematic things on his mind. His wife was in the hospital, dying. If he didn't very quickly come up with more money, she would not have a chance at another clinical-trial treatment that might stave off her raging cancer. Even the best health-care programs didn't pay for the unproven treatments of clinical trials. The technician winced every time he imagined trying to raise his daughter alone.

The answer, it seemed, had just landed in his lap—in the form of a moral dilemma. The official-looking man in the perfect suit who'd visited him at his home offered money. Big money. All the technician had to do was, effectively, flick a switch when asked.

He had warily allowed the man in the perfect suit into his home while his daughter played in the backyard. He had listened. At first, he had resisted. But the man in the perfect suit reminded him of his wife's condition. Then told him the sum. A hundred-thousand dollars for rendering a computer program unusable. A whole year's salary. The technician thought about that. He was confident he could cover his tracks after making a simple change in the computer code that would take days to discover. Nobody would know he had done it. But could he live with the knowledge that he had disrupted the flow of information to the National Hurricane Center?

Could he live without his wife?

He had looked out into the backyard, at his four-year-old

daughter who had no idea of the weird scene taking place in the living room. She didn't even understand that her mother was dying.

He said nothing to the man in the perfect suit. Just nodded that he would do it.

The man in the perfect suit then gave him ten crisp one-hundred dollar bills. A down payment, he'd said. And then he'd explained the little test they wanted to do, the simple blip he was to create in the GFDL program. The test had gone well.

Nobody suspected much once the program began functioning normally again.

The man in the perfect suit had called to congratulate him. He said the real job might come soon. In fact, the call might come one day this week.

CHAPTER 19

ABOARD HUGO,
LATITUDE 23.9 NORTH,
LONGITUDE 72.0 WEST
8:30 A.M. (12:30 ZULU)

Captain Glen Barnes chewed fiercely on his flavorless Doublemint gum. The roar of the four Allison engines was dulled by his headphones, which filtered the noise to a loud, constant drone. It usually gave Barnes a headache three or four hours into the flight. But the crew of Hugo had been flying for more days in a row than Barnes could remember. What a season. More flying time than in any year since 1995.

Including the refueling stop in the Bahamas, they were into their eighth hour, and the headache was like a familiar but unwanted companion now, an acquaintance who tags along until you give up and just try to ignore him, knowing he won't go away.

Hugo had made four passes through Harvey's eye. Each had been rougher, with more lightning and turbulence, and the pilot knew there was only enough fuel for one more pass. Heavy lightning had prevented a run through the northeast quadrant, but the on-board Doppler radar showed a small window, and the crew was about to make their fifth pass. It was starting to get bumpy. Barnes turned to his copilot, who sat calmly awaiting the heavy turbulence they both knew was coming.

"You sure you want to do this?"

"Got to save the planet," Duggan deadpanned.

Barnes grinned at his copilot. He could be an irreverent sonofabitch, but he was good. Barnes trusted him. He switched his microphone to communicate via satellite with the mission director.

"Control. Teal One Niner. Looks like we got a storm up ahead," Barnes said. "We're thinking of taking a look."

"Roger Teal. That'd be a good idea. Thanks in advance for a job well done."

"Lightning is close and frequent," Barnes said. "We're hearing six or eight zaps a minute on the radio. We're going to watch closely."

"Not worth wasting a good airplane over. Stay safe and keep us posted."

The frequency was silent for eighteen minutes before Barnes spoke again. "We're cheating west a little. Wild light show ahead. Looks like the Fourth of July... Oh, my! This is the most incredible lightning. It's constant from up here. Wish you guys could see this back home. Ah, we're about thirty miles off the progged position, between cloud layers now."

"Is it possible to stay on that course and give us a fix by 1300 Zulu? That last pass didn't go so well. Central pressure reading was only an extrap."

The aircraft's sensing devices sometimes extrapolated pressure readings when they couldn't get a direct measurement. It wasn't a perfect reading, but it was better than nothing for the forecasters at the Hurricane Center.

"We'll take a shot. Lots of convection now. We're starting to get tossed around a little. The newsies ought to be sick any minute."

Barnes smiled at Duggan. Few things were routine on a Hurricane Hunter mission, but a journalist throwing up was one thing you could count on. They flew on in relative silence for another twenty minutes.

"See the hook?" Duggan asked.

"I see it," Barnes said. The hook on the Doppler indicated a probable tornado. Not even a Hurricane Hunter wanted to mess with a tornado. The radar also picked up a nearly solid wall of lightning.

"I don't know about you, but I got better things to do than play Dorothy."

"Would be different if we had imminent landfall on the East Coast," Barnes said. "But this one's still two, maybe three days away. It might take a shot at the Bahamas, but we've done our job. I say we save our asses for another day."

"Roger that."

Barnes spoke to CARCAH again. "Change in plans. The window has pretty much closed. Looks like it's covered by a curtain of lightning now. And we got a hook. We might dodge the tornado and get in, but I don't want to get stuck in there. We're about six miles from the center."

"OK Teal. Don't risk it. We could have used the fix, but we've got another plane en route anyway. Maybe Harvey will calm down a little."

"We're bouncing around pretty good now. It's time to get out. See you at dinnertime."

Barnes wondered if he would have tried to poke through if Harvey were closer to shore, more of an immediate threat. He knew the answer, but for now he pushed the thought out of his mind. There was still a lot of flying to do. Hugo carved a wide arc through the clouds and headed for home.

CHAPTER 20

NATIONAL HURRICANE CENTER
9:00 A.M.

When Amanda had her mind buried deep inside the anatomy of a hurricane, it always surprised her to find the sun shining. She shielded her eyes from the bright sunlight as she walked toward the single-story shoebox she called the Bunker. With its cinder-block construction, ten-inch thick walls and small windows, the building had been constructed specially to house the National Hurricane Center after Andrew had rocked the former building in Coral Gables in 1992, taking out communications equipment and breaking the wind gauge. The array of antennas on the roof of the Bunker, poking into the deep blue Miami sky, were better protected, and a backup power supply ensured the center would operate through any storm.

Amanda walked into the Bunker, poured a cup of coffee and went to her cubicle.

She hung up her straw-colored linen jacket. She had her work clothes on: Loose-fitting blue jeans and a simple, white cotton t-shirt. The Bunker was mostly a man's world, and Amanda felt relatively comfortable being one of the guys. Comfortable enough that she felt no need to play any games about hiding her femininity. Her T-shirt was snug fitting and had a deep v-neck.

Greg Chen stood up in the cubicle next to hers. "My hero," Chen said.

"We'll see," Amanda said. She knew that Chen, like the other forecasters, was worn out. It had been a busy season.

"You're a warm body," he said. "And you're here. If you know anything about wind, that's a plus. Hey, what happened to you?"

Amanda didn't want to talk about the bruise on her face or about Gert. She was especially in no mood to chat it up with her least favorite forecaster. "Had good luck with Gert. A little too good, but that's history now. Which way is it blowing?"

"You're certifiable, you are. The wind? You saw the eight o'clock?" Chen said.

"I saw it."

"No changes. Harvey is just magnificent, isn't he? Anyway, the GFDL is doing fine, so we're sticking with it. No reason to change right now."

Greg Chen had just delivered a small professional dig to Amanda, and she understood it. It was a subtle reminder at the handoff: *Don't change models if you don't have to.* Most storms moved predictably across the tropics and were forecast using one particular model that was based on history. It worked this way: It knew where a storm had been in the past few hours and what direction it had been moving, and it assumed that the storm would continue that same basic movement in the short run. The model relied on a vast databank of historical storms to predict the movement of a storm in a given location at a given time of year with given characteristics.

Typically, as a storm moved out of the tropics, the GFDL model took over, producing the most accurate forecasts. But there were other models, and the forecasters used their judgment in determining which to rely on.

It was tempting sometimes, when a forecaster started the shift, to take a fresh look at the models and add the vital but dangerous element of intuition and decide it was time to switch, that another model would do better under the changing conditions.

But unless something unusual cropped up, the GFDL would likely stay in charge.

Amanda wanted to remind Chen that she understood her job. "Windshield-wiper," she said flatly.

Hurricane forecasters were always worried that changing the forecast—it's going here, now there, now here again— would make them look wishy-washy and erode public confidence. They called it the windshield-wiper effect. The antidote was a smooth, even transition in the forecast and a tendency toward sticking with the one you inherited.

"Yes," Chen smiled bleakly. "Well, I didn't mean to tell you how to do your job."

Chen put his coat on and headed out. Amanda sat down without saying goodbye.

Frank Delaney stuck his head over the wall of her cubicle. "Morning," he said.

She didn't look up, didn't want him to see the bruise. She curled her fingers into a fist to hide the bandages.

"Morning Frank. You get any sleep last night?"

"Couple hours," the director said.

"Stay here?"

"Yep," he said.

"How's Harvey looking to you?"

"C'mon, Amanda. I've been worried sick. You didn't even call. How bad was it?"

Amanda regretted her flash of anger as it happened. Everything—Amanda and Jack and Juan nearly drowning in Gert, her father in the hands of Kim Butler, and now a sensation of longing for Jack Corbin while still missing Sarah— it all welled up into a fountain of frustration, and she let it out with a sharp attack.

"You're not my damn father, Frank. Butt out."

Delaney stood there, waited. Amanda took a deep breath. "I'm sorry." She turned her head to face him.

"Apology accepted. I'm not trying to be your father. But I am your employer, and you could have used some rest instead of doing what you did. I'm also your friend, and I was worried. Nice bruise."

"I'm a bundle of nerves, Frank. What I need is to get back to work. What's up with Harvey?"

"Couldn't see the eye on satellite a few hours ago," Delaney said. "Recon reported that it enlarged to about fifteen miles during the night, but it's tighter now."

Not every hurricane had the characteristic eye associated with the storms. As a storm developed and changed, the eye grew and shrunk, normally ranging from ten to twenty miles across. A small, circular eye usually indicated a healthy storm, one well organized and likely to strengthen. Forecasters likened the shrinking eye to a twirling ice skater, who spins faster and faster as she pulls her arms in.

"Mission controller said the pilot on this morning's recon pass swears it's concentric, though kind of sloppy," Delaney said. "But he didn't get a very good look."

The rare concentric eye, or ring inside a ring, often indicated a temporary weakening while the storm reorganized. Other conditions—a warm sea and absence of upper-level shearing winds—would likely contribute to that reorganization.

"What's the pressure?" Amanda wondered if the Hurricane Hunters had already transmitted new readings since the eight a.m. advisory was produced. "Latest is 942, but that's an extrap. My gut tells me it's accurate."

"So he's reorganizing," Amanda said.

"Looks that way," Delaney said. "I was hoping the whole damn thing would just fall apart. It's going to be a long day. Listen, Amanda. If this heats up, I'm going to really need you to be fresh tomorrow and Friday. No fourteen-hour crap today."

"I'm fine, Frank."

"No you're not. You're tired, just like me, just like Chen. Just like everybody. Thing is, we can all handle this storm when it's a thousand miles away. When it gets close, *you* are in the hot seat, and I want you rested. Understand?"

Amanda thought for a moment. She ran the next two days

through her head. If Harvey did take a turn to the north, she would call Joe Springer and make sure he would evacuate early, before the rush. Then she thought of her father in the Seaside Nursing Home out on Coney Island. She didn't want to think about him, but she couldn't help it. She knew how vulnerable his building would be in a hurricane. Guilt pounded at her temples for having ignored that thought for so long. She wondered if Kim Butler had figured out the evacuation. She reminded herself to call Kim. Her father was nearly helpless on his own, and Amanda more than anyone knew the danger he might face. If Kim Butler failed, there was no one else who would help him. She wondered if she could find the courage herself. He could be ornery and difficult to deal with. Then again he was so sweet yesterday.

"OK, Frank, I won't kill myself today. But there's just one thing. You know my dad's up on Coney Island, and—"

"Harvey heads that way, I'll push you out the door myself," Delaney said.

"Thank you, Frank."

"And, listen, I need a couple favors from you, too."

"Anything," Amanda said.

"CNN wants to do an extended spot for tomorrow afternoon. They're devoting a full hour to the storm and the whole season, at three p.m., and they want somebody to explain Harvey."

"Oh, Jeez, no."

"But you're the only one…"

"I know. I'm the only person who can do it. Frank, c'mon. You've got half a dozen people here who can explain perfectly well what's going on with Harvey. You know how I hate television. Jeez, I'll probably pass out."

"It'd be all taped at around noon, nothing live. You can do it three times over if you need to."

"C'mon. Why me? Really."

"Because I've got the same fears you do about this storm, Amanda. I know the spin you'll put on your description. I know the message that will come through loud and clear, between the lines."

"OK. I'll do it. But if we're going to bother, don't give it to CNN exclusively. Let the other networks in, and the Weather Channel. Now, what's the other thing?"

"You know the New York weather emergency coordinator?"

"Leonard Lassitor," Amanda said in a dull voice. "Wouldn't know a hurricane if it blew him off his feet."

"That's him. I know he's a thorn, but he's the only weather emergency coordinator we have."

"Jeez, Frank. He's been sitting on the damn evacuation report for a year, at least. Nobody's even seen it."

"I know. But we have to work with him anyway. I want you to call him today, tell him to keep his eyes on Harvey. Don't engage him beyond that, just give him an early heads up."

"OK, I'll do it. Hey, Frank. About the blip in the GFDL last night. You think it was just a glitch?"

"What do you mean?"

"I don't know. It's never happened before. What if it was on purpose?"

"Christ. We've got enough to worry about around here. Let's not make it worse by inventing conspiracy theories."

"I'm not inventing anything. It was just a concern."

"Well, let's leave it at that, then."

***

As it did whenever a storm was threatening, activity in the Bunker picked up as the day went on. Reporters started to call. TV crews wanted to come in and get footage. More forecasters came in, some to work, some because they couldn't stay away when a monster like Harvey was gearing up.

Amanda had compared notes with each forecaster, soliciting opinions and engaging in a hurricane forecaster's version of shoptalk. Millibars, wind speeds, vortexes, intensification. She'd learned nothing she didn't already know about Harvey. She was back at her cubicle, dreading her next task.

Amanda reached for her phone, hesitated, then picked it up. It was eleven, and she'd put off calling the weather emergency coordinator as long she could. She wanted to talk to Leonard Lassitor like she wanted to stick needles in her eyes.

Weather emergency coordinator was a new post in New York. The mayor, a brusque man who many said was involved in things way beyond the politics of the City, had finally capitulated to repeated recommendations to improve the City's hurricane emergency plan. The Army Corps of Engineers, the National Hurricane Center and a slew of emergency officials had pressed him to create a central clearinghouse for information and operations in a storm emergency, an entity that would act as an umbrella for decision making over the dozens of agencies that would need to coordinate.

Somebody had to run the new agency, which would operate within the Mayor's Office of Emergency Management. The choice had turned political, and Leonard Lassitor was owed more than a few favors. One of those favors was connected, by a distant thread, to promises the mayor had made during his campaign. The well-paying position was given to Lassitor, a wide politician with a wide political reach who had held various posts in City government. Nobody had been happy with the appointment, mainly because Lassitor had no formal training or experience in meteorology or emergency management, but those who had shouted for the position to be created were powerless to affect the choice. And nobody knew how effective the position would be, anyway, as the extensive hierarchy within the Office of Emergency Management threatened to suffocate the new department. The bureaucracy had so far managed to keep outsiders in the dark about how the department functioned. Not even Amanda Cole knew if Leonard Lassitor wielded much power. He might merely be a pawn of the mayor or a weak shadow in a process that would sidestep him in the event of a real weather emergency. All she knew for sure was that he was the official contact.

Amanda punched in Lassitor's number. A secretary

answered the phone, said Lassitor was over at the Mayor's new Emergency Operations Center in the World Trade Center Complex, and connected her.

"Hello?"

"Hi, Leonard. Amanda Cole."

"Amanda, how wonderful to hear from you."

Amanda gritted her teeth, ignored the insincere pleasantry. "What are you doing in the Control Center? I thought it was only for use during emergencies."

"It's quieter here," Lassitor said. "Besides, with all these hurricanes you keep saying are coming my way, I figured it's easier to stay here."

"One hurricane, Leonard. One. And Gert *had* a good shot at you."

"But she didn't come here, and once again you've scared the residents of New York for nothing."

Lassitor's tone was caustic, vindictive, as if it were Amanda's fault that Gert had veered into the Carolinas.

"We did our best. You know that."

"And I'm beginning to wonder if that's good enough. Should I really be listening to you folks?"

"Leonard, jeez, we gave you small odds on Gert coming there, issued nothing more than a watch. No warnings, no panic. We were appropriately cautious."

"We all have our opinions. Anyway, what do you want now?"

Amanda wanted to hang up on him, but she remembered what Frank Delaney had said: *Don't engage Lassitor, just give him an early heads up.* The conversation had already gone on too long.

"I just want to tell you that we're keeping a close eye on Harvey," she said. "He's wide, he's powerful, and he's got a shot at the Northeast."

"And what would you have me do, Ms. Cole? Near as I can tell, Harvey is more than forty-eight hours away from anywhere. Your own computer model shows a track into South Carolina. Not that that means much. Hell, I know enough to know that it might just go out to sea and not bother anyone."

"It might," Amanda said. "But my conscience wouldn't be clear if Harvey wipes you out and I didn't mention the possibility as soon as it occurred to me. I've done that, so I'll say goodbye."

She slammed the phone down. "Jeez," she said out loud. She wondered how New York City's own weather emergency coordinator could be so flippant about something so deadly serious. He must simply not recognize the danger. So many officials didn't. The U.S. Army Corps of Engineers and the National Hurricane Center had been shouting—loudly—since 1994 when their comprehensive report was issued on the possibility of a major hurricane striking the metro area. Little had changed since. Dozens of agencies, from transportation to police, would be working without a master plan, with little or no coordination, to inform millions of people whether or not they should evacuate and where they should go. It was, Amanda knew, a recipe for chaos. Leonard Lassitor was supposed to spearhead the development of a plan to coordinate the agencies. For three years now he'd been working on that plan, and nobody had heard a thing about it. New York was not prepared.

***

Amanda ignored the first two rings on her phone. She picked up the receiver reluctantly. It was Jack Corbin.

"How's your leg?"

"Sore, but it's no big thing," she said.

"Well, it looked great with that black dress last night."

Amanda didn't say anything.

"I guess that was a stupid thing to say."

"Kind of," Amanda said. "But I'm smiling."

Amanda wished she had all day to talk about nothing with Jack Corbin, but it wasn't that kind of day. "Jack? I'm kinda busy."

"Sorry. I just saw that Harvey went Cat 4. He's not screwing around."

"No, he's not. I told you that."

"Tomorrow's Thursday. You said Harvey could be here on Friday. What should I write?"

"Official forecast is still the same."

"Charleston, I know. What about the LORAX?"

Amanda hesitated, stood and looked around the room to make sure none of the other forecasters were within earshot, sat back down.

"C'mon, Jack, I told you I can't talk about it."

"OK. I won't box you in. Let me ask you this: How much confidence do you have in the GFDL forecast right now?"

Amanda let out a sigh. This was turning into a dance, Jack looking for a juicy quote, Amanda not wanting to say anything that might tip her hand. She thought fleetingly about whether she could get in trouble for kissing a reporter to whom she was giving information. The thought made her chuckle.

"What?"

"Nothing," she said.

Amanda was concerned that she not let her infatuation with Jack influence their professional relationship. He had always shot straight with her, never twisted stories around, always been clear about what was and what wasn't on the record. If Harvey became a worst-case scenario, there were thousands of lives at risk. Jack could help. Besides, her career seemed small in comparison.

"Talk shop a minute?" she asked.

"I'm all ears."

"Frank Delaney would kill me…"

"I won't say a word."

"They hindcasted Gert today."

"Hindcasted?"

"Ran the data through the LORAX. Hindcasting lets us see how the LORAX would have done."

"Let me guess," Jack said. "Last-minute strengthening?"

"You got it. And remember that dogleg Gert made a few

hours before landfall? Well, LORAX called that too."

"Has it been that good all year?"

"No. First storm of the season it did terrible. We tinkered with the code a little, found some problems. After that it did better. We kept tweaking the algorithms after each hindcast, and it got better and better. Two of the last three storms it beat all the other models, hands down."

"And now?"

"It shows a turn to the north, a curve out to sea."

"But you're not using it for your forecast."

"Officially, we can't. Besides, it could be way off base. Each storm presents its own unique problem. We don't have enough storms under the LORAX's belt to trust it on any one storm."

"Why are you telling me all this, then?"

"Because I'm scared to death Harvey will split the difference, run right down the middle between the two forecasts. Look, Charleston is a good call at this point. Odds are with it. Thing is, people in the Carolinas know how to evacuate. We say 'boo,' they run. But what if Charleston isn't the spot? We say 'boo' to New Yorkers and there's millions of dollars at stake in lost tourism, things like that. In my official capacity, I can't say 'boo' to New York right now."

"But I can," Jack said.

"If you're careful. You say it too loud and my butt is history. And anyway, the GFDL is a solid model. It's done well. Harvey may very well hit the Carolinas. Thing is—we still off the record?"

"Until you say otherwise."

"I had a strange conversation this morning. You know Leonard Lassitor?"

"Weather emergency coordinator," Jack said. "Word on him is everything from political snake to ineffectual slob. I'm still trying to figure out if his post means anything."

"Me, too. I called him this morning to tell him we're worried about Harvey running north, that we're keeping an eye on it. He shrugged it off like it was a small thunderstorm that might rumble through, but probably wouldn't. I've never known a more arrogant SOB, but even for him it was way out of line."

"Has his hands in a lot of pies," Jack said, "and doesn't seem to take too many orders. Maybe the mayor's pet, or maybe they just filled the post for appearances and don't have plans to make use of it, or him. He's a friend of my editor, Walter Beasley, and Beasley says he's a straight shooter. I'm not so sure."

"That's why we need you, Jack. Even though we can't say 'New York' right now, we've got to have something in the *Times* tomorrow morning."

"I can do that. I'll get some other meteorologists to talk, you won't be mentioned. Tell me, though. What's your biggest fear?"

"Too many to count," Amanda said.

"Give me a couple. It's been awhile since I wrote about the threat."

"Time is our worst enemy. The ocean is warmer than normal this summer. If the steering winds take Harvey north, he could accelerate to phenomenal speeds."

"Like the 1938 hurricane?"

"Just like the 1938 hurricane," she said. "Forward speed of sixty miles an hour when it hit Long Island. The 1938 storm was only a Cat 1 by landfall, though. And still the storm surge was more than twenty feet. Harvey could be stronger."

"How much stronger?" Jack asked.

"Depends. Soon as it moves north of Hatteras—if it does—it will begin to weaken as the ocean gets cooler. But there's a chance that it could be Cat 5 by then. If so, and if it's moving fast, it could race to New York in seven hours and might still be Cat 3, just through sheer momentum. This is all hypothetical, you understand. It *will* happen someday, but it may not happen with Harvey."

"And if it does?"

"First problem is evacuation. Just in Manhattan and Brooklyn alone there's more than a half a million people we consider vulnerable. Thing is, they don't know who they are.

Lots of people who aren't in danger will probably panic and try to leave the City, plugging the bridges and tunnels. Even if everything went smoothly, it would take anywhere from five to nine hours to evacuate Manhattan. But we may not know where Harvey's going until early Friday morning. People could wake up to clear skies and learn a major hurricane is just a few hours away."

"OK," Jack said. "Now, what if it hits? What happens?"

"Bridges go first. Unusable once winds reach gale force, well before the worst of the storm arrives. That compounds the evacuation problem. People have to be moved several hours before the center of the storm actually arrives."

"Storm surge?"

"You won't have to use any imagination to frighten people," Amanda said. "We're talking flood heights like New York has never seen. Start at Fire Island. On average, it's a few hundred yards wide, and in only a few spots is it higher than five feet above sea level. We're looking at a storm surge of fifteen feet or more. As the surge moves into New York Bay, the bathymetrics of a rising bottom and narrowing shores act like a funnel. The water has nowhere to go but up. So, at Coney Island the surge could exceed twenty feet and extend three-quarters of a mile into Brooklyn."

"Even in Manhattan the surge will top twenty feet. Lots of people will see water on the second floor, and it will rise incredibly fast, almost like a wave. There are a couple dozen institutions in Manhattan—nursing homes, hospitals, jails and so on—that will flood at least on the first floor. There's at least that many in Brooklyn. Some face the water down around Coney Island and aren't built to withstand the wind. My father is in one of those buildings."

"I'm sorry, Amanda."

Don't bore him with how much it hurts. "I went to see him yesterday. Told the assistant manager that if she didn't figure out how to evacuate the place she'd have some pretty serious lawsuits on her hands. I don't know if it will help, but it made me feel a little better."

"It will help," Jack said. "Hey, you just reminded me. You think of anyone who might know which insurance companies have how much exposure to East Coast hurricane risk?"

"It's not too hard to find out, in general at least. Annual reports usually summarize exposure, talk about what a company is doing to spread risk."

"What about specifics?"

"A little harder to come by. You'd have to be inside the company to know exactly what their exposure is. Why?"

"Well, I got a tip from our business editor, said somebody sold short a big chunk of Global Insurance Company a few hours before Gert made landfall. Seems GLIC, as it's known, has some pretty strong exposure in North Carolina."

"Could just be somebody who was thinking on their feet," Amanda said.

"Doesn't look that way. I've been poking around about the people who made the trade. Perez family in the Dominican Republic. Then I got a visit from an FBI guy. Don't know how the hell he knew I was looking into it, but he wanted to know everything I knew."

"What'd you tell him?"

"Not a damn thing. I feed it to him and we lose a story and a good source. Anyway, my gut tells me something is going on."

CHAPTER 21

GODDARD SPACE FLIGHT CENTER
5:55 P.M.

The technician in Building 28 scratched his head. He'd hoped the call would be from the man in the perfect suit. When it turned out otherwise, the technician had been almost relieved. He was still wrestling with his conscience over the commitment he'd made to the man in the perfect suit.

Either way, it was a big break from procedure, but Frank Delaney was the director of the National Hurricane Center. The technician hadn't argued.

It was nearly time to shut down the LORAX; Harvey would soon be within thirty-six hours of landfall. The GFDL model had it heading for Charleston. But instead of shutting the LORAX down, as they'd done at this juncture with every storm before, Delaney had asked him to keep the LORAX running real-time. No explanation. The technician shrugged and obliged. Didn't make any difference to him. He entered it in the logbook, mentioned it to the technician who came in to work the night shift, then headed off to the hospital to visit his ailing wife.

CHAPTER 22

MANHATTAN
6:45 P.M.

The Palisades of New Jersey were reflected like a mirror image off the tranquil evening waters of the Hudson. Walter Beasley sat in his chair on the rear deck of the *Slow Times,* his feet on the stern rail, and studied the reflection for inconsistencies while he sipped a glass of red wine and dreamt about the young, small, well-proportioned woman who had given him such pleasure last night. He was pleased with himself, pleased with what his friend had arranged for him.

"Walter, it's so peaceful down here. Why haven't you invited me before?"

Beasley was surprised to hear another voice. The marina security was tight, and only boat owners were allowed through the keyed gate. He turned his head toward the voice and peered through his thick lenses.

"How'd you get in, Leonard?"

"Friends, Walter. I have friends everywhere."

"Well, join me then. Wine?"

"Surely."

Leonard Lassitor labored to climb into the trawler, which listed with his weight.

Beasley went into the cabin and took the wine bottle from a

cabinet. He felt a sense of unease at the sudden appearance of his friend, making his first visit to the *Slow Times*.

But Leonard Lassitor *was* his friend. Walter Beasley didn't have many friends. He poured the wine and thought about how little the two really had in common besides a shared love of good food and wine. They ate together often, cynically discussed City politics, the media. Lassitor was a low-level official, but he had a wide view of what went on in New York City, and Beasley enjoyed his company.

Beasley returned to the rear deck with the wine and an extra chair. He set the chair down and Lassitor fitted himself into it. Even with Beasley's thin stature, the two of them tied up most of the space on the small deck. Beasley handed his friend the glass of wine.

Lassitor held the glass up to the low sun and peered into the ruby liquid. He swirled it, took a sip, then set the glass on his stomach. "Still drinking the French stuff, I see."

"Drink the best, if you can."

"How many bottles a day are you up to, Walter?"

"Hardly ever more than one."

Lassitor laughed. It was a hearty laugh, between friends. Beasley turned to sit down. He saw a broad-shouldered man just inside the marina gate, standing with his arms folded and feet wide apart. Beasley recognized him as Lassitor's limo driver. He was keeping watch. Lassitor was one of those people who always seemed to have other people doing things for him. They were alike that way, and Beasley respected his friend's ability to manipulate others. He sat down.

"Well," Lassitor said, "wine can become a helluva habit, but it's not addictive in the true sense, I don't think."

"Certainly not."

Lassitor leaned back and tried but failed to put his feet onto the stern rail. They slid down the white fiberglass, leaving black marks. He sniffed and took a drink of his wine. They both looked at the reflection of the Palisades.

"You ever get addicted to anything, Walter?"

"Not yet," he said, looking at the black marks on the

fiberglass.

"Ever do any drugs?"

"Some pot back in the sixties," Beasley said. "Tried cocaine once."

"Never heroin?"

"Never."

"Good for you, my friend. Stuff's a bitch. I don't do it myself, but I hear it's awful, awful stuff. They say it bears a strong resemblance to chemicals in the brain that simulate sexual pleasure."

Beasley shifted in his chair, didn't like the direction of the conversation. He could feel Lassitor looking at him now. Beasley stayed quiet.

"You get used to the heroin though, I've heard, and you need more and more of it to produce the feeling. I guess the brain kind of marinates in this euphoria. Now that I put it that way, it sounds pretty good, doesn't it?"

"If that's all there were to it," Beasley said.

"True. Well, anyway, it's probably good business for somebody, wouldn't you think?"

"I suppose."

Lassitor took another sip. "So long as you don't use the stuff yourself."

"Definitely. "

"Or get involved with it directly."

"That would be risky."

"You're a smart man, Walter."

Something had just happened. Beasley wasn't sure what. He said nothing.

"How was the little trick last night, my friend?"

Beasley smiled.

"Thought so. Asian, was she?"

Beasley nodded, breathing deeply. He'd always wanted an Asian girl. This one couldn't have been a day over twenty, and she was very good at her craft. Beasley had just let her do it, no money had exchanged hands, and she left. He didn't feel the guilt he had expected. He did feel a small swelling in his pants at the thought of her.

"Consider it my treat," Lassitor said.

"Thank you, Leonard." It was a reflex by now, he realized. *How many times have I said that?*

"Don't mention it. I know if I ever needed anything, you'll be there for me." He cupped Beasley playfully on the shoulder.

Beasley didn't agree. But he didn't disagree.

***

The sun set over New Jersey, taking the reflections from the Hudson with it.

Thunderheads threatened to bring a shower before midnight. Leonard Lassitor had been gone about an hour, and Beasley was still trying to figure out their conversation. Lassitor was going to ask for something, he was sure, but he had no idea what. All the talk of drugs bothered him. It was a topic they'd never discussed before. If there was one thing about Lassitor he was sure of, it was that no conversation was meaningless.

A soft, deep voice startled Beasley from his thoughts again. "I was told you'd be expecting this."

Beasley looked up to see a large man in a tight t-shirt with short black hair, coarsely greased back, and steroid muscles, four large gym bags under his arms. He'd never seen the man before, but he knew instantly who had sent him.

"Who the hell are you?"

"Let's just say I'm the messenger. Heat's on a little too heavy. Your friend says you'll keep this safe for a couple days."

"What the hell is it?"

"I'm just the messenger. Where shall I put it?" The man smiled amiably, began to step aboard. "Somewhere where it won't be in your way."

"Jesus Christ." Beasley's mind raced. "Get the hell out of here."

The muscular man moved swiftly, maintained a friendly tone. "Here, I'll carry them in for you." He stepped onto the rear deck, smiled. "Your friend speaks very highly of you, mentioned how much he loves having you as a dinner partner."

Something dreadful was happening. Steroid Man was being far too polite. Beasley thought about all the free meals Lassitor had provided him. If there was one thing a journalist wasn't allowed to do, it was to take freebies from anyone, especially a City official. If he needed to, Lassitor could call Beasley's boss and explain how he had been buying meals for Beasley on a regular basis over the years. The information would never become a story—for it would make the *Times* look bad—but Beasley would suffer from it, might be demoted or even asked to leave. Lassitor wouldn't suffer one iota. And there would be no way Walter Beasley could retaliate without further eroding his own standing at the paper. Without even bringing it up directly, Steroid Man was making it clear that Beasley didn't have much choice.

"The sonofabitch," Beasley said out loud. His legs were shaking.

Steroid Man was moving past him, into the cabin. He pointed at the bed. "Hey, this looks like a good spot. Shall I put them here?"

"No," Beasley said as forcefully as he could. It came out like a whimper.

"Bet you and the Asian trick had a ball last night, huh? Right here on this very bed. I hear it's a gas, fucking on a boat." He grinned widely. "You're a lucky man. And you have a good friend. Be a shame if the girl talked. Spoil everything."

"Holy shit." Lassitor had him by the balls. If that got around, his career would be ruined. He pondered whether or not his career was really that important to him. The girls were, that was for sure. If he didn't help Lassitor, he'd lose his career and the girls and the meals. But he couldn't help Lassitor. *Jesus. What will happen if I don't help?*

He looked back up at Steroid Man, who smiled and waited patiently. Beasley's eyes drifted down to the handle of a small revolver protruding above the man's belt.

Beasley backed up. Steroid Man stashed the gym bags under the bed, then came back out and stepped onto the dock.

"How... how much?" Beasley stammered.

"Seven figures somewhere. Doesn't matter. You don't touch it anyway. Someone will be back for it in a couple days. You'll get a nice reward."

Steroid Man smiled again, squeezed his bicep. "Great view of Jersey you got down here. Wish I had a boat. Well, you have a nice evening." Then he turned and left. Beasley stood and watched him walk away.

"Fuck you, Leonard Lassitor," he said under his breath.

Beasley eased himself into his chair. He wondered how he ever got himself this deeply involved. His whole future could be ruined. He could go to jail. Beasley was scared to death of jail. He shuddered when he considered how a thin, frail man like himself would fare behind bars. Thoughts lashed out from the dark recesses of his mind with depressing images of dark prison cells, thick bars, frightening cell mates who could do unthinkable things.

Maybe I'll get off with probation, turn state's witness or something. Hell, I can't even prove the heroin is Lassitor's. The slippery bastard.

He could go to the police. He had to go to the police. But what would he tell them?

There's some heroin on my boat, but it's not mine? Well, see, it belongs to Leonard Lassitor. No, I can't prove that.

He couldn't go to the police. Not yet. He needed to think. His next thought was that he now hated his only friend in the world. He went into the cabin of the *Slow Times* and found a bag of potato chips and the half-gone bottle of red wine, then grabbed another bottle and returned to the deck and slumped into his chair.

***

Using Walter Beasley had been another stroke of brilliance, Lassitor thought to himself as he walked down the ramp, crossed over to the B-dock and walked all the way to the end.

Nobody would have any reason to come snooping on Beasley's boat, and Beasley was too weak of spirit to call the cops. Lassitor had tolerated Beasley's whiny personality for years, cultivated him, always knowing that he would use him one day. Lassitor would retrieve the packages Friday morning, before the hurricane did whatever it was going to do. The City would likely be in a state of confusion. Nobody would notice. Lassitor stepped cautiously off the dock, onto the stern deck.

Beasley peered through his thick glasses, fear, anger and confusion on his face like a boy in trouble for saying a dirty word without knowing what it meant.

"What are you trying to do, Leonard?"

Lassitor spread his hands. "What do you mean? I thought we were friends, Walter. Now pour me a glass of wine, will you?"

Beasley half-stumbled into the cabin, returned with two full glasses. "Sit down, Walter."

"But…"

Gently, with a smile and nod: "Sit down. I've always been good to you, Walter. I've done you a lot of favors over the years."

"And now you've ruined it."

"Oh, goodness. I'm surprised you feel that way." Lassitor stood, put a hand on Beasley's shoulder. "I'm sorry. I thought we were friends."

"We *were.*"

"Walter. You hurt my feelings. C'mon, I'll fix things up as soon as I can. One, maybe two days. Then it's over, forgotten, and I'll never ask you for help again. C'mon, what do you say?" He nudged Beasley with his shoulder.

"And what about me?"

"You have nothing to worry about. Nothing at all."

"Bastard."

Lassitor smiled. "You really are angry, Walter. I feel terrible now. Terrible."

"Angry is an understatement. What if I just throw the damn bags in the water? Fuck you and whatever it is you're up to."

"You wouldn't do that to me, would you? C'mon, everything's going to be fine. See that building over there?" Lassitor pointed to a mid-size apartment building across the West Side Highway, overlooking the marina. "There's a man in a room there with very good eyesight and large biceps. He's keeping an eye on you. You know, for your own safety. Nothing to worry about. Now, I need one other small favor from you. You have a reporter on your staff, Jack Corbin."

"Cocky son of a bitch," Beasley said.

"Then you won't mind getting him out of the City for a couple of days."

"Why the hell should I do that?"

"Because I'm asking you to. We wouldn't want to have to arrange any visits to the *Slow Times,* would we? I mean, we don't want the cops down here, or even our friend with the big biceps. C'mon, Walter, help me out for two days and I'll leave you alone."

"What's Jack Corbin got to do with this?"

"Oh, you don't want to know. I can tell you don't really want to be involved. Now, I'll call you in the morning. I want you to tell me that he's on his way to somewhere far from here." Lassitor dropped the jovial tone, looked directly into Beasley's eyes. "Understand? "

Beasley stared, tried to look defiant with his delicate shoulders pulled back. His eyes dropped first, then his shoulders. A sigh. Then a weak nod.

~ ~ ~

EXCERPTED FROM
HURRICANES: HISTORY AND DYNAMICS,
BY DR. NICHOLAS K. GRAY,
HUMBOLDT UNIVERSITY PRESS (1998)

When the hurricane struck Corpus Christi in 1919, Robert Simpson was just six years old. It was Sunday, so he did not go to school. He was one of the lucky ones. The school was used as a shelter, but it collapsed and many of those who had sought refuge there died. Robert Simpson recalled helping to evacuate his grandmother, who was strapped into a cane wheel chair, from their home. They floated her out.

Forty-nine years later, after hundreds of reconnaissance flights into hurricanes, Simpson became director of the National Hurricane Center.

Soon after, he teamed up with a Florida engineer named Herbert Saffir to create a simple scale for measuring the damage potential of hurricanes. The 1919 storm that devastated Corpus Christi became—after the fact—a Category 4 storm on the Saffir-Simpson scale, a hurricane with winds between 131 and 155 miles per hour and capable of causing major damage to structures near the coast and extensive damage to inland buildings, both through extreme winds and severe flooding.

The highest category on the Saffir-Simpson scale is Category 5, when winds exceed 155 miles per hour and can overturn small buildings and blow them away, as well as destroy large buildings. Storm surges from a Category 5 storm can extend several miles inland in low-lying areas. Only two such storms have made landfall in the United States since 1900: Camille in 1969 and an unnamed storm in 1935.

~ ~ ~

THURSDAY, AUGUST 26

CHAPTER 23

NATIONAL HURRICANE CENTER, MIAMI
8:15 A.M.

Though Amanda had expected it, she could hardly believe what had happened overnight. History had been made. She poured a cup of coffee and went to her cubicle, said a gruff hello to a smiling Greg Chen and read the bulletin he'd just put out. It was an historic forecast; she felt cheated that he had issued it instead of she:

BULLETIN
HURRICANE HARVEY ADVISORY NUMBER 54
NATIONAL WEATHER SERVICE MIAMI FL
8 AM EDT THU AUG 26

… LARGE AND DANGEROUS HURRICANE HARVEY BECOMES CATEGORY 5 … THREATENS EASTERN U.S. COAST…

A HURRICANE WARNING IS IN EFFECT FROM SAVANNAH GEORGIA TO CAPE HATTERAS NORTH CAROLINA. PREPARATIONS IN THE HURRICANE

WARNING AREA SHOULD BE RUSHED TO COMPLETION. RESIDENTS SHOULD HEED ADVICE FROM LOCAL EMERGENCY MANAGEMENT OFFICIALS.

A HURRICANE WATCH IS IN EFFECT FROM JACKSONVILLE FLORIDA TO SAVANNAH GEORGIA.

A HURRICANE WATCH IS IN EFFECT FROM CAPE HATTERAS NORTH CAROLINA TO CAPE HENLOPEN DELAWARE. THE HURRICANE WARNING COULD BE EXTENDED NORTHWARD INTO THIS REGION TOMORROW. RESIDENTS OF THE NORTHEAST SHOULD PAY CLOSE ATTENTION TO NEWS REPORTS TONIGHT AND INTO THE MORNING.

AT 8 AM EDT... 1200Z... THE CENTER OF HURRICANE HARVEY WAS LOCATED NEAR LATITUDE 27.90 NORTH... LONGITUDE 74.45 WEST OR ABOUT 560 MILES... 900 KM SOUTH OF CAPE HATTERAS NORTH CAROLINA.

HARVEY IS MOVING TOWARD THE NORTH NEAR 16 MPH... 26 KM/HR. A GRADUAL TURN TO THE NORTHWEST IS EXPECTED DURING THE NEXT 24 HOURS.

MAXIMUM SUSTAINED WINDS ARE NEAR 160 MPH... 260 KM/HR. HARVEY IS A DANGEROUS CATEGORY FIVE HURRICANE ON THE SAFFIR/SIMPSON HURRICANE SCALE. SOME WEAKENING MAY OCCUR DURING THE NEXT 24 HOURS.

HURRICANE FORCE WINDS EXTEND OUTWARD UP TO 150 MILES FROM THE CENTER... AND TROPICAL STORM FORCE WINDS EXTEND OUTWARD UP TO 300 MILES FROM THE CENTER.

AT THIS TIME… HURRICANE HARVEY IS MORE POWERFUL THAN ANY LANDFALLING U.S. HURRICANE SINCE CAMILLE IN 1969.

LATEST MINIMUM CENTRAL PRESSURE REPORTED BY A HURRICANE HUNTER PLANE WAS 907 MB… 26.78 INCHES.

CHEN

Amanda pulled up the graphic showing the green line of the GFDL forecast. Like a giant C the green line curved out into the Atlantic, no longer aiming at Charleston but instead brushing Cape Hatteras. Chen had issued the watches and warnings anyway. Either he'd stopped trusting the GFDL model or, more likely, Frank Delaney had forced him to do it. If it had been her, the watches would have extended to New York.

She overlaid the red line representing the LORAX and gasped out loud. She headed straight for Frank Delaney's office, closed the door behind her.

"Frank. The LORAX's track has moved into New England."

"Christ. But now the GFDL has it curving out to sea," Delaney said. "Bermuda High is starting to weaken. The storm could slip right around it, nice and neat."

"That'd be nifty," Amanda said. "If it happens."

"What's LORAX thinking?"

"Harvey has consolidated, pulled his arms in a little while he strengthened. He's going to accelerate, plow ahead on the current course, not be swayed by the external steering winds."

"How fast?"

Amanda pulled up a sea of numbers from the catalogues of her mind, studied them, eyes toward the ceiling. "Twenty-five by morning."

She could almost hear Delaney calculating in his head.

"That gets it abreast of Hatteras before the high weakens…"

"And shoots it straight up. Now, the LORAX barely touches Cape Cod, but it doesn't take much of a difference to, well, you know."

"Amanda, you know we can't go with an official forecast for anywhere in New England, let alone New York. Not with the information we have, especially not on the basis of a test model that disagrees with all the others. Christ, it'd be both our careers if we end up wrong and anybody ever found out."

"I agree that it's too early for a warning, but we can issue a watch. Jeez, we've got a Cat 5 on our hands. We've got to do everything possible. And Frank?"

"Yeah."

"I don't care about a damn career that much."

CHAPTER 24

NEW YORK TIMES NEWSROOM
9:50 A.M.

Walter Beasley was the kind of journalist Jack Corbin could do without. Beasley started as a copy boy in 1964 after graduating from NYU, and despite a general lack of news savvy managed to find himself in a deputy metro editor position. Even at the biggest newspapers the talent pool was thin, and there always seemed to be room for an astute ladder-climber to ascend a few rungs without a lot of talent.

Beasley was thin and soft-spoken—some said sneaky was more like it—with a penchant for sloughing blame to those below and beside him in the hierarchy. He had pasty white skin all over except for a summer burn on his balding head. He wore Coke-bottle glasses that didn't seem to help his eyesight too much.

Jack walked into his editor's office after having successfully avoiding him all week. Beasley, hunched forward and inches from his computer screen, didn't look up. Jack sat down.

"At least you were in the right spot this time, Mr. Corbin."

Beasley's voice was high-pitched and nervous. Jack hated the voice. And it seemed slightly higher today. Jack couldn't put his finger on it, but there was something strange in it:

Anxiety. Or fear.

"Too close," Jack said.

"Yes. Well, you made it out alive."

It was a statement of fact. No pity, no congratulations. Jack waited.

"I've procured you a seat on a Hurricane Hunter plane, Mr. Corbin."

"You what?" *What the fuck? Are you trying to kill me?*

"You know, the gentlemen who fly into the storms. It's an angle we haven't done this year, and with such a busy season, it seems we ought to do a feature on them."

"But..." He was going to remind Beasley of his only two big fears in life—heights and flying—but he thought better of it.

"But what?"

Jack's mind raced.

"I got a tip from the business editor this morning. Looks like somebody might have sold short the shares of an insurance company just before Gert made landfall. I want to pursue it."

"That's not a weather story. Let business handle it."

"OK, how about this: I should be on the ground to cover Harvey. It's what I do."

"We'll have a whole team of reporters on Harvey if it comes ashore. You're the right person to give us a view from the air."

The right person. What the hell does that mean?

Jack was tired. His muscles still ached from the fight with Gert. He admitted to himself that he wasn't in the mood to chase into the maw of another storm, especially a Cat 5.

Beasley waited for an answer.

"When?"

"You're supposed to check in at Keesler Air Force Base tonight," Beasley said. "Your flight leaves at midnight. I prefer that you get down there right away, get some color."

"Night flight?"

"They make the rules. That's when they had a slot. Seems

it's getting to be a rather popular assignment for journalists."

"I get one big vacation after all this, right?"

"Of course," Beasley said in the high voice. He looked down, indicating the conversation was over.

CHAPTER 25

7 WORLD TRADE CENTER,
MANHATTAN
10:00 A.M.

A hurricane watch had been issued for New York City. Not a warning, just a watch. The vast emergency command and control center might have filled up, but it was the second time in a week that a watch had been issued. Emergency officials knew the drill, and they'd just been through this part.

Leonard Lassitor, the City's weather emergency coordinator, did a quick head count: About half the people who should have been on the twenty-third floor had actually showed up. That suited him just fine.

The PC on his desk cast an ethereal glow into the dimly lit corner office.

Leonard Lassitor typed *nhctest1* into the password field. He didn't know if the password, given out to emergency coordinators during a demonstration of the LORAX during the National Hurricane Conference back in April, would still work. He hit his return key.

The LORAX home page came up. Lassitor smiled. He chose "72-hour forecast" from the menu. A map of the

Atlantic scrolled onto his screen. A red line headed toward northern Florida, curved upward and out to sea, but not before brushing the eastern edge of Long Island.

"Sonofabitch," Lassitor whispered. Amanda Cole was looking at the LORAX. That's why she had called and told him to keep an eye on Harvey. From the Hurricane Conference, Lassitor knew something of the LORAX's capabilities. It was expected to eventually become the premier program in the Hurricane Center's suite of models. In a year or two, after full testing.

She's watching it right now.

Leonard Lassitor had no soft spot for Amanda Cole, but he knew she was good at her job, that she'd designed the LORAX, and that she was a hotshot forecaster.

Now that Amanda was using the LORAX, Lassitor would have to revise the plan a bit. He picked his phone up.

CHAPTER 26

NATIONAL HURRICANE CENTER
11:45 A.M.

Hurricane Harvey was picking up speed, moving north at eighteen miles an hour. The storm was holding strength, but all the models predicted a gradual weakening as Harvey moved into cooler waters during the next twenty-four hours. Frank Delaney stopped by Amanda's cubicle, which overflowed with rough sketches on large sheets of white paper.

"You're going to use markers and paper? Why not use the computer graphics? The guys can have them camera ready in no time."

"Because then the networks control how it's presented," Amanda said. "You ever notice how television graphics are often beautiful, but don't tell you anything if they aren't accompanied by an explanation? Just arrows and colors. Noise, really."

She wanted her explanation to be simple. She wanted Hurricane Harvey to unfold before people's eyes, so the threat would become real, not just a pretty picture.

"Your call." Delaney shrugged. "Just one thing. I know you're going to make it clear that the Northeast is in danger. I want you to. But the models still don't point that way."

Amanda stood up and looked around to make sure nobody was within earshot. "LORAX does."

"The watch already extends north to Massachusetts, per your suggestion. I'm not going to issue a warning unless we get something on the GFDL. Not this afternoon or this evening, anyway. Just do me one favor: Don't say New York, OK?"

"I won't say New York."

Delaney nodded. "Listen. One last thing. I got a call from Goddard. Somebody used the old test access account and peeked at the LORAX."

"Who?"

"No way to know," Delaney said. "All we have is the domain name that somehow tells us it was a computer within the New York City government. Could have been the mayor, could have been a sanitation worker."

"Jeez, I can't believe they didn't deactivate it. This is spooky. You think it's related to the blip in the GFDL?"

"I don't see how. Anyway, it's been deactivated now. Just thought I'd mention it. Hey, how's Sarah doing?"

Amanda had mixed emotions about the change of subject. She sighed. "She's OK. Misses me. But I talked to her earlier and she seems to be having a good time."

"You OK with it?"

"She needs to know her father. Spend time with him. Yeah, I'm OK with it. Just hurts like hell."

"Hang in there," Delaney offered. "She'll be home soon."

***

Amanda was surprised to see Greg Chen show up just before three p.m.; he'd pulled the overnight and wasn't due back in until eleven.

She stood and said hello and noticed that two other forecasters who weren't supposed to be in were across the room getting coffee. They all knew history was barreling toward the East Coast. The lure was too strong.

A fresh batch of reconnaissance data was on Amanda's

AWIPS computer. She sat down and began studying it while Chen turned his computers on.

"What's the pressure?" Chen asked. His quick pace and sharp tone was of one who'd decided to take charge. Amanda bristled.

"Extrap of 913, up from 909 this morning." It was good news, meant that Harvey was finally beginning to weaken. She smiled at the knowledge that it would be a drop of rain on Chen's parade.

"Rising. Too bad. It was just starting to get interesting."

Amanda closed her eyes before she rolled them, so that Chen wouldn't see her disgust. "Still plenty healthy, though," she said. "Core temperature is ten degrees above the eyewall. Humidity in the eye holding steady at eighty-seven percent."

"Good. Structure?"

"Let me see." She read on. "Closed wall, blue sky above. Circular, six miles across."

Harvey's eye was completely surrounded by a ring of thunderstorms. The eye formed a perfect circle with a small diameter. All indications of a healthy storm.

"I like this storm," Chen said. "Could run north on us. Of course, that could make me—*er*, us—look bad. Whenever they run north it spells trouble. You know, last winter I did a review of all my forecasts for the past fifteen years. I worked back from landfall and looked at the forecast I'd made twenty-four hours prior, then had the computer figure out what I was close on and what I missed, you know, location, direction, strength. You know what my biggest error was on all storms north of Hatteras?"

"Speed," Amanda said without hesitation.

Chen's eyebrows arched in surprise. "How'd you know?"

"I did the same study two years ago, but included *all* of the forecasters at the center." Amanda shrugged. "I was curious."

"Well, yes, I suppose that was a smart thing to do. Um, so you know we have basically no clue how much this thing will accelerate."

"We have a clue. A lot. It will accelerate a lot."

Chen frowned. "I don't like the GFDL right now. You know, I pulled your LORAX up before I issued the eight o'clock, and it's…"

"It's just in the test phase." Amanda tried to sound firm. The way he had emphasized LORAX was as if it tasted bad in his mouth. Her project was a sore spot for Chen, who wasn't on the small team producing the new model.

He tried again. "I realize its performance isn't proven, but it did well with Gert, and with Harvey it's been right on the money so far."

"It's not in the forecast suite."

"But this is a helluva storm. And I might be the one on duty when the critical bulletin goes out. Has Frank seen it?"

"Greg." Amanda was standing.

"Yeah?"

Her phone rang. She ignored it, looked Chen straight in the eye. "LORAX is just in the test phase. Don't ask me any more, OK?"

Chen squinted, then his face relaxed and tilted slightly upward as realization dawned. He smiled wide, blinked long and nodded once.

Prick. She picked up her phone.

"Amanda… Hi, it's Jack."

"Jack. Where are you?"

"On my way to Biloxi."

"Why, for God's sake?"

"I'm not really sure. My editor booked me a flight with the Hurricane Hunters. I get to see Harvey from the inside."

"I thought you were afraid of flying?"

"I am."

"Well, don't worry. Those guys are the best. It might get a little bumpy. Well, OK, it might get *real* bumpy. But it's safe."

"Thanks a lot."

"Why in the world did he want you in the air instead of on the ground? This is the biggest storm in decades."

"I don't really know," Jack said. "It felt like he was trying to get rid of me. Probably more like he just doesn't know what the hell he's doing."

"Why didn't you tell him no?"

"I don't know. Maybe because I've been missing so many stories this summer. This one, flying into this giant beast, will be a shoo-in. And, to tell the truth, I'm not much in the mood to go swimming again right away."

"I don't blame you," Amanda said. "And I'm glad you won't. Go swimming, that is. Hey, did you learn any more about the insurance thing?"

"Haven't had much time, but I did a little digging. GLIC could be in trouble. Hard to tell. How badly they fare probably depends on lawsuits as much as anything else. Property damage is quantifiable, a known risk. Lawsuits have virtually no ceiling."

"Lawsuits over what?"

"Say somebody dies in a place that was supposed to be safe. A shelter or something. Family sues for wrongful death. Insurance company might settle out of court, but they're still stuck."

"I get it," Amanda said.

"Another unknown is what's called business interruption, or stream of revenue insurance. Commercial policies. GLIC doesn't seem to have too many policies like that. But that idea made me curious, and I found another company that is heavily weighted with commercial policies. Planes, trains, ships and big buildings. Outfit called PrimeCo."

"But the trade wasn't made on PrimeCo," she said.

"PrimeCo's policies aren't in the Carolinas."

"Aha. Let me guess."

"You got it," Jack said. "So, what's your feeling on Harvey right now?"

"That he's huge. I'm glad you wrote about it today. Nice job, by the way."

"Thanks. Still think the City has a shot?"

"Yep. Maybe I should sell short some shares of PrimeCo."

"I think you might go to jail for that," Jack said. "My sources aren't exactly giving out public information."

"OK, I'll keep my money in the bank. When do you take off?"

"Midnight. If I get back in time, I'll call you, get one last guestimate out of you, maybe chase the storm on the ground."

"If you don't catch me here, try my cell phone," Amanda said.

"Where will you be?"

"I'm worried about my dad. I'm going to head up there, fetch him if I need to. I'll stay with Rico."

"Now I *know* where Harvey's going," Jack said. "I'll call you if I get the chance."

"OK, good. Jack?"

"Yeah?"

"Be careful. I'd like to see you in one piece when this is over."

"Me too," Jack said. "I mean… I want to see you."

"On the other side, then."

"Like Play-Doh."

Greg Chen was leaning over her cubicle. Amanda hated it when he eavesdropped, which he usually did.

"I hear you talking about PrimeCo?"

"Forget it."

"I know about that company. What's your interest in—"

"I said forget it, Greg. I've got a lot to do before the TV shoot."

"OK. OK." He raised his hands and patted the air, retreated into his own space and disappeared behind the cubicle wall. "I was just curious."

***

Dozens of lights blazed in her eyes. NBC, ABC, CBS, FOX, the Weather Channel and CNN all crowded into a conference room in the Bunker. Frank Delaney said they were going to make an instant celebrity of Amanda.

She sat next to a large easel with sheets of white paper, a black marker pen in one hand and a red one in the other. Five microphones crowded the table in front of her. Cables snaked throughout the room. On the first sheet of paper, she had drawn a decent outline of the United States with a green pen. On it she had labeled Charleston, Cape Hatteras and New York.

After a half-hour of fiddling with lights and cords and microphones and plugs, during which time Amanda repeatedly refused make-up, the crews were ready. The cameras rolled.

Amanda drew a large red circle well off the coast of Florida. "This is Hurricane Harvey," she said. To the right and slightly above, further out in the Atlantic, she drew a black circle. "This is the Bermuda High, an area of above-average atmospheric pressure. Winds rotate clockwise around it as they are pushed outward." She drew an arrow to indicate the direction. "Harvey is curving around the edge of these winds."

Then, over the Midwest, she drew another black circle roughly level with the Bermuda High. "Another area of high pressure is moving east across the country." She drew an arrow pointing to the right.

Then she drew a long arching line that curved up from the southeast, from far out in the Atlantic, gradually turning northward until it touched the red circle that represented the hurricane.

"The hurricane has been pushed westward across the Atlantic by prevailing winds high in the atmosphere. They're known as the trade winds. We call them steering winds. Between these two areas of high-pressure areas is a trough of low pressure, which is very strong and extends far south. As predicted, Harvey got sucked into this trough and began moving northward. What happens next depends on how fast Harvey moves. If it moves very rapidly, it could hit somewhere between Charleston and Cape Hatteras by tomorrow morning, before the area of high pressure moving across the country has time to kick it out to sea. Or, it could overpower that high pressure system and move inland anyway."

She drew a thin red line that crossed the C in Cape Hatteras.

"If it moves slowly, there's a good chance it could get kicked out to sea. Some of our computer models show this path."

Another thin red line curved out into the North Atlantic toward Norway. "Now." She pointed into the air with her red marker. "It's also possible that the two areas of high pressure act like a child's fists on a tube of toothpaste, squeezing Harvey and spitting it right out the top." She never said New York, but she drew a thick red line that ran right between "New" and "York."

She tore the paper off, revealing another sheet with a green outline of the United States. Again, Charleston, Cape Hatteras and New York were labeled.

"There is a strong possibility that Hurricane Harvey will head for the Carolinas tonight and make landfall or nip the coast sometime tomorrow morning. But it's equally likely that we'll wake up and find the storm a couple of hundred miles off of Cape Hatteras and moving north very rapidly."

She drew a small red dot 200 miles east-southeast of Hatteras.

"If that happens, there might be very little time for people in the Northeast to react, since the storm could begin moving as fast as a car on the freeway. Keep in mind that we're talking about where the center of the storm would be. Winds faster than thirty-nine miles an hour extend nearly three-hundred miles outward from the center of the storm."

She drew a large red circle with a 300-mile radius around the dot. The circle touched Cape Hatteras and reached halfway to New York.

"Hatteras is in for strong winds and waves no matter which path the storm takes. Now look at how close the thirty-nine mile an hour winds are to the Northeast. If the storm moves north, it's this circle of winds we have to keep an eye on. Once they arrive, and it could happen by early afternoon tomorrow, evacuations would come to a standstill. Bridges become unsafe, roadways begin to flood, and debris can be tossed about, making it unsafe to be in transit."

Without mentioning New York City, Amanda figured she had done as much as possible to prepare any sensible New Yorker for a possible evacuation, which might be issued before morning. Before anyone was listening.

The CNN reporter jumped in quickly with the first question. "When, at the earliest, could the hurricane hit New York City?"

"We're not saying that would be the path," Amanda said, "but if Harvey picks up enough speed the eye could be in, say, Atlantic City by the evening rush hour tomorrow. Or it could be in Rhode Island by sunset."

"Then why not issue a hurricane warning for the Northeast?" the reporter bored in.

"None of our official computer models show the storm taking that track." She did not want to lie, but she hoped none of the reporters would pick up on her qualification.

The CNN reporter shouted another question, but Amanda fielded one from another reporter. "How fast are we talking? How fast could the storm be moving?"

"It's possible for a storm to reach speeds in excess of twenty miles an hour as it moves north of Hatteras. The 1938 hurricane that hit Long Island was moving at *sixty* miles an hour when it made landfall."

She watched the reporters scribble the date she had purposefully dangled in front of them. They'd all search the archives on the 1938 hurricane now. She made a mental note to throw together a press kit for them.

"Doesn't that make a storm more dangerous? When it moves faster?"

"Yes," Amanda said. She tore off another sheet of paper, thinking quickly. With her red pen she drew a circle the size of a basketball. Then put the numbers of a clock around the rim of the circle and drew a large hand pointing to eleven and the small hand pointing to the two. Five minutes to two.

"Think of the hurricane as a clock moving up the coast. Imagine its hands moving backwards, counterclockwise, representing the internal winds of the storm." In the center she drew another red circle the size of a quarter. "Here's the eye. That's where the air pressure is the lowest. So not only are the winds rotating backward, but they're being sucked in toward the center. Imagine the hands of the clock shrinking as they go around."

To the left of the clock, she sketched a coastline running north-south. "Let's say the hurricane is moving north, toward noon. It makes a slight left turn, to eleven o'clock, and hits the coast. On the large hand that pointed to eleven o'clock she wrote "50."

"The storm is moving toward eleven o'clock at fifty miles an hour." On the small hand, pointing to two o'clock, she wrote "130."

"Internal winds are 130 miles an hour right near the eye. On this side of the eye, at two o'clock, the internal winds are moving in the same direction as the forward motion of the storm. So the effective wind speed that you feel on the ground is fifty plus 130. 180 miles per hour."

Amanda glanced up and caught Delaney's eyes. His smile told her she'd just secured at least fifteen minutes of fame.

***

Back at her desk Amanda had one more call to make. Joe Springer.

"Joe, it's Amanda. How's Sarah?"

"Fine. What do you want?"

Amanda sighed. *Get to business:* "I want you to watch the news tonight. I'm on it. I want you to listen to what I say, what's between the lines."

"Let me guess. Harvey."

"Joe, you should get out of there now, beat the rush."

"You saying it's coming here?"

"Don't know for sure yet, but it's starting to look like it might."

"Every year you guys say a hurricane is coming to the Jersey Shore. Every year we get all scared. My whole life I've never seen one."

"Harvey is different, Joe. I want you to…"

"Don't tell me what *you* want. I'm on vacation. You've done your motherly deed for the day. I'll watch the news."

"And you'll get out."

"I'm not stupid," Joe Springer said.

CHAPTER 27

OUTSIDE SANTO DOMINGO, DOMINICAN REPUBLIC 3:30 P.M.

Maximo Perez was in a better mood. His investment was starting to pay off. Now he was impatient for the Octopus to call. Perhaps they really were going to be able to place that big bet on New York City. The phone rang right on time.

"Nombre?"

"Octopus."

"My friend. Our shares in GLIC are falling nicely today. It looks as though your scheme has worked."

"Did you doubt me?"

"I always doubt everyone. Now, it's nearly four o'clock. We have little time left before the market closes." Maximo realized he was getting a little excited. He reminded himself that he was in charge. He should sound so.

"I think we have plenty of time," the Octopus said. "Some people are poking around about the GLIC trade. Sounds like somebody at LateNet raised a flag. We need to be careful. I think we—er, you—should wait until tomorrow to place your bet on PrimeCo, assuming Harvey heads for New York. Wait until the last minute so that we're sure, and so that there's less time for people to look into it."

"Very well," Maximo said. "I will trust you. With your life. If you give me the go-ahead, I plan to sell short a very large sum."

"And become even richer."

"And become even richer." The hearty laugh turning into a hack. "And I'll be counting on you to secure the situation."

"Maximum death and destruction. Don't worry. I'll deliver. We'll soon be contacting our technician friend at Goddard again."

"Fine. Now, I have a question for you. How will people be leaving New York once the evacuation begins?"

"I told you, don't worry. I'm going to make sure…"

"I will worry about what I goddamn well want to worry about. Now how will people leave?"

"Some might take the trains," the Octopus said quickly, "and a lot of people will try to cross the bridges and tunnels into New Jersey. But I don't see why this is relevant."

"You don't need to see." Like many of Maximo's people, the Octopus made the mistake of thinking he was more important to the organization than was true. Maximo took pleasure in hinting at an element of the plan that the Octopus was not privy to. But the job was not over, and he did not want to alienate the Octopus. "You've done well, my friend. If all this works out, you'll get your wish to spend the rest of your life drinking piña coladas and enjoying our Dominican women. On me, of course."

"I'd be honored."

Maximo set the phone down and motioned to Terese to get out of the pool. She was naked again, a habit of late that he did not discourage. She stood before him. He watched the water run down her body, curling up between her legs and dripping on the deck.

Terese put her hands on her hips and cocked her head to one side, impatient.

Maximo smiled at his own power, and at the way she defied

it. He worried, though, that she was pushing the limits of his tolerance. She would have to be careful, or she'd lose her privileged position in a heartbeat. He spoke gently at first to soften her. "I wanted to thank you for your advice. I'm going to arrange a few accidents across the river from your hometown. It will be my insurance for the plan. And we'll get some technical assistance from a contact at the Goddard Space Flight Center."

Terese nodded, seemingly disinterested.

Maximo had expected some appreciation. He changed his tone, spoke sternly. "I want you to pick someone out and prepare her for the arrival of our new guest."

"The Octopus?"

"Yes. If all this works out, we'll have to get him out of there rather quickly. And we'll owe him a good time. I want to, how do you say it, *butter him up* for awhile, then send him to San Francisco to run the new show there. I want him to get laid so often that he *wants* to leave."

"He's a fat ugly slob," Terese protested. "I can't prepare one of the girls for that."

Maximo ran out of patience. He considered standing up, but his true power came from the confidence with which he wielded it, not from overt intimidation. Anyway, he needed Terese at least for a few weeks. He hated dealing with the girls directly. He remained reclined on the lounge chair, reached for his glass of rum, took a sip, then set it down slowly.

He spoke in a low and deliberate voice that he'd never used with Terese.

"Pick a fucking bitch," he said, "and prepare her. Unless you would rather that I pick."

Terese stood firm, looked into him. He watched the confusion cross her face. He had to drive the point home, turn the confusion into fear to ensure she would do as she was told. "There are more disposable women around here than you imagine, my love."

He knew it would hurt her, that she would eventually turn against him. It was the beginning of the end for her as his favored confidante and sexual partner. He knew, because it always started this way. They became close, they became confident, then they crossed the line, and finally they became bitter. He would pick another, but he wondered if he'd ever find one who could make him as happy as Terese.

With a hidden mixture of triumph and sadness, he watched the proud girl's spirit sink, then he watched her firm butt wiggle away. He felt alone again, just like the last time and the time before. He just hoped he would not have to kill her.

CHAPTER 28

UNDER MANHATTAN
9:25 P.M.

The hole in the dirt floor of the Block House was about two-feet square and eight feet deep. At the bottom, it turned and ran north toward the abandoned construction tunnel. The wall couldn't be more than a foot or two away.

The space was barely large enough to work in. But it was as big as an escape tunnel needed to be. Sleepy and PJ took turns digging in four-hour shifts, working every day since Hammer had first been spotted nearby. They rested at night.

Sleepy couldn't rest tonight. As soon as Jonathan fell asleep, he instructed PJ to keep a close eye on things and he set out. It had been quiet since Hammer killed the old man. Too quiet. He wanted to take a look around.

He made his way up the ladder, moved the steel plate aside, put it back in place. He did the same with the plywood that blocked the passage to the small entry space, then he moved down the abandoned tunnel, through the crawl space into the active tunnel, and on to the subway platform. He caught the train north to 42nd Street, then transferred and traveled cross-town to Grand Central Station.

PJ had explained where Hammer's hangout was. Sleepy

headed for the subway platform that led into the dark lattice of tunnels that he would have to navigate. At the end of the platform he was about to hop off when he saw the pitted, grotesque face, the claw hammer at the belt. Hammer was talking with someone, a fat man, twenty yards up the platform. The fat man moved little, except for a quick turn of his head from side to side every few seconds. His back was to Sleepy. Hammer moved nervously, the cat out of doors in a strange environment. Sleepy couldn't hear their conversation, but the furtive movements told him it wasn't about the weather.

He wondered if Hammer could recognize him. *By the scar, maybe. Otherwise, no. I've seen him, he has never seen me. But he'll have heard of the scar.*

Sleepy stayed out of sight behind a group of loud teenagers, waited until the next train came. Hammer and the fat man looked around, nervously, then they got on the train.

Sleepy barely made the doors of the next car. The train left the station. Sleepy followed a woman through the doors between the cars. He walked with his head turned, kept the scarred side of his face away from Hammer and the fat man. They sat next to each other, Hammer on the far side, not looking at each other so as to appear not to be together. Sleepy approached slowly, stopped and pretended to scan the map on the wall, then turned his back to Hammer and moved quickly past him.

As he went by, he heard a snippet of conversation.

"Again tomorrow morning at nine," the fat man said.

"I'll be here," Hammer said as Sleepy moved out of hearing range.

Sleepy stopped at the next pole and grabbed it with one hand. Hiding his scar, he swiveled his head to look at the fat man.

Holy shit!

He felt a wave of dizziness. Time became distorted. The fat man was Sleepy's brother. The brother who beat him. The brother he'd threatened to get even with.

His own brother was Hammer's supplier. No other reason

for them to be talking to each other. He wasn't surprised. He had suspected his brother was moving drugs into the city. But his next thought hit him like falling bricks: *You sonofabitch. You killed my woman. Your goddamn drugs killed my woman.*

The train pulled into the next stop. Hammer and Sleepy's brother continued talking, didn't get up. Sleepy wanted to kill them both right there, make the world safer for himself, for Jonathan, for all the mole people. He wanted to put his thumbs into his brother's neck and squeeze the life out of him. He felt his fists clenching at his sides, fingernails digging into his palms.

Can't do it here. Can't do anything here. Don't get caught.

People got off, people got on. What had his brother said? *Tomorrow morning at nine.* They were going to meet again. What could he do about it?

The train doors were closing.

Sleepy darted through the doors just before they slammed shut.

***

An unexpected sense of urgency, borne of fury, came over Sleepy. Seeing his brother and Hammer together, and not being able to do anything about it, angered him, made the *way out* seem even more important. He needed to think, and so when he got home he went back into the hole and started digging.

The first foot, on Tuesday, had been the hardest to dig. The dirt floor was compacted after years of foot traffic so that it felt more like concrete than dirt. The rest of the way down, bricks and lengths of pipe and other construction debris slowed progress.

On his knees, Sleepy backed out of the horizontal crawl space and stood in the hole. He rubbed the base of his spine. His whole body ached. *I'm getting old. This should be my last construction job. I should be doing social work, raising a family.*

The dreaming would get him nowhere. There would be no

next job, no social work, no anything, if he didn't finish this tunnel. That's the way he had come to view the project. It would never have gotten done if he saw it merely as an important safety measure. The work was too hard, the conditions too cramped and dark, and he would have given up by now. A rough idea was taking shape in his mind for how he might get rid of Hammer. The tunnel was the key to it. Sleepy had tacked a crude sign scribbled on cardboard onto the wall above the project. *A way out,* it read. The sign summed up everything he wanted, and the escape tunnel became a symbol for his dreams. For PJ, the work held much less significance. He worked because Sleepy told him it was important and PJ trusted him.

They were close now, he thought as he closed his eyes and stooped, reached out with the small, rusty shovel and dug out another scoop of earth in the dead black.

Sleepy found the work meditative. In the darkness, he could close his eyes or leave them open, it did not matter. He had always appreciated being alone, and his four hours in the hole every day was for Sleepy a relaxing stretch of isolation.

His shovel hit something solid, and he reached out with his fingers to work around it. It was another chunk of brick or cinder block that would slow him down. As he dug his fingernails into the cold earth, eyes blind, Sleepy suddenly felt that he truly was a mole. The thought made his heart sink. He never liked the term. It sounded so subhuman. *We're not animals. We're men and women and children. We live and breathe and think and work and love.*

And hate and fuck and fight and scratch. The obstruction was large. He felt its rough surface and knew it was a brick. It might take ten minutes or more to get it out. He dug with the shovel in a widening circle, looking for an edge to pry on. Sleepy tried to let his mind drift back into the Zen-like state he often enjoyed down here, but he couldn't maintain it: His brother and Hammer kept taking over his thoughts.

He had a nagging feeling that Hammer would act sooner rather than later. In the past few weeks, the campaign to enlist more pushers and get cheap heroin on the streets had begun to work. Once Hammer had enough addicts buying from his pushers, he began raising prices. It was time to reap some profits now, and he would want to make sure he had found all the pushers he could summon. He had already stepped up his recruiting efforts, targeting more distant underground dwellings. He was invading homes occupied by more than two men, where the odds were riskier.

Sleepy had seen it all before. He knew Hammer's business tactics would become even more aggressive.

He sighed deeply in the darkness.

Then his fingernails dipped into the indentation between one brick and another.

Mortar. Where there's mortar there is more than just debris. He had found the wall of the old construction tunnel.

His mind leaped for joy. His head followed, and he bumped it on oak plank that supported the earth ceiling of the horizontal section of the escape tunnel. He rubbed his head, and then his mind began immediately to work on the new problem. It might take a full day to chisel a hole through the wall. Then there was the question of whether or not there was any way out of the construction tunnel. It might have been cut off on both ends, after its abandonment, by the actual construction areas it served. Sleepy felt a sinking feeling with this thought, one he hadn't allowed himself all week. If he had not assumed there would be a way out, he could never had mustered the energy to dig every day. PJ never thought that far, and the question had never been raised.

Sleepy felt a new pressure. All week, he had known it would take a long time to dig the escape tunnel. He had not made a deadline, but had focused on the daily schedule. They didn't have the men or the energy to keep up a more rapid pace, at least not for long. But now they were close. And so was the danger. He felt Hammer nipping at his heels. He stared into the darkness at the bricks, ran his fingers over them. *The way out. We'll double our efforts.*

CHAPTER 29

KEESLER AFB,
BILOXI, MISSISSIPPI
11:32 P.M.

The tarmac was quiet, the distant sounds of night bugs and animals mixing to form a barely audible hum. The moon was full and it cast an eerie blue light on the tarmac. Jack was standing near the WC-130, listening to nervous jokes made by a stringer Beasley had rounded up to take Juan Rico's place, and two other journalists Jack didn't know. They were all waiting for the flight crew.

Jack felt like a piece of him was missing without Rico around. He called him on his cell phone.

"On my way to face death again," Jack said. "What're you doing?"

"Watching Leno," Rico said.

"Lazy ass."

"Hey, wasn't like I wanted to break an arm."

"You going to chase Harvey?"

"I dunno. Maybe I let him chase me."

"He might," Jack said.

"Wanna bet?"

"Yep."

"Double or nothin'?"

"Sure," Jack said. "I could use a hundred. Where's your pick?"

Rico thought. "Topsail Island."

"Oh, c'mon. That's a throwaway. Betting with you is like taking candy from a baby."

"Topsail Island," Rico said again. "Where you pick?"

"I'm here. You're there. I pick New York."

"Fuck you, man! I'm a one-armed bandit. Can't even defend myself."

Jack saw the erect silhouette of Captain Glen Barnes emerge from the hangar, followed by a crew of five.

"Gotta go, pal. Looks like we're on our way."

"Take pictures for me," Rico said.

"Sure."

Jack hadn't gotten access to Barnes all day. Resting, the PR woman said. The whole afternoon and evening had been a waste of time. The Captain reached the clutch of journalists, extended his hand and introduced himself and his crew.

Jack took Barnes' hand. "Jack Corbin, *New York Times*."

Barnes grumbled.

Jack had met the pilot briefly last year at the National Hurricane Conference. His recollection of a short man with a condescending tone was correct. They had shaken hands, Jack saying something polite about maybe doing a story about the pilot someday and Barnes, returning the politeness, saying its always nice when reporters acknowledge the work of the hurricane hunters. It was the way he emphasized *reporters*. *As though he were talking down to me. Clear tension, like I smelled his asshole and he smelled mine and we could tell we were from different packs.*

Barnes was unimposing, average height and build. But he looked as though he contained a bridled, boundless energy, as if he'd managed to drink seven cups of coffee and yet keep a grip on his nerves for some possible future moment when superhuman energy would be needed. *Air Force guys. Gung ho about everything.*

Jack pointed to the stringer. "This is Harvey Miller, our photographer."

The pilot seemed unimpressed. "Harvey. Humph," Barnes said, casting a glance over his shoulder at his wiry copilot, who flashed an internal-joke grin. Barnes looked back at Jack. "I hate coincidences, Mr. Corbin. Glad we're flying into Irene, sir."

"We're what?" Jack had forgotten all about Hurricane Irene. Everybody had, it seemed. But she was maintaining Category 1 strength, barely-chugging along in relative obscurity in the Gulf of Mexico, existing in the media shadow of her larger cousin. Irene, a small storm with a tight wind radius, had been inching across the Gulf toward Brownsville, Texas, near the Mexican border, with landfall predicted in two or three days. The Hurricane Center was taking her seriously, as they did every hurricane that might affect land, but the media had all but ignored the storm.

"Irene," Barnes repeated. "We're flying into Irene, sir."

"But I thought we'd be going to Harvey. Jesus, I just assumed. I mean, it's the biggest storm in years, and we're going to miss it?"

"You might be missing it, Mr. Corbin, but we've been there already. With all due respect, we're quite pleased not to be going back. It's been a long season and Harvey is a helluva storm, sir."

"But there's no story in Irene. Damn. What the hell am I supposed to write? 'During the Storm of the Century, Captain Glen Barnes was pleased to be flying into wimpy little Irene.'"

Barnes studied Jack. He took a stick of Doublemint chewing gum from his shirt pocket, unwrapped it and stuck it in his mouth. He wadded the wrapper up and flicked it with his thumb and forefinger, narrowly missing Jack's shoe. Neither man looked down.

"Mr. Corbin. This is the military. We take orders from CARCAH, not from reporters. Not even *The New York Times* can tell us where to fly. I'm the pilot. Full authority to throw your ass out of the plane if you cause problems. Now, you coming, sir?"

No one else had said a word yet. Jack let out an exaggerated breath of exasperation and shook his head, then rolled his eyes and threw up his hands in acquiescence.

"Copilot Duggan here will tell you what to expect during the flight." Barnes pointed with his thumb at Duggan and walked briskly toward Hugo.

Duggan clearly had a memorized spiel designed for the benefit of the journalists and the stories they would be writing. "The WC-130 here has 65,000 pounds of fuel on board, enough to be in the air safely for ten or twelve hours. It's in the big tank you'll see in the middle of the fuselage. We'll ask you to remain seated and buckled in during takeoff and for much of the time while we're in or near the hurricane, as we never know when it might get bumpy. Cap'n will let-you know when it's safe to get up and walk around. In the eye, of course, you'll all have a few minutes to enjoy the view. Now, safety. Laptop computers are fine unless Cap'n asks you to turn them off, then we request you do so immediately. Transmissions of any kind are not allowed. There are no parachutes on board. If we have any problems, which of course we don't expect, we'll ditch the plane. There's a life preserver under your seat and a twenty-man life raft filled with survival supplies stowed in each wing. The dropsonde operator will show you how to get at all that stuff. Hopefully we won't need it. Hugo here is a pretty trusty old plane. If there's any mechanical problems, we usually spot them on the ground. We've got a couple of decommissioned WC-130s around back of the hangar that we strip for whatever parts we need to get the old bucket of bolts up in the air."

Duggan grinned. Hurricane Hunter humor. Jack wasn't amused.

Duggan reminded the guests there were no stewardesses on board, no dinners served. "You all board in five minutes," he said.

Jack quickly tried to call Amanda on his cell phone, but she was not at the Hurricane Center and did not answer her cell phone. *A long day for her, too.* He had a brand new laptop with him. He sent her a quick email:

```
Luck runs out again. Flying into Irene
instead. Due to take off at midnight.
See you soon. Wear black.
Jack.
```

The dropsonde operator had strapped the other three journalists in. Barnes was shouting. "You coming or not, Corbin?"

"Shit," Jack said under his breath. "I'm coming."

~ ~ ~

EXCERPTED FROM
HURRICANES: HISTORY AND DYNAMICS,
BY DR. NICHOLAS K. GRAY,
HUMBOLDT UNIVERSITY PRESS (1998)

On July 27, 1943, Colonel Joe Duckworth of the Army Air Corps bet a highball that he could fly his single engine AT-6 Trainer into a hurricane approaching Galveston. He did it with one navigator. He did it without official permission. Duckworth was the lead instructor at Bryan Field, training British pilots—many of whom were already World War II aces—in the nascent field of instrument flying.

Word spread that the AT-6 "Texan Trainers" might have to be moved out of the storm's path. The British pilots scoffed at the implied frailty of the plane. Duckworth, tired of the ribbing, proposed the wager. He collected on his bet that night, becoming the first known person to fly into the eye of a hurricane, an adventure he described as similar to "being tossed about like a stick in a dog's mouth."

Duckworth's mission eventually led to the creation of the 53rd Weather Reconnaissance Squadron. The Hurricane Hunters.

~ ~ ~

FRIDAY, AUGUST 27

CHAPTER 30

ABOARD HUGO
6:57 A.M.

You never knew what a storm was like until you got inside. That was the only constant with hurricanes, Captain Glen Barnes believed. So far the flight was smooth and uneventful. But the pilot was nervous. Not only did he have his usual headache, but his jaw was sore from the furious chewing he gave the gum. Hugo and its crew were about to make another attempt at their first pass through the eyewall. Several previous tries from the south and west had been aborted because of strong thunderstorms. They were now taking a shot from the north.

"Control, Teal One-Niner. We're about 200 miles out, right on progged position, everything smooth so far. Hope to be in the eye by 1200 Zulu."

"Roger, Teal. Fate of the universe is in your hands. Stay in touch."

"Everybody's a fucking comedian," Barnes said to his copilot.

Duggan smiled. "Lighten up, Cap'n. It's just another storm. We've been here before."

"I know. That's why I won't lighten up."

It bothered Barnes whenever his copilot said anything

without a joke or obscure reference. When Duggan sounded serious, it meant there was probably a real problem to consider. Barnes ran the whole mission through his head, ticked off the sequence of preflight checks, made sure nothing had been missed. His argument with the *Times* reporter was eating at him. Mission control's holding Hugo on the ground for an hour while they made their minds up was eating at him. His superstitions were eating at him.

"*New York* fucking *Times.*"

***

They had been in the air since one in the morning. It was broad daylight now, but Jack Corbin wished it were still dark, for the view was one he did not enjoy: thick angry clouds and a frothy sea. Hugo's giant rear end gaped open. The dropsonde operator pushed a button and with a loud click the small torpedo-looking metal canister slid out the back of the plane.

Jack had been forced to remain buckled in while the crew went about its work. He tried his best to interpret what they were doing and take notes. The weather officer made periodic visual observations of wave heights to estimate wind speed. The flight engineer kept his eyes on an array of gauges, monitoring Hugo's health.

The navigator told Jack that Hugo would fly an Alpha pattern through the storm, crossing through the center several times in what from above would look like a giant X. Each leg of the X would be 100 to 200 miles long, plus a little extra now and then to avoid severe thunderstorms.

As they approached the eye, the navigator's radar screen showed the characteristic spiral bands of thunderstorms wrapping around the bright red ring in the middle: the eyewall, a nearly solid circle of thunderstorms in which the crew was searching for holes.

As the large steel door at the back of the plane closed, Hugo hit a rising current of air. The dropsonde operator landed on his back, scrambled to his seat and strapped himself in. Jack looked out the window. Visibility dropped as they flew into another band of thunderstorms. Sheets of rain streamed across the windows.

"Sorry about the bump," Barnes said over the intercom. "Everybody sit tight and hang on. We're starting our descent now to 850 millibars—five thousand feet—prior to eyewall penetration in about thirty minutes. It's going to be rough."

Jack knew just enough about airplanes and flight dynamics to be scared. He knew the WC-130 had no special reinforcement, no structural enhancements to prepare it for the ferocious winds it tackled. Jack's sweaty hands turned white. The roar of the four Allison engines penetrated his green headphones.

Jack's stomach rose into his throat as a stiff downdraft dropped Hugo hundreds of feet in an instant. Hugo rose as quickly as it had fallen and Jack threw up on his brand new laptop.

CHAPTER 31

MANHATTAN
7:09 A.M.

Already it was like wearing clothes into a steam room. Amanda's jeans still stuck to the back of her legs from the sweat produced while sitting on the vinyl seat during the taxi ride in from the airport.

Amanda had taken the first flight she could get out of Miami. She used the key she still had to let herself in to Juan Rico's apartment. Rico was gone already. She called the newsroom, but he wasn't there. Amanda had a million things on her mind: Harvey, Jack, Sarah, Ed Cole, even the mole people. And now Rico.

She was determined that things would be different this time. Hurricane Gert had fooled her as a forecaster and then nearly killed her and two people she loved.

Hurricane Harvey was far more dangerous. But Amanda would not be pushed around. She would not chase Harvey foolishly, but she would *face* the storm. And win.

As soon as she cleared some business away, she'd go fetch her father out on Coney Island. There had been a thread of a connection with him this last time, frayed as it was. She wanted to hang onto that, build on it. Anyway, she wasn't comfortable leaving her father in the hands of Kim Butler. At last look, an hour ago from her laptop on the plane, the LORAX showed Harvey's path nipping the eastern tip of Long Island. The damn forecast kept moving west.

Amanda had been so busy watching the storm she hadn't checked her email. She downloaded it. There was a message from Jack:

```
Luck runs out again. Flying into Irene
instead. Due to take off at midnight.
See you soon. Wear black.
Jack.
```

Amanda was relieved. Irene was less intense, and though that was no guarantee, it would probably mean a safer flight. *One less person to worry about.*

The eight o'clock bulletin would be going out from the Hurricane Center in less than an hour. Amanda set up her laptop and downloaded the latest.

Though she half expected it, Amanda couldn't believe her eyes. While all of the other models still showed a curve out to sea, the LORAX was pointing due north, hitting Long Island dead center.

The LORAX's forecast had marched farther west, toward Manhattan, each time she'd pulled it up. *Why?* Amanda typed in a command, downloaded the sea of data that went into the computer model's algorithms. It could take her an hour or more just to catch up with the LORAX's thinking. She glanced at her watch. *Don't have an hour. Get going.*

But first she had to call Leonard Lassitor.

***

"You smug bastard."

"Flattery will get you nowhere, Amanda."

"What makes you think you can ignore the experts? We're talking about thousands of lives. This isn't a game anymore, it's not about you and me. It's not about whose job is what. It's about life and death."

"I promise you I'll talk to the forecaster in charge—Chen I think is his name. You've got nothing to do with this as I see it."

"I've got everything to do with it," Amanda shouted. "It's my goddamn storm!"

"Ms. Cole. You folks warned me about Gert, too, and it didn't come our way. Now. Haven't we had our big hurricane for the year? Besides, the Hurricane Center hasn't issued a warning. I'm not a fool. I'm not going to tell millions of New Yorkers to leave town just because you tell me to. Especially not because you tell me to. You're not even at the Hurricane Center, for God's sake."

"Look, Leonard." She was calmer, but still with the edge in her voice. "I'm sifting through the data right now, as we speak. I'm certain that Harvey has a good shot at New York. I'm going to call Frank Delaney as soon as I pin down a couple of things. He's going to issue a warning at eight o'clock, I'm sure of it. Now, it'll take up to nine hours to clear Manhattan, fifteen for Brooklyn. Harvey could be here in ten or twelve hours. What the hell are you waiting for?"

"Ms. Cole, I'm tiring of this conversation. Now. It's time for you to run off and do whatever it is you do when you're on vacation. I'll worry about my job. "

"You should worry."

***

Lassitor was pretty sure it was the LORAX that had Amanda so fired up. At any rate, he had just about all the information he needed. He wanted one last look at the computer model. He pointed his Internet browser to the site, typed in *nhctest1* in the I.D. and password fields. A message flashed on his screen:

```
The password "nhctest1" is not valid.
Please try your password again.
```

Lassitor understood. They'd locked him out. Now he was *sure* the LORAX was going to be the basis for the official forecast.

CHAPTER 32

GODDARD SPACE FLIGHT CENTER
7:12 A.M.

The technician was sweating. His wife had taken a turn for the worse last night.

Possibly just another dip in the roller-coaster ride of a cancer patient. She would probably feel better by afternoon. But maybe not. Either way, she was still dying. He'd spent the night trying to put food in her. His daughter was staying at her grandmother's, again.

All that on his mind, the man in the perfect suit had called. The technician had raced to Goddard, slipped unnoticed into Building 28. His shift didn't start for another two hours.

The technician's fingers hovered over the keyboard. He hesitated.

A hundred thousand dollars.

The commands were simple, though he'd had to rewrite them slightly for the LORAX. They would be buried deep within the computer model's code. Nobody would find them for at least a couple days, wouldn't even know what they were looking for. And they'd have no way to trace how they got there. The technician would act just as surprised as everyone else. In the meantime, the computer model would be inoperable. But what would that matter? The LORAX wasn't in the official forecasting suite anyway. Still, he'd gotten that strange request from Frank Delaney to keep the program running.

But surely they wouldn't make an official forecast with a test model.

The technician took a deep breath, thought about the evil cancer sucking the life out of his wife, thought about raising his daughter alone. He typed the commands and hit the enter button. He tried to swallow but found no saliva. He grabbed his coat and headed out of the building. He had a meeting with the man in the perfect suit in an hour. Pick up the money. Home free.

CHAPTER 33

MANHATTAN
7:17 A.M.

Amanda pored over the data, squinting. The latest measurements from the Hurricane Hunters, including a critical extrap that fixed the hurricane's current center, completed a vital piece of the complicated puzzle she had in her head: Harvey was picking up speed faster than even Amanda expected.

Other data showed her that the high-pressure area moving across the country, which she had hoped would kick Harvey out to sea, was weakening and slowing down. The LORAX understood the gravity of these measurements, taken far in front of the storm. The other models did not.

It was decision time now. She knew what the LORAX was thinking. Harvey was expected to make a sharp dogleg to the west and squeeze between the two areas of high pressure, just as she'd explained on TV: like toothpaste out of a tube squashed between a child's fists. She needed only to check it one last time and make sure that the LORAX's forecast was in line with what she had deciphered. During the time it had taken her to comprehend the data, the LORAX should have moved its forecast in line with the one in Amanda's brain. The red line ought to be pointing directly at Manhattan by now. She pointed her Internet browser to the LORAX's site, entered her password.

Once inside the non-public area, she clicked on a link to the forecasted track. A message flashed on her screen:

```
Document contains no data.
```

"What the hell? Not again!"

She returned to the previous page, clicked on the link again. Same message. *Oh, Jeez. Not now. Not the LORAX.* Something was terribly wrong. Amanda called Frank Delaney. The director sounded tired and rushed.

"Frank, what happened?"

"I don't know," Delaney said. "I went to look at the LORAX a while ago, and there was nothing there."

"You call Goddard?"

"Yeah. They don't have a clue," he said. "Tried to get it back online but couldn't. Said it might be a few hours."

"A few hours! We need it right this minute. I've been going over the data, and I think I know what's going on. Jeez, I just wanted to confirm what I already suspected."

"Chen has to spit out the eight a.m. in a few minutes. He's recommending we go with the GFDL, of course. I'm going to personally approve the bulletin. Christ, maybe I'll write it myself.

"That would be smart, Frank." He'd know what she meant.

"Regardless of what we decide, I'll get on the horn to New York, call all the emergency officials I know there and tell them what's going on. Chen has a couple of close friends up there, too. He can make a couple calls. But they're so damn disorganized, you know? I don't know who the hell is calling the shots. It's really the public bulletin that will count."

"What's your plan?"

"Still trying to decide. The dogleg is a possibility, but…"

"It's a big storm," Amanda said. "It's running on adrenaline now. I'm not even sure the LORAX would understand it. When it ran the last data set, it seemed to think the trough has enough oomph to carry the storm due north. If I understand the model at all, it figures Harvey is going to bully right through the continental high. Right now the red line would be pointing at Manhattan. If it were running."

"Amanda. It's your model. Your storm. You know them both better than anyone. And we know the dangers, either way. If I pick New York as the official track when none of our operational models do, it could be the end of my career. Yours too. We both know what happens if I'm wrong the other way. It's time, Amanda. Decide. Your call."

"You can't do that to me, Frank."

"I just did."

It was the one thing she was afraid of, though she'd never told Delaney. *Tell me to guess where a storm's going, and I'll go out on a limb, make that educated guess, place my bet.*

She thought about the bet she'd placed on Harvey, the email she'd sent to herself back on Sunday. It had been a long shot, a small amount of science and experience mixed with big doses of intuition and guessing. But now it was looking like she might actually win that dinner from Frank Delaney. The idea of betting on the storm suddenly made her nauseous. Now she had to make a decision, and it wasn't about winning or losing dinner. It was about people's lives. *We tell everybody that the storm's coming to New York City, people could die trying to evacuate. We don't issue the warning, more people could die.*

"Amanda?"

Something in Delaney's voice, the urgency, made her mind up for her.

"Do it."

"Done," Delaney said.

CHAPTER 34

OUTSIDE SANTO DOMINGO, DOMINICAN REPUBLIC 7:55 A.M.

Maximo was pacing around the pool, alone, clutching his cell phone. He was peeved. Terese had avoided him last night, but that was to be expected. He was surprised this morning, though, to learn she had left during the night. No one left the Perez estate without permission. And she'd taken her passport. She was fleeing. It was a transgression he could not allow. She would have to be punished, and that fact was responsible for his foul mood.

He admitted to himself that he was in love with Terese. He was regretting the way he'd treated her yesterday, and now his show of power had escalated out of his control. One thing about power was certain: Once you made a show of it, you could not back down or you would lose it forever.

He should have known the strong-willed girl might do this. He wished he'd thought to have someone watch her last night to keep her from running off. Given a day or two to sulk, she might have forgiven him and they might have continued their relationship. But not now.

He had his two best men out looking for her, and he

considered how they would treat her. One of his most effective tools for maintaining allegiance was that everyone in the organization feared being hunted down by Maximo's men. Maximo let them do as they wished, and he never got involved in the details of punishment. It was one aspect of the organization about which he never asked.

He kept pacing around the pool. In his mind, he pictured Terese standing in front of him yesterday, naked and dripping. Thoughts of what his men would do to her flashed through his mind, and he winced.

Finally, the cell phone rang. "Nombre?"

"Octopus."

"I'm getting nervous, my friend. A nervous Maximo is not a pleasant Maximo. Now, what do you have for me?"

"Our technician friend at Goddard has done his job. Things are in a great state of confusion. Don't pay attention to the news. The Hurricane Center knows this one is heading to New York."

"You wouldn't think of deceiving me."

"Of course not, Maximo. Then you'd have to kill me."

Maximo didn't laugh. "You learn well, my friend. Now, one last time. Do you see everything just as you've told me before? Is this PrimeCo the right company?"

The Octopus' reply was cold and certain. "Bet the farm, Maximo."

Maximo rounded a corner of the pool and faced his huge home. A compound, really. It was among the finest haciendas in the Dominican Republic, all built with the sweat of his own labor. Not physical labor, but the labor of calculated intimidation, the labor of organization, the labor of leadership. Only a few men were born leaders, and Maximo Perez had always considered himself one of them. Nobody had ever given him anything. He'd earned every dime he had made, no matter how illegally.

But the political costs of the drug business took their financial toll. The payoffs were steep and had kept Maximo from his goal of being not just among the richest Dominicans, but *the* richest. At forty-seven, he figured he had only a few years' worth of energy left to get there.

The Perez compound sat atop the highest hill for miles, and afforded a splendid view of the mountains outside Santo Domingo. But there were others on the island that were bigger, more lavish, with more land and more servants and more women. Maximo wanted to buy them all.

Betting a big chunk of the farm on Hurricane Harvey would be one large step toward that goal. Maximo steeled his mind, made his final decision.

"I plan to do nearly that," he finally replied. "And if we win, I'll have a delightful young thing waiting here to give you more pleasure than you've ever imagined. Now, yesterday you told me that a lot of people would try to leave through the bridges and tunnels."

"Yes, but…"

"What would be a good time for an *accident* or two to suddenly close these bridges and tunnels?"

"Maximo. Are you taking out a little insurance against me?"

"You ought to have known."

"Yes, I guess so. Well, if the storm speeds up as expected, I'd say around three or four o'clock would be good."

"Very well." Maximo cleared the line without saying goodbye, then he dialed a number in New Jersey. He might trust an American to help plan a scheme, but to secure the outcome he chose an old Dominican friend.

***

"The 7:42 flight to Miami is running a little late," said the woman at the American Airlines ticket counter. "It's boarding now. If we hurry, you can still catch it."

With nervous, shaking hands, Terese gave the ticket agent her American passport and a wad of cash. She looked around furtively while the agent processed the ticket. She hadn't seen anyone she recognized yet.

Terese had ridden half the way toward the northern coast

of the island in the back of a truck loaded with sugar cane. The driver hadn't even seen her hop aboard in the predawn darkness. As soon as Maximo realized she had fled, he would have sent his men looking for her. They would most likely check Las Americas airport in Santo Domingo, less than an hour's drive southeast from the Perez estate. So she went north toward the more distant La Union airport in the resort town of Puerto Plata. She thumbed the final two hours, hitching two rides over rugged mountains and through lush valleys, then took a taxi for the final stretch. There wasn't much traffic so early in the morning, and it had taken a while to catch the rides. It had all taken longer than she had hoped. For all she knew, Maximo's men might be right on her heels.

Her mind was spinning in an adrenaline overdrive. She needed to get on that plane. And she wanted to warn somebody.

To hell with Maximo. The fucking slave owner.

Maximo's empire had always fed off the weak, the helpless, those who were least capable of scraping together the money needed to buy their next fix. Terese knew all about those kind of people. She'd been one of them.

That was all after she left New York, after she left the only man who'd ever treated her like an equal. He was good to her. And he loved her. But he was so content living each day as it came. That worked for Terese for a while. But he was older, settled, a working man. Terese was young, and she wanted to hold the world in her hand, live the good life. She ran off to the Caribbean to look for it, left her man behind. Now she would give anything to be back in those warm, confident arms.

Maximo never really loved her. Not the way she knew it could be. And now he was going to kill innocent people. Thousands of them.

The agent smiled and handed the ticket over. Terese did her best to look composed, took the ticket, then turned and scanned the airport as she headed toward the gate.

The flight was nearly finished boarding. Terese wanted desperately to tell someone about what she knew was going to happen. Not telling would make her an accomplice, she reasoned. But she could not think of anyone to call. Who would believe her? Who could do anything about it? There was only one person. She went to the pay phone and dialed the number in New York with shaky fingers.

***

"Hello?"

It was a woman's voice on the other end of the crackly connection, and it threw Terese off balance. Her heart dropped. Her mind was still thinking in Spanish when she finally spoke.

"Puedo hablar con Juan?"

"What? Hello?"

Terese realized the woman didn't speak Spanish. "I'm sorry. Is Juan there?"

"No," the woman said. "I was hoping this was Juan calling. Do you know where he is?"

"No," Terese said, confused. "Who's this?"

"Amanda Cole," the woman said. "Um, can I take a message?"

Terese had heard of Amanda Cole. But was she Juan's girlfriend now? In a deep recess of her mind she had held onto the romantic idea that he would always wait for her, even though she had left him so abruptly, so coldly. She had to know.

"Amanda, are you his, his…" she couldn't say it, and the question hung.

"No. I'm just a friend," Amanda said.

Terese exhaled. She spoke cautiously: "Tell Juan I'm… I'm coming. That I'll…"

"Listen. I'm really busy right now. There's a helluva storm coming this way and, well, I guess I'm in charge of it. But I can't find Juan, and I'm worried about him. So if you hear from him, please tell him to let me know he's OK."

"That's what I'm calling about," Terese said. "I wanted to

tell Juan that, well, I don't suppose you'll believe me."

"Believe what?"

Terese pulled the receiver away from her ear and strained to hear the airport loudspeaker. The flight to Miami was making its final boarding call. She glanced around. Far down a long hallway she saw two men walking briskly toward her. She couldn't make out their faces, but it made her nervous. She thought for a second. Who was this woman? Was there any point in telling her? Did she have time?

"You said you're in charge of the storm?"

"Yes, I'm a forecaster."

"Maybe it's better to tell you, then. My name is Terese. I'm in the Dominican Republic. There's a man there who's going to try and ruin the evacuation."

"Who?"

"The Octopus is all I know him by. He's got help from some place called Goddard. And there's going to be some accidents."

"Accidents?" Amanda said. "Where? What are you talking about?"

The two men down the hallway were moving more quickly. Terese recognized them. "Shit," she said into the phone. "I have to go."

"Wait! Who's the Octopus, where does he work?"

Terese didn't hear Amanda. The phone swung from its cord as she rushed toward the gate.

CHAPTER 35

ABOARD HUGO
8:01 A.M.

Jack used his sleeve to wipe the puke from his computer. The ride was getting worse. Hugo pitched and tossed so violently that Jack wondered why the wings didn't just fall off. He tried to focus his eyes on something, the endless colored wires and tubes running along the ceiling of the fuselage, the galaxy of flashing lights from computers and airplane controls and radar screens, the bulky silver fuel tank in front of him. Each time he blinked his vision shuddered, the inside of the plane rippled like the reflection in a pond disturbed by a pebble. If he closed his eyes he felt dizzy and sick again. There was nothing left in his stomach, which was sore from heaving, so he kept his eyes open and waited for the WC-130 to become the first casualty of the 53rd Weather Reconnaissance Squadron.

Jack should have been writing a story, but he couldn't see the point. His computer still rested on his lap, the screen folded open, but he'd stopped taking notes. He didn't want to be here anyway, didn't want to write this story. Hugo jerked, seemed to stop flying, suspending its forward speed. The shoulder harness grabbed him as his head was thrown forward. The plane rocked to the left, dipped and shook. Jack took a deep breath, closed his eyes and squeezed the armrests until his fingernails bled.

Hugo made one last hard shudder before it surged forward into a smooth pocket of air. The four engines relaxed. They were in the eye.

"Free time," came Barnes' voice over the intercom. "Stretch your legs, have a look. Sorry for the rocky ride. Hope everybody is OK."

"Fuck you," Jack muttered under his breath. He undid his seat belt and shoulder harness, made his way slowly, shakily, to a window.

He looked up at the towering, circular wall of clouds that seemed to converge over the top of the plane as if in a photo taken through a wide-angle lens. Blue circle at the top. It reminded Jack of the Colosseum in Rome. The air inside the plane grew gradually warmer with the increased temperature in the eye. The smell of vomit grew with it.

Five-thousand feet below, the sea could be mistaken for the Swiss Alps. Winds swirling inward from all points on the compass pushed waves in every direction, sending them crashing into each other, a war of clashing whitecaps.

The weather officer studied the waves, too. "There's the center," he said. "Calm spot on the water at two o'clock."

The plane banked slightly, leveled off. In the back, the dropsonde operator loaded a canister into the launch tube.

"Winds are dying down," the weather officer said. "Shifting... shifting... Fix it!"

Jack heard a loud clink-chunk.

"Sonde away," announced the dropsonde operator. The navigator noted Hugo's position and the exact center of the storm had been fixed. The dropsonde would return important data to the plane as it fell, then the small metal canister would hit the water and send up a precise measurement of atmospheric pressure at sea level, the most vital statistic indicating the storm's strength.

Jack looked over the weather officer's shoulder. His screen was crowded with meaningless numbers. "High-density data," he explained. "Computer is collecting position and weather information every thirty seconds and encoding it for transmission."

For the first time during the flight, Jack felt calm. He almost smiled at all he'd gone through in the past five days. Seeing Amanda Cole again and falling in love so fast. Facing Gert. Amanda saving his life. Kissing him. Talking obliquely about a life together. *A life together. What the hell am I doing up here?*

Jack wanted nothing now except to get his feet on the ground and find Amanda.

***

Barnes looked at Duggan. "We got everything we need?"

"Yep," said the copilot. "Let's go home. I'm not having any fun today."

"Which way?"

"Wall of lightning ahead," Duggan said. "I vote we backtrack."

"Wasn't exactly a party back that way," Barnes said.

"Known evil versus the unknown."

Barnes considered the options. There was one narrow hole in the southeast quadrant, but it was unclear if it was any better than the spot they penetrated in the north. The rest of the eyewall was rampant with thunderstorms. There was no good way out.

Barnes flicked a switch to broadcast on the intercom: "OK, folks. Take your seats. We're going to do a one-eighty and exit the eye back where we came in. Looks like it's the only soft spot. Hold tight and count your blessings."

"Whaddya think?" Duggan asked. "Record barf-bag count today?"

"Not now," Barnes said sternly. It was no time to play the copilot's game of speculation on how the newsies would fare. Hugo swung a ponderous arc and headed back toward the eyewall. Duggan became uncharacteristically quiet. Barnes chewed his gum, now a tough, flavorless ball of hard rubber. He double-checked the gauges.

"Oh, my. Oil pressure's low on three."

"Shit," Duggan said. "Kill it?"

"Not yet. Watch it, see if it moves. Hang on."

Hugo was seconds from the eyewall. Barnes couldn't avoid entering it now if he wanted to. There was nothing to hang around for anyway. Many times he had witnessed birds taking refuge in the eye, following the storm until it made landfall or dissipated. A parrot might end up in Boston. Hugo didn't have enough fuel to consider that option.

"Still dropping," Duggan said.

"Shit. Hugo, you bastard." Barnes spit his gum at the sea of instruments in front of him, glanced at the oil-pressure gauge. It was sinking, slowly but steadily. "Shut it down."

***

Jack barely noticed the difference when four engines became three. But in the brief instant before hitting the eyewall, the drop in sound level was unmistakable. The plane shuddered with the initial impact, as winds suddenly changed from nothing to the strongest in the storm. Jack's computer, not yet a week old, rose from his lap as though suspended by an invisible wire, then fell to the hard metal floor and broke into two pieces.

He struggled against his shoulder harness to see if the props were turning, but he couldn't see far enough out the wing. Sheets of lightning illuminated the scud of clouds. Visibility was zero. A strange feeling welled up, something that must have been claustrophobia, though Jack had never felt it before. The plane was over the sea, wrapped up in a storm made mostly of water. And now, down an engine, Hugo was being kicked around like a tin can on a playground. Jack Corbin suddenly felt that the airplane he was riding in was nothing more than a huge metallic coffin.

CHAPTER 36

TRIBECA
8:13 A.M.

The tunnel was twice as creepy without Juan Rico to hold her hand. She wished she could have got a hold of Rico so he could do this. Somebody had to. She wrote Rico a quick note about Terese, that she was coming. Amanda had known of Terese, but on the phone there hadn't been time to say so. She was still trying to make sense of the phone call.

Now she was beginning to question her decision to come into the tunnels. She hadn't heard the rats yet, but it *felt* like they were there. She was a hundred yards down the abandoned tunnel, wondering if she could even find the small hole in the wall. The stench was worse than it had been before, and she had on only a thin t-shirt with a low-cut neckline—nothing to pull over her nose. She felt vulnerable, walking through a pitch-black abandoned subway tunnel filled with rats and human waste.

As she got nearer to where she thought the opening should be, she felt the same eerie unease that she was being watched.

Her flashlight barely reached the dismal opposite wall, but Amanda found the opening. She crossed the tracks, careful of the third rail. It was surely disconnected, she thought, but she couldn't remember if Juan had said so or not. She clambered up the opposite side onto the thin platform and was about to pull the fresh plywood cover off when she heard a voice in the darkness.

"What you want, scientist lady?"

There was fear in the voice, but also a menacing streak that sent a chill through her.

"Who's there?" She had meant to sound mean or confident, but her voice was feeble and frightened.

Louder, the voice said again: "What you want?"

"I came to warn Sleepy."

"'Bout what?"

"There's a hurricane coming."

"Fuck you, scientist lady. We got bigger problems."

"Can I at least talk to him?" *Who is this man? Where is he?*

There was a long pause. Amanda listened. Her flashlight was absorbed in the grease. She could not see the wall in front of her, and she had the sensation that it was very near to her face and getting closer. Finally the man spoke: "You move to the side, lady."

She moved about ten feet away from the entrance, along the wall. She was afraid for her life. *Jeez, a hurricane is going to destroy the City and I'm going to die down here before it even hits.*

The plywood was pushed out from the inside. The man in the darkness spoke again: "Is the scientist lady. Says a hurricane is coming. Should I pipe her?"

Amanda had no idea what that meant, but it didn't sound good. She mustered what little courage she could find and spoke toward the head in the hole. "Sleepy, it's me, Amanda Cole. I came to warn you."

"PJ, back off. Amanda, come on in. Sorry."

***

Sleepy waited impatiently for Amanda to come down the ladder. *Just what I need today.*

"What's this about a hurricane?" he asked. Jonathan stood behind him, quiet.

"It's coming this way, I'm nearly positive."

"How big?"

"Huge."

Sleepy had his hands full today. He had just started his shift down in the escape hole. They hadn't broken through the brick wall yet. His whole plan hinged on that. He really didn't have time for this. But what if she was right? What if a hurricane really did come this way, and what if the room flooded? They might all die while they were trying to dig deeper into the earth. But Hammer was coming soon, he could feel it, and they had to have a way out.

Sleepy was still working on exactly how to fight Hammer and then the idea hit him. "Jesus Christ," he said aloud. "When?"

"This evening sometime."

"When exactly?"

"I can't say for sure."

"How close can you be?"

"Look," she said, "I came down here to warn you. I risked my life doing it. Your friend out there scared the daylights out of me. Now I know as much as anyone about this storm, but not even I can tell you its exact arrival time. You're smart, you ought to know that. My best guess is around six, but I could be off by an hour."

"I'm sorry. I only hoped you might be able to predict the time. I'm very grateful that you came down here. You've probably saved all our lives." He looked back up at Amanda and let his eyes apologize, too, then he thought of his plan and how it was beginning to mingle with Amanda's work. A dreadful thought flashed into his mind. He blurted out, "You going to be able to save the City?"

"I'm going to try."

"What if you had to do it without anyone in charge?"

Amanda looked confused. "What do you mean?"

Sleepy decided he'd said too much. Who knew if he could really trust Amanda? Though he wanted to, he'd always survived by *not* trusting people.

"Never mind," he said. "I'm just babbling. Anyway, thanks for coming down."

"It's OK," she said, the confusion still written across her face. "I'm just glad you listened."

Amanda studied him. She bit her lip, glanced around the room. "You know where Juan Rico lives?"

"Above Chez Henri," he said. "We eat there all the time."

"Sixteenth floor, first door on the right," she said. "Entrance is on Washington. You go there."

Sleepy couldn't imagine accepting the offer. They'd find some safe place to evacuate to without imposing on anyone. "Thank you," he said, "but we'll be fine."

"But you'll leave," Amanda persisted.

"We'll be fine. PJ will follow you out, make sure you're safe. Don't be afraid of him, by the way."

"A little late for that," Amanda said, smiling. Then her face seemed suddenly consumed with other worries and she hurried up the ladder.

A rush of elation ran through Sleepy. It was a crazy thought, really, an outside chance. But at least he had a plan, and the escape tunnel would be his backup.

To Jonathan he said: "I'm going out for a while. You stay here. When PJ gets back, tell him to find a crowbar, quickly, and start in on the bricks."

CHAPTER 37

SUBWAY TRAIN
NEAR GRAND CENTRAL STATION
9:02 A.M.

Sleepy hid his face behind a newspaper, but he was close enough to hear.

"Ice worked," his brother said to Hammer as the train pulled out of the station. "Package is cold. Will arrive today at five."

Hammer said nothing, which meant he understood. He got up and walked to the other end of the car and disappeared through the doors into the next car.

Sleepy lowered the newspaper to peer over the top and watched Hammer disappear. He was sitting right across from his brother.

He probably wouldn't be recognized—it had been twenty-five years—but he didn't want to take chances. He pulled the newspaper back up and waited for the right subway stop.

CHAPTER 38

TRIBECA
9:08 A.M.

Amanda's mind felt like a captured fugitive being quartered by horses. Though the other models still showed Hurricane Harvey going out to sea, she was certain it was going to run smack through Manhattan. But things were happening quickly, and could change in the blink of an eye, perhaps requiring at any moment a change in the forecast. And the LORAX was still down, so she was doing her best to get into Harvey's mind, to think for the LORAX and speak for the storm.

The mother in her worried about Sarah. She'd called Joe Springer's number and gotten no answer. That was good, meant he'd evacuated ahead of the rush. She left a message, just in case.

The daughter in her worried about her father. She planned to go and get her father if necessary, at least get him back to Manhattan, to Rico's apartment, where they'd be relatively safe.

Some other part of her brain—a part she wished she could ignore—worried about the whole city. There still had been no evacuation order, in spite of the warning issued by the Hurricane Center.

It almost seemed as if somebody were trying to stall the

evacuation. But she had no clue who, or why. She ran what she knew through her mind.

First, the LORAX had gone down. After the blip in the GFDL program earlier in the week, she was pretty sure that was no accident. Somebody hacked into the program. Then there was the odd question from Sleepy about saving the City without anyone in charge. *In charge of what?* She tried to connect the two thoughts, but couldn't.

She thought back over the jumbled conversation with Terese, who'd said she was in the Dominican Republic, and that someone *there* was trying to ruin the evacuation. Someone where? In the Dominican Republic? In the United States? In New York?

And why?

Amanda felt her brain about to burst. It was already full of Hurricane Harvey data, and now she was trying to use it for something for which it wasn't trained. She was no private investigator. She decided to focus on what she did best. Forecast the storm and issue warnings. It was time to talk to the mayor.

She dialed the Office of Emergency Management. She learned that the Hurricane Center's warning had had at least one effect: The phone lines were being taxed. After three failed tries to get through she gave up, threw a stack of backup data and scribblings in her leather briefcase, and headed out.

***

Amanda had learned long ago that if you wanted to get into a government building, you could usually do it by simply acting as though you belonged there. So long as security wasn't passing visitors single file through a metal detector, it usually worked. She strode into 7 World Trade Center with resolute purpose and headed for the elevators.

A security guard wandered lazily toward her while she waited for the elevator.

Damn. Not now. Not today.

"Ma'am? You supposed to be here?"

Amanda suspected the building had been busier than normal all morning. One more weather person wouldn't be a surprise.

She gave the security guard a bored look, careful not to be condescending. It was a look any government employee would recognize: I don't *want* to be here; I *have* to be here. She reached into her bag and pulled out her security card from the NHC, flashed it. "Hurricane Center. Mayor called me in. Looks like it's going to be a doozie out there, huh?"

"Yes, ma'am. Let's hope not." The guard smiled and wandered off. The elevator doors opened, and Amanda stepped in, pushed the button for the twenty-third floor. The doors closed. Amanda smiled. The mayor had spent $20 million on the 46,000-square-foot operations center. He'd stocked it with enough food and water to house thirty people for a week. He'd supposedly made it bomb-proof and hurricane-proof, and he'd even put a heliport on top to allow stealth entry and exit. Yet anyone with a good story and an official-looking card could just walk in.

The elevator doors opened, and Amanda stepped into a vast room buzzing with activity. Fifty or so people sat hunched over computers, talking on the phone, or shouting at each other. She spotted the mayor across the room. His face was red, his sleeves rolled up, his tie loosened. He was on the phone, but he slammed it down and looked around the room as though something important were missing. Amanda threaded her way through the maze of desks and walked up to him, stuck her hand out.

"Mr. Mayor. Amanda Cole, National Hurricane Center."

He didn't shake her hand. "What the hell are you doing here?"

"I was in the neighborhood. I know you're busy, but you need to listen carefully. An evacuation should…"

He cut her off sharply. "Amanda?"

She nodded.

"Amanda. Listen to me. I don't know how the hell you got

in here. But I just got here myself. I'm trying to find my goddamn staff, get a briefing, and decide what to do."

His staff isn't here? She looked around the room, but there were so many people she had no idea who might be missing.

"That's what I'm trying to help you with," Amanda said after a brief hesitation. "An evacuation should already have been called."

"Big help," he said curtly. "I'll add that to my list of suggestions. Now listen. I've got fifteen people right now shouting fifteen different opinions at me. You folks are no help. I saw the forecasted track a couple hours ago. The storm was going out to sea. Now suddenly you say it's coming directly at us! I'm not an expert in meteorology, but I've got some people on staff here who're pretty sharp, and they tell me there's nothing in the computer models that supports that track. What the hell's going on?"

"I could explain it to you," she lifted her leather briefcase toward him, "but it's awfully technical. Point is, it's coming."

"I heard you the first time. Look, I'm swamped here. Unless you can prove it to me in about ten seconds, I'm going to have to ask you to leave."

Amanda felt the whole room looking at them. It was time to come clean, and it would mean putting her career on the line. Frank Delaney's, too.

She lowered her voice so that only the mayor would hear her. "We're using a new, non-operational computer program. I believe in it. So does Frank Delaney. Pointing right at you."

The mayor studied her. He glanced down at the floor, then out the window at his City. Amanda noticed the irony of the bright sun and the perfectly blue sky. Finally, hands still on his hips, he pointed with his head toward an office. Amanda followed him in. The mayor sat down, motioned for her to do the same, but she remained standing. "Tell me more," he said.

"It's the LORAX. You've heard of it?"

"Yes. Supposed to come online in another year or two."

"Well, it's the only program that can understand a storm like Harvey," Amanda said. She went on to give a brief technical explanation to back her claim, part of a strategy that sometimes worked with government officials: Confuse them with scientific details and show them how little they know, then punch them in the nose with the reality. "I've rechecked all the data manually, and Harvey is coming this way. I've got nothing to gain by telling you this. Anybody finds out we used it, I lose my job. Unless I'm right. Even then…"

"I don't much care about your job, Ms. Cole."

"Neither do I at this point. I'm just trying to show you that I'm risking everything for what I know is true."

The mayor played with his thumbs, twirling them around each other. He looked past Amanda, out into the room. "Calling for an evacuation is a huge economic commitment. Businesses close, tourists leave."

"You don't do it, and the business people and the tourists will just be dead. C'mon, have some balls, Mr. Mayor. It's your city. You're going to wake up tomorrow with enough problems. You don't need more deaths."

He let out a deep sigh, still didn't look at her. "I'd have to confer with several people."

"No. Forget everyone else. This is about you. If you don't declare a citywide emergency and begin evacuations this minute, you are going to be responsible for thousands of lives. The storm is ten hours away, maybe less. I give you my word on that. The Army Corps study shows it'll take nine hours to clear Manhattan, up to fifteen for Brooklyn. You're already behind the curve."

"Thousands of lives," the mayor said.

"Thousands. Maybe more."

"OK, I'll call everybody in and we'll make a decision by nine-thirty.

"Make it now."

"Don't push me, Ms. Cole. That's my answer. You want to stay for the meeting?"

"Nope. I've got other people to take care of. This is your job." Amanda moved to her left to catch the mayor's gaze. "I hope you don't screw it up, Mr. Mayor. Harvey is going to kill a lot of people today."

She turned to leave. "I'll find my way out."

CHAPTER 39

NEAR THE CANAL STREET
SUBWAY STATION
9:42 A.M.

His brother wasn't moving his wide body as the train approached the Canal Street station. Sleepy would have to move it for him. He dropped the newspaper that had been covering his face, stood up and stepped across the aisle and faced his brother.

Sleepy hadn't faced his brother since he fled their childhood home, but he'd kept track of him over the years in the newspapers and through the underground gossip mill, and he supposed now that his brother had kept track of him through Hammer and some of the other underground drug dealers. His brother had probably gotten an account of the night Sleepy killed the intruder. Sleepy didn't like what he'd read and heard about his brother. He had been a bully as a child, and now he was a bully as an adult. Back then, though, it was usually only Sleepy who suffered.

His brother scanned the *Daily News,* didn't notice Sleepy. Sleepy stared at him. With an irritated flick of the *Daily News,* he looked up.

"What." It was a demand, not a question.

Sleepy didn't say anything. He hadn't formulated a speech in his mind. His anger welled within him and choked his thoughts. His brother looked back at his newspaper. *He doesn't recognize me. The sonofabitch doesn't even recognize his own brother.*

Sleepy wanted to give him immense but invisible pain, to make him suffer in ways that would garner no sympathy from others. He wanted to slap the skin on his body red and punch him in the stomach and stamp on his toes, the way his brother had done when they were boys. He wanted to punch him in the arm until it was black and blue, then hit the other arm for awhile and then come back to the first, just as the pain began to subside, and pound on it some more. Sleepy wanted to shake his brother until his brain came loose. He became nervous with the excitement of the thoughts, and his left eye began to twitch.

Then he remembered his plan—a plan that wouldn't get him into trouble if it worked right. He spoke just as his brother glanced back up with a look of irritated impatience.

"Hello, brother," Sleepy said. "Comfortable?"

Sleepy saw the recognition sweep across his brother's face, then he saw it replaced by cold fear. That made him feel good. Fear was part of his plan. *I'm much stronger than you.*

Sleepy hadn't realized how tense he was. His fingers hurt from squeezing them into fists. He relaxed his body some and concentrated on his idea.

"What do you want?" His brother was trying to be dismissive, but his eyes were still full of the cold fear.

Sleepy reached deep into his memory of childhood beatings, called up all of the anger inside him and focused it all in the muscles and tendons of his arms, making them taut and straight like the cables of the Brooklyn Bridge. He let his eyes simmer and shrink. Then he spoke in a low voice, controlled and barely audible.

"I'll tell you what I want," Sleepy finally said. "I want you to come with me. I have something to show you."

"Not now. I've got business to take care of. What is it you want?"

Sleepy rubbed the scar on his face for effect. "You can't hide from me. I live beneath you, invisible. I haunt places you don't know. There is nowhere you can go—no apartment, no cafe, no taxi, subway or tall building where I cannot sneak up behind you and squeeze the life out of you in less time than it takes to grab a rat by the tail and fling it against a wall. Right now, I have something that's more important than your business. Something you need to see. Something you will see. You're coming with me."

A corner of the *Daily News* twitched, then began a rhythmic shaking. Sleepy knew he had won. His brother had given into the fear, and now there was only defeat in his eyes. They stepped out of the train, onto the platform, and Sleepy prodded him off the platform, into the true bowels of the city, and they headed north along the tracks.

CHAPTER 40

NEW YORK TIMES NEWSROOM
10:05 A.M.

The managing editor had called a special meeting to go over hurricane coverage. Walter Beasley, deputy metro editor, slinked into the conference room and sat next to the metro editor, wanting to escape from the meeting with as little responsibility as possible. His mind was on the *Slow Times*. The boat had become his whole life, consumed him like the passion for a beautiful woman, and this hurricane threatened that new life. Worse, Leonard Lassitor and his bags of drugs threatened everything.

He put a legal-size pad on the table in front of him and began studying his shoes.

When everyone was seated, the managing editor spoke curtly from the head of the table: "Where the hell's Jack Corbin?"

Everybody looked at Walter Beasley, who was Jack's assigning editor. There was little he could do but tell the truth. "He left Biloxi, Mississippi, at midnight to fly into the hurricane. I sent him out with the Hurricane Hunters."

"You did *what?* Goddamn biggest weather story to hit New York in decades and you sent the beat reporter *out* to cover a secondary story? Jesus Christ, Walter, what the hell were you

234

thinking?"

"I didn't know the storm would come this way. We made the arrangements a couple days ago." *But I could have pulled him in last night. Oh, shit. I'm in trouble.*

"When's he due back?"

"He's scheduled to land in Mississippi sometime this morning." Beasley looked at his watch. "He may already be there."

"Great," the managing editor lamented. "Just great. Walter, your job is to find Jack Corbin. If he can get here, bring him in. If not, have him work the phones from wherever he is." The man stared into Beasley's eyes, as if to say, "Don't blow this, or else."

The managing editor shook his head in disgust and turned to the metro editor and began laying out a plan for coverage. Beasley sensed he would not be involved, that he had but one job he was now trusted with.

Beasley was shaken. Succumbing to Lassitor's request to get Jack Corbin out of the City had been a mistake, and now it had forced a blunder that he could not have foreseen and could not control. He had put himself in hot water at the *Times*. Scalding. The only way out was to find Jack Corbin, which was the last thing he wanted to do, and somehow get him back to the City before the storm hit.

This is all Lassitor's fault. It's gone too far.

What Walter Beasley really wanted to do was say the hell with it and head down to the *Slow Times* and secure it against the storm. *There's that loose stern line, and I really should check all the lines, maybe secure it better with extra lines front and back. Damn, maybe I should have just sailed upriver last night after all. Too late for that now. Screw this job. Screw Jack Corbin. Screw Leonard Lassitor.*

CHAPTER 41

TRIBECA
10:13 A.M.

The mayor had finally issued an evacuation. New York City residents would now be struggling to evacuate without a plan. No one was in charge. Agencies would scramble to make decisions—when to shut down services, whether or not to add extra services. Residents wouldn't know if they should stay in their apartments, leave the area, or go to a shelter. They wouldn't even know where the shelters were. Some simply wouldn't have enough time to get there.

Amanda knew that the evacuation would not go smoothly. She also knew that she knew more about the danger, and more about how the City should be evacuated, than anyone, including the mayor and his whole staff. A voice inside told her that people would die if she didn't stay at the Emergency Operations Center and advise them.

Another part of her mind was still working hard to understand the conversation with Terese, but it was going nowhere.

She forced the scientific part of her brain to relax, allow all her thoughts to focus on the people close to her. She still hadn't heard from Joe Springer. She tried his number again but there was still no answer. She tried Kim Butler at the Seaside

Nursing Home and could not get through—all lines were busy, the recorded voice said.

"Damn."

And what about Jack Corbin? He should be back from his flight with the Hurricane Hunters by now. He said he'd call. But maybe his call couldn't get through. Maybe he'd email.

Amanda unpacked the portable satellite setup from her suitcase. She fired her laptop back up, used the satellite dish to connect to the Internet and download her email. Quick scan of her inbox: Nothing from Jack.

He should be back by now.

But there was a message from Joe Springer. He had never e-mailed her before. She opened the message.

```
Amanda:
Got your message. We were out on the
boardwalk. Tried to call but couldn't
get through. Sarah says to say she
misses you. She's excited about the
hurricane. We've decided to ride it out
here. She insisted, said that's what Mom
would do. Probably won't come this way
anyway.
Joe
P.S.: Saw you on TV yesterday. You
looked great. What's with the cuts on
your face?
```

"Goddamn you Joe Springer!"

Amanda couldn't control her rage. She picked up the nearest thing she could find—besides her computer—and tossed it across Juan Rico's living room. The glass of orange juice shattered against the wall.

"What the hell are you thinking?" *Oh shit oh shit. What do I do now? Why didn't he get out? Damn him. What do I do now?*

She picked the phone up nervously, fumbled it to the floor, chased the receiver across the kitchen and picked it up again.

Punched in Joe Springer's number.

"We're sorry, all circuits are busy."

Amanda yanked the phone from the wall, hurled it toward the splatter of orange juice and it smashed into pieces.

All of Amanda's thoughts became focused on one thing: getting to Sarah. Joe Springer lived in Point Pleasant Beach, down on the Jersey Shore. A two-hour drive on a good day, when traffic was flowing in two directions. Today, assuming emergency coordinators did their jobs, traffic would be flowing in one direction only, away from the Shore.

Amanda remembered her father. A fiery stab of remorse cut through her chest.

She shook her head. Ed Cole was on his own now. She had no choice. She found the keys to Juan Rico's Dodge, packed up her new laptop and the suitcase with the satellite dish, and headed out the door.

***

A man in a smart-fitting business suit crossed Washington Street carrying a four-by-eight sheet of plywood. The breeze was light, the plywood like a sail, and the man struggled with the awkward weight.

There won't be enough plywood. Most people won't know what to do with it anyway. Probably do more harm than good. There'll be a bunch of poorly nailed plywood flying around the streets, too. Anyway, how do you secure plywood over a third-floor brownstone window?

A homeless man lay curled up along the dull, bare industrial wall of a nondescript four-story building on Watts Street. It was the homeless man who seemed to have less to worry about today, Amanda considered. Then she imagined him shuffling at the last minute into a subway station.

She thought of Sleepy, PJ and Jonathan. She wondered if they would evacuate in time. Something about an accident knocked at her conscience, but she couldn't let stray thoughts in anymore. Amanda closed her eyes and rested her forehead on the steering wheel of Rico's immaculate white Dodge.

She withdrew from the world, watching as a spectator. All thoughts funneled into the tiny universe of her relationship with her daughter.

Get to Sarah. Get to Sarah.

Rico's Dodge, its pearl white exterior waxed up and its black interior glistening with care, idled at the stop sign in front of Chez Henri. Amanda was impatiently trying to turn right onto Watts, which led straight to the Holland Tunnel three blocks away. Traffic was backed up from the entrance to the tunnel.

Amanda assumed a line of cars stretched for many blocks outward, winding around myriad main streets, blocking and being fed by many smaller ones. Like anyone else familiar with the nightmare problem of evacuating New York City, she had no idea how people would actually react in a crisis. Some people who should find shelter would not. Others who lived in relatively safe buildings above the storm surge would try to flee the City. Amanda realized she was now one of those, contributing to the problem. She had done all she could as a professional, now she was just Amanda Cole, visitor to New York City, mother desperate to find her daughter.

A small gap opened between two cars on Watts Street as a driver became preoccupied with his fighting children in the back seat. Horns blared. Amanda screeched into the opening. Fifteen minutes later she was heading down into the tunnel. Traffic was stop and go. It was another ten minutes before she emerged on the other side of the Hudson River in New Jersey. Here, too, people fled low-lying areas, spilling onto the highway from Hoboken and Jersey City. The New Jersey Turnpike was jammed. Moving slowly south, Amanda looked up at the curly wisps of cirrus clouds nearly 40,000 feet overhead, first sign of the hurricane's approach. To the south, lower in altitude, a thicker, webby batch of cirrostratus clouds was moving in. The car was stopped. She turned off the air conditioning, rolled the window down and stuck her arm out. The breeze was stronger here on the open asphalt plains.

Amanda shivered. She tried to think of something besides

Sarah. She flicked on her radio, which was already tuned to WCBS.

"...when the mayor declared a state of emergency City-wide at a press conference earlier this morning at City Hall. Again, the mayor has asked that people complete preparations as quickly as possible and find a safe place indoors. We expect to have a list of shelters for you in a few moments. Now for the latest on the storm, here's meteorologist John Turner in the WCBS Weather Center."

"We've just got a fresh update from the National Hurricane Center," Turner said. "As predicted, Hurricane Harvey has made a sharp turn to the left during the past couple of hours and is picking up speed. We're starting to get a clearer picture of the storm now as it moves into the range of Doppler radar stations along the northeast coast. A large area of deep red around the eye indicates very strong thunderstorm activity. The storm *has* begun to weaken as it moves over cooler water, just as we expected. The Hurricane Center has downgraded the storm to a Category 4 now, still a dangerous, dangerous storm. Sustained winds near the center still exceed 150 miles an hour. Now, what we commonly see with a storm like this is further weakening as it moves north. I wouldn't be surprised if Harvey is a Category 3 by the time it makes landfall. That would still be the strongest hurricane to hit the region in decades, enough to cause a devastating storm surge along the coast of New Jersey, in Manhattan, and right on out to Long Island. Remember, this is a broad storm, and damage is likely to occur over a wide area. I can't emphasize enough that residents who live in low-lying locations within the listening area should evacuate immediately. OK, as to the storm's path. The Hurricane Center is picking Atlantic City for its official track. Interestingly, all of the official models they use show the storm going out to sea. I just spoke with one of the hurricane specialists there and he told me that Harvey is an unusual storm, difficult to forecast because of its intense strength, large size and its rapid forward speed, all of which can overpower other weather systems that might normally steer the storm. In such a hurricane, the forecasters rely more on experience and judgment. They've certainly called it right so far on this one, as this morning's abrupt turn to the left shows."

The lead newscaster stepped back in. "John, when do you think we can expect to see the effects of this storm?"

"We're already seeing some high-level clouds move in. Those will drop down and begin to thicken over the next hour or so. I think that by noon we'll see these light breezes we're getting turn into steady, sometimes gusty winds, and the first raindrops could arrive about an hour later. Now, the tide is just about low right now, so residents aren't going to notice as the surge from the storm starts to gradually move in by mid-afternoon. But Harvey is moving very quickly—near thirty miles an hour now. That speed is expected to increase, so things are going to happen very quickly."

"And when will the worst of it hit?"

"The eye may arrive just about the time it gets dark, maybe sooner. Though we should note that there's still a chance the storm could change course and veer out to sea. We'll have a better handle on it as the day progresses."

"OK, thank you John Turner in the WCBS Weather Center. Uh, we've got a report just in. The AP is reporting that a Hurricane Hunter plane may have gone down in the Gulf of Mexico, in or near Hurricane Irene. Now these are the guys who fly…"

Amanda's chin clenched into a knot and her bottom lip began to quiver.

"…cites Air Force sources saying the plane's last contact with the center was earlier this morning and that it has not returned to its base as scheduled. Hurricane Irene is a Category 1 storm currently moving…"

Traffic was moving again and she tried to focus, but everything in front of her was a blur. Not wanting to pull over, she cleared her tears with a sweep of a finger, over and over again.

"Dammit!" she said aloud. *No, no, no.* "God dammit!" Amanda felt suddenly cut off from her world. *I've left my daughter in danger while I tried to save the world. My God. I don't know if I'll even be able to reach her. I'm driving into the biggest hurricane of my life. And now Jack is...*

She couldn't allow herself to think it. The Hurricane Hunters had never lost a plane. She had to hope the report wasn't true, or that Jack was somehow not on that plane. What should she do now? She couldn't do anything about Jack. For the first time in her life, Amanda Cole hated the weather. She felt alone, hanging on to one thin hope. She focused on the only goal that mattered.

Get to Sarah.

CHAPTER 42

NEAR THE CANAL STREET
SUBWAY STATION
10:19 A.M.

The crowbar was heavy and cumbersome, but it was effective against the brick.

Sleepy wished they'd found one sooner.

The slow, backbreaking work was destroying his spirit. It seemed he would never break through. His shoulders felt a sharp pain with each swing, and his back had developed a persistent dull ache. Even his ears hurt from the constant *clang-clang* of his efforts. He had to rest. He dropped the crowbar and climbed out of the hole.

Jonathan was eager to take his turn. It would do little good, but PJ, who was out in the tunnel keeping watch, was tired too, and any progress was better than no progress. He decided to let the boy go at it for a few minutes while he rested, then maybe he could summon the energy to go back in. Jonathan thanked his father profusely and jumped into the hole and began chipping away.

Sleepy took a long drink from a jug of water. His body slumped onto the small ramshackle bed. He rolled onto his back and closed his eyes.

His brother was tied up in the corner.

"You were going to deliver a package to Hammer this evening," Sleepy said. "You arrange that yet?"

The bound man spat on the dirt floor.

Sleepy stood slowly, shuffled toward his brother, glanced back to make sure Jonathan was in the tunnel, then pulled a heavy boot back and kicked his brother in the ribs with all his strength.

Deep, all-body exhale of pain. He doubled into himself, a ball of stretched fabric over thick flesh.

"I told you this day was coming," Sleepy said. "Talk and it'll be easier."

He allowed him just enough time to catch his breath, then he pulled his boot back again. His brother spoke through clenched teeth: "Still... have to... arrange delivery. You... prevented that."

"One more question. Hammer wants this place. You got any other dealers who might be interested in it, anybody working this area?"

Still gasping for breath: "One... or two."

"OK, here." Sleepy untied his hands, gave him a worn notebook and a pencil. "Write this note: 'Have control of Block House near Canal Street station. Pick up package there at six p.m.' Then sign it."

He wrote the note. Sleepy took it from him, looked at it. "It better work."

"It'll work," He exhaled. "He... does what I... tell him to."

"Good. Because if he doesn't, you and my boot are going to spend a lot of time together." He tied his hands back up.

Just then Jonathan squealed.

"Father, I broke through!"

Sleepy raced into the hole, nearly stepping on Jonathan as he lowered himself. Sure enough, the boy had created a small hole through the brick, barely enough for Sleepy to stick a finger into. There was nothing but air on the other side. His mind raced. The final piece of his plan was nearly in place. *How long will it take to make the hole big enough to fit through? The work will go faster now, and even faster once we get one brick out.*

Sleepy sent Jonathan after PJ. Then he spoke again to his brother, who had regained his breath but the pain in his ribs was still etched on his face.

"How will Hammer come?"

"Tunnels."

"You sure he won't go above ground, take a taxi or just walk?"

"Police know him, he hates it up there. He'll stay down."

PJ arrived. Sleepy turned to him.

"I want you to take this note to Hammer."

"You fuckin' crazy, man," PJ said. "He kill me right there on the spot!"

"No he won't," Sleepy said. "Trust me."

It was too much for PJ to understand, and Sleepy was afraid his friend might screw it up if he gave him the whole plan now, so he kept the rest to himself.

"We goin' to just give up then?"

"PJ, we've been friends a long time. I've always looked out for you, and I've made good decisions for the group, right?"

"So far," PJ said guardedly.

"I need you to trust me. Hammer might try to get more information out of you. If he does, you just tell him that's all you know, that his boss here just asked you to deliver this message. Don't say another word. OK?"

PJ sniffed and ran his fingers nervously through his hair, then looked at Sleepy for a long stretch. "OK," he finally said. "But you better got somethin' up your sleeve."

"Repeat it to me, PJ, what you're going to tell Hammer."

"I tell him his boss send me with this message. Don't know nothin' else."

"That's right. Good. Don't say another word to him. Don't mention that his boss is my brother. Don't tell him he's here. Don't tell him anything."

PJ looked agitated, and Sleepy worried whether he would get the message right.

PJ climbed up the ladder and disappeared. Sleepy looked

over at his brother, pain still etched in his face. He expected a sense of satisfaction to wash over him. He had hurt his brother. He would soon let him die.

But he felt nothing that resembled satisfaction. He felt dirty. He felt evil. *Like Hammer.* It was one thing to kill a man who was hunting you. It was another thing to kill a man for the sake of revenge over something that happened decades ago.

Sleepy's resolve faded. He looked away and sighed. Then he walked over and squatted in front of his brother.

"I hate you. I've always hated you. I was going to kill you. But I'm not like you. I don't have the evil in me." Sleepy untied his brother. "Go. Out of my life."

His brother brushed himself off, reached for the ladder.

"Just one thing," Sleepy said. His eye twitched. He rubbed his scar. "Let Hammer come to me. I have a right to meet him on my terms, to protect my son. You fuck it up and I'll hunt you down again, and I promise you it will be the last time. I will kill you, and I won't do it quickly. You understand?"

His brother's hand shook visibly. He gripped the ladder to steady it, then he nodded that he understood.

CHAPTER 43

CONEY ISLAND
1:27 P.M.

Kim Butler was ordering everyone around again. She was always ordering everyone around. Ed Cole didn't like to be told what to do.

He opened his window. The wind blew his tuft of white hair back. The sand rode the wind, felt scratchy on his face. He squinted to keep it out of his eyes. There were lots of days like this at the Seaside Nursing Home.

Ed Cole liked the wind. He leaned out into it, looked up the beach toward the amusement park. The Wonder Wheel sat idle. The Cyclone didn't seem to be running either. *Good. Hate the damn place.*

The boardwalk was mostly deserted. Flashing lights indicated more beach patrol vehicles than normal. Clouds had moved in from the south and settled.

Looks like a good storm brewing. Kim Butler's afraid of it. Not me.

The bus was leaving in five minutes. Ed Cole decided what he would do.

He left his room, followed the Easter green wall to the elevator and went down. Everyone was in a long, snaking line in the lobby. Kim Butler was checking names off on a clipboard. Ed Cole found Betty Dinsmore, moved in next to her.

He whispered in Betty's ear: "Going to be nice and quiet around here. I'm gonna slip out after the head count, stay here. You?"

Betty Dinsmore grinned.

Kim Butler checked his name off. She finished with the line, went to the lobby doors and led everyone to the two buses waiting outside. Ed Cole slipped away, walked quickly to the back of the lobby, turned to make sure no one noticed him, then hid in the rear hallway.

CHAPTER 44

NEW JERSEY
3:11 P.M.

The Route 34 drawbridge over the Manasquan River would not open again for boat traffic until after the storm had passed. All four lanes of the swelling Jersey Shore artery carried outbound traffic only. Amanda had expected it and taken side streets through small towns to get to the last onramp before the bridge. The sobbing had subsided. She was resolute and tense.

She was stuck in traffic again, this time behind half a block of cars on Union Lane in Brielle, waiting to get on Route 34 and head west, inland. Amanda had been traveling four hours. And she had moved forty-two miles toward the storm. During that time Hurricane Harvey had moved eighty miles in her direction. The light breeze had become a good sailing wind. Clouds were thickening.

The first squall line moved in with the outer bands of the hurricane, a brief downpour the storm sent out in front, a warning signal. She turned on her wipers and lights and pulled the white Dodge across the double yellow line, spun the tires on the slick road up to Route 71. She honked and motioned that she wanted to cross the road, not enter the traffic. A small opening was allowed, and she crossed Route 71 and sped, parallel to Route 34, to the river.

At the base of the bridge she found a small seafood restaurant and a gravel parking lot. There were half a dozen other cars in the lot. *My God, they're eating lunch.* She turned toward the base of the bridge, scraped the front bumper against the gravel incline and left the Dodge about ten feet above water level. She took her cell phone, locked the car and ran up the twenty-foot incline to the bridge, where the wind was blowing strong enough that she had to lean into it. She wore a cotton t-shirt and jeans and her canvas deck shoes, and she suddenly realized she had not brought anything to block the rain. The temperature had dropped, and a chill swept over her.

Amanda cursed and began walking across the bridge. As she had done a dozen times on the way down, she tried Joe Springer's number on the cell phone. All lines are busy, the recording said again.

"C'mon," she groaned.

All the way down, amid dwelling on the dangers that faced her daughter and Jack Corbin, Amanda had thought vaguely about her suspicions that someone had stalled the New York evacuation. A gust of wind slammed into her and seemed to pack realization. She stopped cold on the bridge.

What if somebody was placing a bet, like in the Carolinas?

Anybody in the chain of command, from Frank Delaney to Greg Chen to a local emergency official, could have found out the degree of GLIC's exposure in the Carolinas.

But it was a Dominican who had sold short the shares of GLIC just before Gert made landfall at Topsail Island. Maybe someone there was working with someone in the States.

Maybe the whole thing was being orchestrated from the National Hurricane Center. The possibility appalled her. She was stunned, deadened by thought that someone she knew might be carrying out such an evil plan.

For a brief second she considered Greg Chen. *No way. And not Frank Delaney, either.* She couldn't allow herself to think that either of them would betray the people they were hired to warn. She ran the other forecasters through her mind, ticked them off one-by-one and shook her head at the thought of each one.

Amanda didn't know who it was. Could be the mayor; everybody said he was into more than just running New York. But he was so proud of his City; the king wouldn't destroy his own kingdom. Could be Lassitor, but she had a hard time believing he could orchestrate anything so complicated, and she didn't even see him at the Office of Emergency Management. Could be someone else in the City's vast hierarchy of emergency decision-making. Could be someone from the outside, hacking in.

Or someone from the Hurricane Center.

The thought wouldn't go away. But none of it mattered. She understood something about what was going on, about why the evacuation had been stalled: Someone was manipulating the odds, increasing the chances for his bet to pay off. By delaying the evacuation, he could guarantee chaos, more damage as ships and trains and cars were stranded. And more deaths. More deaths, more lawsuits. More financial impact to the insurance companies.

What was that other company Jack mentioned, the one that was overexposed in New York? PrimeCo.

She began walking again. It was more difficult now and she crouched. She called *The New York Times.* Surprisingly, the call went through. She groaned that luck would put this call through but not one to Joe Springer's house. She got patched through to the business editor.

"Bob Drucker."

"Hi Mr. Drucker, my name is Amanda Cole. I don't have much time. Listen carefully. You gave a tip to Jack Corbin the other day about some Dominicans selling short the shares of Global Insurance Company."

"Jack shouldn't have... who the hell is this?"

"I'm a forecaster at the National Hurricane Center. Please listen to me. It's possible that the person who provided the Dominicans with the information about GLIC has told them about another company. PrimeCo."

"I'm listening."

"I don't give a damn about the story, but I'm sure you'll be interested. Here's what I need: I have to know if a trade was made on PrimeCo this morning, and if so, when."

"Why?"

"Because PrimeCo is overexposed right here in New York City, and I'm pretty sure someone tried to slow down the evacuation to pad his bet."

"Who all is involved?"

"You answer my question, I'll make sure the *Times* gets the story."

"Not easy to find out about trades."

"Thousands of lives are at stake."

Bob Drucker was quiet.

"And a great story," she said.

"I'll call you right back," Drucker said.

Amanda clicked the phone off and struggled against the wind. She looked back toward the river's edge under the bridge. The tide was still rolling in, but already the water was lapping at the horizontal line that scored the mud flats, marking the most recent high tide.

Still nearly 200 miles away, Harvey was beginning to push a mound of water toward the shore.

***

Bob Drucker called back, just as Amanda reached the other side of the bridge. She sat down against the railing and cupped her hand over her ear so she could hear.

"Looks like we've got a story all right," he said. "René Perez, same guy as before, made two short sells this morning on PrimeCo. First one was at 7:59, a pretty good chunk for after-hours trading. Second one was at 9:32, just after the market opened, and it was much bigger. Overall, he sold $10 million worth of PrimeCo."

"How much can he make on that?"

"Depends on how much the stock drops," Drucker said. "Let's say it's cut in half."

"Then he buys the shares back for $5 million and pockets a profit of $5 million."

"Thanks," Amanda said. "That's all I needed."

"Hey, what about our deal? Who else is involved? Who's feeding Perez the info?"

"I'm still sorting it out. I said the *Times* will get the story, and I'll keep my word. Jack Corbin's going to write it. I'll make sure he has all the information he needs."

Amanda knew she had something now, but she still wasn't sure exactly what. Somebody might still be hampering the evacuation somehow. She needed to get back to the City. But Sarah was first. Amanda got up and started off again in a crosswind that nearly lifted her off her feet.

***

The cab driver cursed as traffic stopped on Route 495 in northern New Jersey. "You see that accident? We don't get to the tunnel. They make everybody go to Weehawken. Tunnel closed. Shit. I fucking tell you."

He slipped the cabbie another twenty, the third he'd given him since leaving Penn Station in Newark an hour before. They hadn't been able to get close to the ramp for the Holland Tunnel, so they took the Turnpike north to the Lincoln. "Use the shoulder. Get to that off-ramp. I'll get out there."

"You crazy," the cabbie said. "I can't get over. Everybody want that off-ramp. We fucking stuck now. Maybe we spend the night here."

"Listen, pal. I started my day in Biloxi, Mississippi, sitting on the tarmac at an Air Force Base in a beat-up old airplane, waiting for some guy in Florida to decide which hurricane to send us into. Then after an hour in the plane I think I'm *lucky* when he changes his mind and diverts us from the sorry little excuse of a hurricane in the Gulf of Mexico to Hurricane Harvey, where I puke all over myself, break my computer and practically shit my pants. Then we lose an engine. You hear me, pal? We lost a fucking engine in the middle of a hurricane 200 miles out in the middle of the Atlantic."

"I got problems too, mister. Right now, you my problem."

Jack ignored the cabbie. "Fucking plane diverts to McGuire. Some nice person—the only one I've met all day—gives me a lift to the train station. I paid him well, you hear me? Then Amtrak stops in fucking Newark and tells us to get off, all inbound traffic suspended. Now. I've got a woman—no, a *wife—to* find in New York. I'm going to get there come hell or high water. You're going to help me."

"How many more bills you have?"

"You get me to the off-ramp, I'll find three more."

The driver to their right honked and cursed as the cabbie cut in front. Five minutes later, Jack got out of the cab in the middle of Route 495 right near the Palisade off-ramp, a half-mile from the large looping downgrade that fed the Lincoln Tunnel.

The wind nearly tore the door off the cab. He gave the driver sixty dollars and ran through the driving rain, up the off-ramp, over a rise and down to a back-door approach to the tunnel.

***

Amanda turned left on Broadway, which led straight to Point Pleasant Beach. To her left she could see Gull Island in the middle of the river, where the brown reeds danced in the surging wind. Remnants of an old wooden boat, submerged in the mud, jutted a foot above the water. She crossed the stalled outbound traffic on Broadway and broke into a run down the strip of motels. At the end of Broadway she crossed over the small wood-piling bridge that traversed the canal. She saw boats in the river. *Curmudgeon, Forewinds, Deep Six.* On the left was the brightly colored *River Belle.*

They'll find them all in Brielle tomorrow.

If it were the Carolinas, these boats would have long since

been sailed to safe havens. But there hadn't been time.

***

A broken patchwork of sidewalks led to the toll plaza, a battery of small grimy booths under a tall, simple roof. It wasn't a place people usually walked into.

All lanes were streaming outbound.

Jack knew the security guards wouldn't let him in. He also knew there was no way to slip in unnoticed. If he ran in, he might be viewed as a threat to security. But he was pretty sure they wouldn't stop the evacuation to chase one crazy reporter. He walked casually up to the rightmost tollbooth, where a security guard was using the phone. He flashed his press card, slipped a $5 bill through the window—enough to cover the auto toll—then broke into a run. It was only thirty yards to the tunnel entrance. Any overzealous security guard who wanted to catch him would have to do so on foot. He was fairly confident they wouldn't shoot.

***

The stretch of sand in front of Joe Springer's house was intact. The wide beach was nearly flat from the boardwalk out about a hundred yards, where it dropped steeply into the ocean. On a normal summer day, you couldn't see the waves, which were hidden below the drop-off. Joe Springer had a great view of the beach, but his view of the *ocean* on a calm day started about fifty yards offshore.

All that was changing. From the boardwalk Amanda could see the tops of the growing waves, their quick curls before they crashed down against the berm, out of sight. She looked north toward the dilapidated concrete-and-boulder jetty, a lip that defined the mouth of the Manasquan River, where normally there would be the bobbing masts of boats going in and out of the harbor. The waves punished the jetty, careened off at an oblique angle and funneled toward the beach.

She jogged south on the boardwalk, noted how many people hadn't evacuated: About every fourth or fifth home still had people in it. *Idiots. They have no idea.* This wasn't going to be an iffy thing like Topsail Island, a house destroyed here and another surviving there. If Harvey stayed on his present course, the whole Jersey Shore was going to be reshaped.

She spotted the American flag flying in front of Joe Springer's house, flapping like a terrified bird. She hurried up the four steps to the deck, looking at the short, brown-shingle house. It was not built on pilings in the manner of coastal homes farther south, like Bill Leaderman's house on Topsail Island. There was no pass-through for the storm surge. She walked across the deck and rapped on the sliding glass door, which hadn't even been boarded up. Nobody answered, so she slid it open, walked in and stood dripping on the wood floor in the living room.

"Mommy!"

"Hi sweetheart. C'mere."

Sarah sprinted across the room and flew into her mother's outstretched arms. "You're all wet," Sarah said.

"It's raining pretty hard."

"I know. Your hurricane is coming, Mommy. Just like you said. Aren't you glad?"

"No, honey, I'm not glad. It's dangerous. Let's go."

"What the hell do you think you're doing?"

Joe Springer stepped into the room from the kitchen.

"Shut up, Joe," Amanda said. She pulled Sarah into her chest. "Don't argue with me. No more. We're leaving."

"Not for you to decide. Sarah's with me. Harvey's going to go out to sea just like all the other hurricanes that come this way."

"No, he's not. Dammit, Joe. This is Sarah's life we're talking about. Not something to play the odds with."

"But I have…"

She knew what he was going to say. She didn't want to hear it. "I don't care about any damn piece of paper you have. I don't care what any judge thinks. I'm her mother. I know

256

what's best."

"What makes you think you know what's best? You're always trying to make every goddamn decision."

Sarah had her hands over her ears, leaning into Amanda. "Stop it, Daddy. Stop it stop it stop it."

Amanda, calmer, teeth clenched, took one last shot at rationality: "It's like a mother lion, Joe. I just know. I don't even have to think about it. It comes from here." She hit her chest with her fist.

"Fine. Take control like you always do!"

She was completely calm now, but ready to explode, scratch his eyes out if need be. "There's a big storm coming. A really big storm. This house is not going to survive it. Anybody who is in this house is going to die. You seem to be content to wait and see what'll happen, like the other idiots down here who haven't left. I'm not ready to let anyone I love die. So I'm taking Sarah with me. I'm done with your irresponsible ass, Joe Springer. Done, you hear?"

"But..."

"Joe, you can stay. Whatever. Must be a guy thing, wanting to play he-man on this miserable little spit of sand. But you no longer have any say over this little girl. Come near me and you'll regret it," she said, never letting go of her daughter.

I'll do it. I'll scratch his goddamn eyes out to save Sarah.

Joe Springer must have understood. His face boiled, looked ready to explode with all the hideous, hateful thoughts that he decided not to utter. He shook his head, threw up his hands and went back into the kitchen.

Not even a goodbye for his daughter.

"Mommy? Are we going to die?"

"No, Sarah, we're not going to die. C'mon."

"What about Daddy?"

"Daddy's a big boy. He's going to make his own decision."

"Is Daddy going to die?"

"C'mon honey, we have to go."

Sarah was confused, terrified. "Daddy, come on!"

Amanda carried her daughter through the open sliding glass

door and out into the rain. She didn't bother to close the door. It wouldn't make any difference.

CHAPTER 45

MANHATTAN
4:07 P.M.

Even a one-armed photojournalist could get *the shot* if he were in the right spot at the right time. Adjust for the light, aim, focus, click. Any good photographer could do it with one arm if he knew what his target was, if it weren't moving. If it were news. Juan Rico had been scouting the City all day, looking for the spot. He hadn't gone home. He'd even skipped lunch. He ended up right where he figured he would, at the Holland Tunnel. It wasn't going anywhere, except under water. Juan Rico wanted the shot.

The wind was whipping outside and the rain was heavy, as it sometimes was during a summer thunderstorm, but steadier. The sky had become gloomy, the way it gets toward twilight in winter. Inside Chez Henri a few nervous patrons with nowhere else to go sipped drinks at the bar. Lunchtime was over. Business had been slow, and the only people left now were the customers who usually drank more than they ate anyway.

Rico sat in a dark corner with the owner, drinking a cola, not much in the mood to talk.

"Have a beer?" said Henri Mouchet.

"Nope."

"You always have a beer."

"This isn't always." Rico stared out the window.

"What is it, Juan?"

"This fucker ain't jokin' around. I know. I been in two." He told Henri Mouchet briefly about his experience in Hurricane Andrew in 1992. He recounted his tale of Gert, told him how he had looked up from under the sea and saw nothing but more blackness, thought he was good as dead, fighting with one arm to find something to grab onto. "Same thing comin' here."

"But this is New York City," said the owner. "It's not like we're on an island or something."

"No?"

"Well, not like in North Carolina. The ocean is, like, ten, fifteen miles from here."

"And the river's two blocks away," Rico said. "Harbor and the river make it worse, push the water up or something. You have to ask Jack or Amanda 'bout it."

"I saw Amanda leave earlier, in your car."

"Yeah? Shit, I missed her. Been out running around the City all day."

"I see you have your gear," Henri said. "You planning on going out in this?"

"Got a score to settle with these storms, know just how to do it. What about you, Henri? You stayin' here?"

"What else? We'll be open as long as someone needs us. Some of these people need me tonight, maybe more than normal."

"You take care, my friend. Keep an ear to the radio." Rico grabbed his equipment, all of it replaced since Gert. He slung his camera bag over one shoulder, a laptop computer for transmitting pictures over the other, then put his rain poncho on. "Henri?"

"Yes."

"Don't be afraid to be afraid."

Henri Mouchet smiled and inclined his head, then stuck out his hand. "Here's your bill."

***

The rain blew sideways down Ninth Avenue, did the same at the intersection and threatened to flip the few cars that braved the streets, mostly cabs now. One of them had a wide black gouge down the side, a wreck that might have happened today.

The cab stopped. Jack held the door open as another passenger got out, then he stuck his head in. The heavyset driver, dark skin, bushy eyebrows, looked to be part of the cab, as though he hadn't got out of the driver's seat in months.

"Tribeca?" Jack said.

"No way, pal," said the cabbie. "I got another fare to pick up. Reserved. Out you go."

"Sixty bucks," Jack said.

"Hop in."

The driver was listening to the radio. Jack leaned forward to hear meteorologist John Turner.

"Hurricane Harvey is moving north-northwest at *forty-five* miles an hour. The storm is now centered about 190 miles south of New York City. Hurricane-force winds extend outward from the center roughly 120 miles and should be arriving within the next two hours. Atlantic City has already reported sustained seventy-five mile per hour winds. That's hurricane force. As the storm's far-flung bands of strong thunderstorm activity move into our area, conditions will change rapidly."

The cabbie cursed and honked as the traffic stopped at 23rd Street. Ahead, Jack saw the reason. The road was flooded and several cars had stalled in the intersection.

Jack fished for his money, asked the driver: "You going home now?"

"Naw. Brooklyn. Too far in this storm."

"Not safe here, either," Jack said.

"Maybe I'll get out of town."

"How?"

"Dunno. Seems like a good idea, though."

Jack handed the cabbie his unearned sixty dollars and jumped out.

***

The subway line was just two blocks east. Jack ran, dodging umbrellas that unfolded helplessly. He rounded a building at the intersection near the subway station and the wind blew him sideways into the street. He bent his knees, got low, and made it back to the sidewalk, then pushed his way down the stairs and into the subway.

The southbound train arrived, brakes squealing, and Jack got in. The rattle of the train seemed peaceful compared to what was going on outside. He thought about what was actually going to happen to New York City. The unthinkable. "The Storm of the Century," the *Times* would call it. Maybe "The Storm of the Millennium." He had been so focused on getting to Amanda that he hadn't been thinking about what the *Times* would be doing. Here he was, the weather beat reporter, not even on the job.

Jack wondered how many other reporters around New York City had abandoned their jobs today. No, not many. That's not the way reporters think. This is it. *The* storm.

Every reporter in New York and New Jersey will write something about it. Analysis, opinion, sweeping conclusions and minute detail, the gamut. Editors will work overtime, assigning hundreds of stories, from the how and why to human interest stories about little old ladies who got trapped in the subway and survived. The vast resources of the *Times* would be scrambled like infantry to question and dig and shove and push, to inform, to fill every available column-inch in the paper.

The scratchy speaker broke his concentration. "Ladies and Gentlemen. The New York City subway system will be shutting down in thirty minutes due to anticipated flooding problems. All lines. Repeat, all lines will be shutting down in thirty minutes. This train will continue on to South Ferry

Station with no northbound service. The last northbound train will arrive in about two minutes."

The train stopped at the Canal Street station and Jack ran to the exit.

But something deep inside called him to the newsroom. It was the same urge that got him into reporting in the first place. He was the weather beat reporter. And now his turf was finally getting nailed, and he was running away from his job. There was one more northbound train, arriving in two minutes.

Jack could no longer stand upright in the wind. He leaned into it. A steel garbage can rolled past him as he crossed the nearly empty street. Jack's mind flip-flopped between his life as a reporter and his potential life with Amanda. An aluminum can whirred by at head level, narrowly missing him as he made his decision.

CHAPTER 46

NEW JERSEY
4:20 P.M.

The emergency vehicle was just as trapped as all the other cars and trucks. Amanda and Sarah had walked, run and finally hitched a ride with this fireman, trying to get to the bridge over the Manasquan River. Amanda had avoided the main evacuation route out of town, Route 88, which was jammed with traffic and ran much farther before reaching high ground. Amanda knew it was a good three- or four-mile drive before they'd be out of reach of the surge, whereas if they could get across the bridge they could take the Dodge the remaining quarter-mile to high ground.

But now a van had flipped on the bridge, the fireman said, blown over by the wind. The bridge had been closed. The evacuation from Point Pleasant Beach in this direction was over.

They hopped out of the vehicle and were nearly blown over. The wind was growing each moment now. Amanda ducked reflexively, looked past the shuttered Spike's Fish Market and across the river at Gull Island. The old sunken boat was gone. The water was inching up into the reeds. On the near side of the river, the grass of the public park was beginning to flood.

There were hundreds of cars backed up with nowhere to go. She wondered how many other people, like Joe Springer, hadn't even left their houses.

Sarah's teeth chattered: "Mommy, I'm scared."

"We'll be OK," Amanda shouted over the growing wind. She tugged at her daughter's arm.

"What are we going to do?"

Can't stay here. Surge will wash right over us. She pointed at the bridge.

Sarah pulled hard against her mother's grip. "I'm not going on the bridge," Sarah said, face set in a firm scowl.

"We'll be safe on the other side. Stop arguing with me, will you?"

Sarah shook her head in fierce defiance.

"Look up," Amanda said.

Sarah did so, and her eyes grew wide. Sepia clouds raced overhead, folding upon each other like kneaded dough and moving with dizzying speed.

Sarah pulled her mother toward the bridge.

A town cop was huddled next to his car, which blocked the bridge. He stopped them and, pressing his face close to Amanda's, shouted: "Bridge is closed, lady. Nobody allowed."

You'll have to shoot me to stop me.

"Everybody on this side of the bridge is going to drown," she said. "I'm crossing."

"No you're not, lady. I got orders."

"You going to arrest me now or shoot me in the back?"

The cop stared at her, thinking. "Drown?"

"Storm surge."

"How do you know?"

"I'm a forecaster at the National Hurricane Center. I know. Water will be fifteen feet deep here. How tall are *you?*"

The cop winced, curled his nose. Rain washed across his face. He nodded his head toward the bridge.

Amanda took her daughter's hand, held it with clasped fingers and started across the 3,000 feet of exposed steel. She glanced back. The cop watched her, nodded once, held his position.

Once up and away from the relative protection of buildings and trees, Amanda realized the difficulty. The wind was blowing at near hurricane force out of the northeast—at right angles to the bridge. There was no way they would cross standing up.

On the wing of an airplane, a stuntwoman in flight. That's how Amanda felt, crossing the metal bridge over the Manasquan River.

The wind, blowing out of the northeast, hit them from the right. She was sure it was at hurricane force now—on the bridge, at least, high over the water. A straggling seagull gave up and was thrown backward.

Amanda huddled against the railing on the upwind side of the bridge, moving forward a few inches at a time on her knees and alternating holds with her hands, always one hand gripping firm. Sarah was downwind of her, arms wrapped around her mother's waist. They crawled together, fingers clutching belt loops.

Got to make it to the other side soon. Can't hold on much longer.

They passed the flipped van that had blocked traffic. Terese's voice filled Amanda's head: *There's going to be some accidents.*

The impact of the thought suddenly hit Amanda. She understood where the accidents would be. She imagined the streets of Manhattan now, gridlocked with people trying to escape. She knew about New York drivers. They would sit and honk and curse and honk some more. And then a lot of them would drown. The nagging thought returned: She should be at the Emergency Operations Center. Just as the mayor had waited too long to start the evacuation, now he would wait too long to stop it. And somewhere, someone was encouraging him to do just that. She had to find out who. She had to warn the mayor.

They were mid-span when the lighting started up again. The wind gusted, and Amanda pulled her daughter flat against the cold steel until the gust abated. Then they continued.

Sarah pleaded every minute or so. "Mommy, I'm scared."

"You're doing great. Hold on tight. We're almost there."

~ ~ ~

EXCERPTED FROM
HURRICANE HARVEY: CHRONICLE
OF DEATH AND DESTRUCTION,
BY NICHOLAS K. GRAY (2000)

Hurricane Harvey sent an advance warning, its first gusts of seventy-four miles an hour, to New York's most famous and most crowded borough during what would have been the evening rush hour at the beginning of a busy tourist weekend. The moon was full, making the tides higher than normal, exacerbating an already deadly situation.

Black clouds descended on the island of Manhattan as water seeped into its edges.

The storm pushed water into the wide mouth of New York harbor, and as the channel narrowed, the water rose, surging over the concrete seawall at Battery Park along the south end of the rocky island.

Three-foot waves pounded a set of stairs that led up to a series of eight engraved stone monoliths honoring U.S. servicemen who sleep forever in American coastal waters. The quantity of engraved names hinted at the remarkable number of people the sea had taken by other means. Harvey would add greatly to that tally.

CHAPTER 47

MANHATTAN
4:38 P.M.

The dock was connected to the mainland by a hinged ramp, which always sloped downward by a slight angle at high tide and a steep one at low tide. Walter Beasley, drenched, held the rail with both hands and walked *upward* to the dock. The rain splattered his glasses, making his narrow field of vision even more blurry than usual.

The dock was secured by steel rings to narrower steel pilings, so that the pilings remained fixed while the dock rose and fell with the tide. The steel rings made a loud *ker-chunk, ka-clink* as the dock lurched a half-inch with the wind and back again.

Beasley had always wondered why, even at high tide, the pilings towered over his head. He reached the dock, shuffled with his feet wide apart for balance against the fierce gusts. The tops of the pilings were at eye level.

The boat rocked dramatically in the wind. With such a deep draft, it took a lot of wind to rock the *Slow Times*. There was no sign of other people.

It was partly the loose stern line that allowed the *Slow Times* to move about so feverishly. Beasley held fast to a teak handle and stepped into the stern deck. He unlocked the cabin door and went inside. Rain was forcing its way through the weather stripping in the windows, dripping onto the small pullout couch. The drugs would be getting wet underneath. He wondered why Leonard Lassitor hadn't sent someone to pick them up. He pulled the couch out, removed the bags and stowed them in the windowless forward bunk. He didn't know why he did it, other than the fact that he was terrified of Leonard Lassitor.

He opened a large cupboard door and found two short lengths of rope and went back outside to secure the boat with extra lines. He finished, and pushed his glasses up onto his nose. Now he had to decide where to ride the storm out, whether to stay on the boat or return to the newsroom.

The sky had lowered, grown darker while he worked. Beyond the feeble breakwall of the marina, the Hudson was a deserted, frothy mess. Lightning flashed down river; the thunder competed with the deafening wind, the *ker-chunk, ka-clink* of the dock, the flapping of loose rope ends, groaning and creaking of taut lines.

He didn't even have time to lunge for them. The wind tore his glasses from his head. They slammed into the side of the boat and fell soundlessly into the river.

Walter Beasley wrapped his arms around himself and looked at his blurry boat, fading at the edges into a circle of darkness. He clenched his eyes and thought of the newsroom, how it would be buzzing right now as every available reporter and editor tried to find something useful to do. He wondered if anyone would even notice that he'd left, just walked out. He thought of Jack Corbin, whom he had failed to find. He thought of Leonard Lassitor, his only friend who was now his worst enemy. He thought of the drugs, a certain fortune, a possible end to his career.

Walter Beasley went inside. The cabin door creaked as it closed behind him.

CHAPTER 48

NEW JERSEY
5:10 P.M.

The sound was deafening. Like metal on metal in a horrific crash. Joe Springer thought at first that two planes were colliding above the house. He reached reflexively to put his hands over his head. Then the hair on his arms and his head stood up, and he felt a tingle run through his body.

This is it. The worst of it. I'm surviving.

Hands shielding his face from the lightning, he looked across the small deck toward the ocean. Waves at eye level, eating into what had been a wide stretch of beach, munching their way toward the boardwalk that sat three feet below his deck.

Joe Springer was still fuming about Amanda taking Sarah. Somewhere deep in his mind he acknowledged that it was all about control. He was bucking Amanda's authority, and now his conscience began to suggest that perhaps his anger had gotten the better of his judgment.

A wave crashed into the boardwalk, lifted the two-by-fours up, spread them like a giant Oriental fan, flipped them over and onto his deck.

He should have evacuated. The thought barely had time to

enter his head when a vast dark shape, taller than the house, filled the window. It looked like some larger-than-life science-fiction wave rolling toward him, but it couldn't be. *Couldn't be.*

He ran to the kitchen, headed for the side door leading to the sand pathway off the dunes, toward town. He jumped three stairs onto the sand, ran two steps and the wave picked him up, hurled him and his house in a frenzy of froth. Odd sounds of wood and glass and water. Slam into the sand. Desperate attempt for air. Only water.

Deathly weight on chest. Push and drag, a leg twisting into an impossible contortion. Darkness. Nothing.

***

Amanda hadn't rolled down a hillside since she was Sarah's age. It was the quickest way down from the bridge without standing up, which they couldn't do. Amanda felt her shirt tear as sharp rocks on the artificial bank cut into her back. She would be bruised from it. They rolled all the way to the white Dodge and leaned up against the passenger side, protected only from the worst of the wind, which now seemed to come from all sides. Like fighting an army. *It's everywhere, a constant barrage. No escape. The restaurant?* She glanced at the red building. The cars that had been there were gone and the place was deserted. *Surge will take it anyway. Run up the hill? Flying debris might kill us.* Amanda fumbled for her keys and opened the passenger door, picked Sarah up and climbed in. The Dodge rocked in the wind.

Lightning was moving toward them, its frequency increasing. Driving, she realized, might be more dangerous than sitting where they were.

Amanda knew she might have only a few minutes before the wind became too strong to venture out into. She needed to know the latest forecasted track for Harvey so she would know what the surge might be. That knowledge might be critical in deciding what she and Sarah should do: It might determine whether or not they lived. She still hadn't figured out how to warn the mayor, but that would have to wait.

She reached into the back seat, opened the suitcase and set the satellite dish up in Sarah's lap. Then she fired up her laptop, connected to the Internet. She commanded her email program to download in the background while she studied the storm. The LORAX was still down, but she knew that even the GFDL model would have figured the storm out by now. She downloaded the forecast.

A graphic scrolled onto her screen and Amanda saw in real time what she had feared for most of her professional career, what she and others had modeled hundreds of times in an effort to predict just how bad it could be, the worst-case scenario for a hurricane in the Northeast. The forecast now had Harvey's eye passing just offshore of Atlantic City-close enough to be considered a direct hit. She would win the bet with Frank Delaney. He'd owe her dinner. It was a hollow victory and no more than a fleeting thought. Harvey was heading north-northwest, headed straight for her.

Manhattan was twenty miles east of the projected path—smack in the middle of the right-side eyewall.

Winds had dropped to 130 miles per hour. But Hurricane Harvey was moving at the speed of a car on the freeway—fifty-five miles an hour—creating an effective wind of 185 miles per hour in the right-side eyewall. It was nearly high tide. The timing could not have been much worse.

She searched the latest land-based radar image for some shred of good news. There wasn't much. A solid wall of red surrounded the eyewall, indicating intense convection and the associated heavy rainfall and intense winds. But in front of the storm, nearly upon them, was a pocket of cooler colors. If they could wait for that to arrive, it would provide a temporary respite from the worst of the wind, just long enough to move to higher ground and find shelter. If they could wait.

Amanda clicked on her email inbox. Still nothing from Jack. But there was a note from Frank Delaney. She could see only two words of the message's subject on her small screen. It read, "Jack is…"

Excited, hopeful, Amanda clicked on the message.
"Mommy!"

Amanda put her hands to her ears when her daughter screamed. Sarah was looking out the back window toward the river. Amanda saw the horror on her daughter's face and glanced into the rear-view mirror. A huge wall of water was racing across the river, toward them, more ominous than anything even Amanda Cole had imagined. There was no time to read the message. There was no time to think.

Amanda reached across Sarah's lap and pushed the door open. They tumbled out, and the computer setup crashed to the ground. Amanda pushed Sarah in front of her and they put distance between themselves and the white Dodge. A wave slammed into the side of the car and shoved it toward them.

They were nearly above the reach of the storm surge, but the next wave was coming, taller than the last.

Amanda grabbed Sarah by the wrist and tried to head up the embankment. Sarah, terrified, froze.

The wave came.

Heavy water pounded Amanda into the ground, pushed her up the bank, then pulled back and dragged her down. One hand held Sarah by the wrist. She dug the fingers of her other hand into the wet earth, tried to keep the high ground she'd attained. But the undertow won and sucked them both into the water.

Amanda managed to pull her daughter into her chest as the two tumbled in muddy darkness.

They struggled to the surface and another wave crashed over them, then pulled them farther from land. For Amanda, it was a hell far exceeding Topsail Island, for now Sarah was in danger. Each time they reached the surface, she struggled toward the shore, but the waves pulled them backward and soon they were in the middle of what earlier had been a lazy river but was now part of the sea. Amanda quit trying to swim to the shore and focused on keeping their heads above water.

And she knew this was neither the worst of the surge, nor the worst of the wind.

CHAPTER 49

IN THE SKIES ABOVE NEW JERSEY
5:16 P.M.

Coast Guard Lieutenant Meg Evans had gotten lucky. She'd gambled on the soft spot in the storm, the lighter shades of green on her radar screen, and stayed in the air an extra few minutes to make one last water rescue. The last thunderstorm band had nearly overpowered her stout Sikorsky HH-60 Jayhawk, but Lieutenant Evans had skillfully put down on the lee side of a hill, safely depositing two old New Jersey men who'd been trapped on a barrier island.

Now the wind had settled temporarily to a manageable seventy knots. Barely manageable. And it would change soon for the worse. No more rescues. It was time to head back to base.

In the right seat, Evans gripped the cyclic in one hand and the collective in the other. The Jayhawk was *her* aircraft. She flew it. The copilot in the left seat was content to let Lieutenant Evans fly in this weather. He knew she was the best.

"Damn!" The copilot's voice rang tinny in Evans's headphones. "Visual, three o'clock."

Evans peered through blurry sheets of rain into the open water below. "Holy Cow!" She corrected the copilot: "Two targets in the water. Mark, mark, mark."

The copilot noted the location in case they lost visual. "You're not going in?" he asked.

"The hell I'm not," Evans said. She looked over her shoulder and barked at the flight mechanic. "Mech: Give me part one!" To her copilot: "Kill outside radio."

"Don't have to, Meg."

"What?"

"Atlantic City just went off the air."

"Holy Cow!" Then Evans settled into the routine. "Give me power."

The copilot shook his head and fell in line. He set the engines for additional emergency power. The flight mechanic and the rescue swimmer put on their gunner's belts and moved to the hatch. The swimmer, wearing fins, snorkel and mask, clipped the D-ring of the hoist to a harness around his blue drysuit.

Lieutenant Meg Evans dove the chopper, shot an approach downwind of the victims, who clutched each other. She lost visual in the heavy waves, then regained it and moved in. In less than sixty seconds the rescue swimmer was ready.

"Flight check one complete," the flight mechanic said.

"Roger," Evans said. "Shotgun approach. Rescue check part two." The hatch was opened, the hoist readied. "Go on hot mike," she said. "Check swimmer."

The mechanic tapped the swimmer three times, signaling the pilot was ready.

Evans descended to thirty feet above the water and held the chopper as steady as she could in winds that switched directions as fast as she reacted.

"Wind is jumping up," the copilot warned. "Seventy-five knots. Seventy-nine. Careful, Meg."

Meg Evans knew she had only one shot. The wind was quickly becoming too much. Even the Jayhawk had limits. She'd once done a water rescue in eighty-six-knot winds—a hundred miles an hour. Much more than that and it would be foolish to risk the lives of her crewmembers. She hovered just downwind of the victims. The rotor wash was blown safely backward. "Deploy swimmer!"

The flight mechanic quickly lowered the swimmer until his fins touched the tops of the highest waves. "Forward and right," the mech instructed.

"Roger," Meg Evans said. The victims would soon disappear from her view, under the chopper. The flight mech was in charge now.

"Forward 100 feet... right... right ten... forward and right... hold!"

Evans could not see the victims now. She focused on the horizon, moved as instructed, and then momentarily held the Jayhawk rock steady like a feeding humming bird. Then a fierce downdraft shuddered the chopper toward the waves and the mech screamed: "Steady! Swimmer's under!"

"Gust of eighty-five, Meg!" the copilot shouted. "Get out! Get out!"

A wave slapped the Jayhawk's tail wheel. Lieutenant Evans added power, pulled up, leveled off, and said a quick silent prayer. "Stay with it," she said evenly.

"Left five... ahead... ahead... hold!"

Below, the swimmer tried to separate the victims and take one at a time. They would not let go of each other. Together, they weighed no more than a large man, so the swimmer strapped his harness around both and signaled the mech to hoist.

In a moment, there were two more people aboard the now-crowded Jayhawk.

Evans immediately lifted the chopper to 200 feet.

"Damn," the copilot said. "One's a little girl."

"Thought so," Meg Evans said. "That's why we went in."

***

Amanda had never felt so blissfully claustrophobic. She clutched her shivering daughter next to her as a starving person protects a basket of food. The Jayhawk vibrated loudly.

A crewmember was trying to separate Sarah and Amanda enough to attach some sort of belt to each of them. Amanda resisted.

"I have to talk to the pilot," she shouted over the rumbling, metallic clatter.

"Victim wants to talk to you," the crewmember said into his microphone. Then he nodded and put a spare set of headphones on Amanda.

"Go ahead," the pilot said. It was a woman's voice, and Amanda recognized it. "Lieutenant Evans?"

The pilot struggled to turn and look into the back of the helicopter. "Holy cow! Twice in one week. Now that's a record."

"Meg, you've got to take me to New York."

"Not a chance. I'm heading to McGuire. Shouldn't have picked you up in the first place, but I saw the kid."

"You see the convection that's coming?" Amanda knew they'd be flying right into a deadly pocket of turbulence that even the Jayhawk couldn't handle.

"We'll beat it," Evans said.

"No you won't. I looked at the radar just before I went in. You *won't* beat it. Head north and you can outrun the pocket. And save a bunch of lives, too."

"New York?"

Amanda explained.

CHAPTER 50

IN THE SKIES ABOVE MANHATTAN
5:39 P.M.

Lieutenant Meg Evans brought the Jayhawk in over the Verrazano Narrows bridge at the lower end of New York Harbor, cruising at 130 knots groundspeed in a strong right-side cross wind. She dropped to 200 feet above the Hudson. The Statue of Liberty slipped by on the left.

Heading north, she had flown faster than the storm. The winds had dropped back down to around seventy knots, better conditions for a tough landing. But it wouldn't last long as the pocket of dangerous convection raced to catch up.

"Helipad right along the river," the copilot pointed. "C'mon, Meg. Use it. Putting them on a forty-seven story building is *nuts*. Orographics might suck us right into it."

Meg Evans was fully aware that buildings acted like mountains, funneling wind over and between themselves into deadly rivers of incredible turbulence. She shot the copilot a stern, determined look. "Done it before," she said.

Evans orchestrated one loop around Building 7 of the World Trade Center, feeling the wind and looking for obstacles. The windsock atop the building flapped madly.

Blue lights ringed a giant, white H adjacent to the only apparent danger—a compact, eight-foot tall protrusion above the roof that housed a staircase into the building.

"Winds sixty-eight knots out of the east," the copilot said. "Gusts to seventy-six. Torque available is one-oh-three."

"Plenty," Evans said. "I'll approach from the west. No-hover landing."

"Roger." The copilot paused, then said softly: "Get it right the first time, Meg."

She started her final approach. "Flight mech con me in."

"Ahead... easy left... easy forward... watch the tail!"

***

Amanda had gotten a good view of the City streets as the Jayhawk approached the Emergency Operations Center. They were clogged with cars, just as she feared.

The helicopter lurched upward and the flight mechanic was thrown to the floor. He recovered as though it had probably happened before. The door on the helicopter was open. Amanda worried suddenly that the door to the stairway might not be. There was a flurry of chatter on the headphones. The Jayhawk lifted, circled, approached, and descended again.

Meg Evans put one wheel on the roof, maintained power and held a no-hover landing. It was the safest way, she had said. They could abort easily if the wind dictated. The flight mechanic unbuckled Amanda and Sarah from their seats. He jumped out the door and disappeared, crouching to keep from being blown off the roof. Amanda and Sarah followed him. He pushed them to the roof and onto their stomachs and helped them crawl to the staircase. Coast Guard rules dictated he escort them until they were out of danger. Amanda didn't mind.

The flight mechanic checked the door. It was unlocked but he couldn't open it against the wind. Amanda helped him and together they pulled it open and it slammed back against its hinges. Amanda and Sarah went inside and crawled down the stairs.

She heard the Jayhawk power up and move away. Evans

had promised Amanda she would head north, staying in the relatively calm pocket of air between bands of thunderstorms until she found a safe place to put down. *Like a bird caught in the storm.* Amanda hoped Meg Evans would have better luck than most of the birds.

***

Once safely on the forty-seventh floor, Amanda decided she didn't want to risk another run-in with security, so she avoided the elevator and carried her wet, weary daughter down the stairs.

On the twenty-third floor, she pushed the door open into a utilitarian hallway with restrooms on one side and boxes of supplies on the other. The hallway ended abruptly to the left, so she went right, past a small kitchenette. Two men were pouring coffee. They stepped back as she approached. Their faces showed the puzzlement.

"This the EOC?" Amanda demanded.

"Yeah, but what the hell?"

"Thanks." Amanda pushed past them. The hallway quickly opened up into the vast room that was the Emergency Operations Center.

She went looking for the mayor. He was not in the main room. Again, people stared at her. She was getting used to it. She marched to the mayor's office. Inside, he and Leonard Lassitor were huddled over a computer. The door was open. She stepped in quietly, put Sarah down. They dripped onto the carpet. Neither man looked up, but the mayor put a don't-bother-us-yet hand in the air.

"Only three evacuation centers left in Manhattan that aren't stuffed full," Lassitor said. Amanda could see his profile. He did not look overly worried. His cheek was bruised and he held his side as though injured.

"So what do we do when those are full?" the mayor asked.

It was Amanda's turn. "Tell everybody in New York to stay wherever they are, get to a higher floor and away from the windows. You have to stop the evacuation."

The mayor spun around. Wide eyes conveyed his surprise. Amanda knew she and her daughter, their clothes soaked and torn, must have been a sight. Lassitor only glanced up, said nothing.

"Well, I'll be damned," said the mayor. "First you barge in and order me to start an evacuation. Now you barge back in and tell me to stop it. Who in the hell do you think you are, lady?"

Amanda didn't answer. "There are thousands of people on the streets," she started, "in cars and on foot, all trying to go somewhere. In the next hour, most of them will die if they don't find cover. You must tell them to get inside and stay inside. Radio, bullhorns, any way you can."

"How in the hell did you get in here?" the mayor asked. Amanda was peeved that he'd ask such an impertinent question. She retorted with more spite than she'd intended.

"Proof that you guys don't know what the hell you're doing," she said. "Just like you didn't know when to *start* the evacuation. Or that you have to *stop* it."

Lassitor kept his cool. Like he didn't really care. Or was avoiding involvement. "We're handling things just fine," the mayor said "And now you've pushed me too far. This is *my* City, and the evacuation is ours to call. Get the hell out."

Amanda had been afraid of this. She wished she hadn't put him on the defensive. The testosterone level on the twenty-third floor of Building 7 was off the charts, and the mayor had lost sight of what was best for his City, and now he didn't want anyone getting in his way. He was running on storm-induced adrenaline—like forecaster Greg Chen—not wanting the fun to stop. But she had to stop it, and now there was no going back to try a softer approach.

Amanda sensed the two security guards that had moved in behind her. She looked at the mayor and Lassitor. She needed something drastic to shake things up, or she was going to be hauled away and nothing would get done right. She wasn't sure who was involved in the stock-market scheme, but she was out of time and out of ideas. It was her only shot.

She looked firmly at the mayor. "Mr. Mayor. Somebody is placing bets on the storm. Whoever it is is trying to make a mess of your evacuation. I doubt you can trust the people around you."

Amanda glanced at Lassitor. He didn't flinch, gave no sign that he might be the one. She gave no sign that she suspected him. She looked back at the mayor.

"What the hell are you talking about?" the mayor said.

As succinctly as she could, Amanda explained the connection between the Dominicans, Global Insurance Company and PrimeCo, and how a botched evacuation would make the PrimeCo stock transactions more valuable.

"The first trade on PrimeCo was placed at 7:52 this morning," she said. "We hadn't issued our bulletin yet. Only someone awfully familiar with the storm could have known it was coming here before eight o'clock. That would be our own forecasters, and the people in this building."

The mayor was listening now, curious. "Who, then?"

"Don't know yet," she said, "but I'm certain it's happening. I'll find out *who* before I'm done." She made a point of not looking at Lassitor. If it was him, she'd figure it out, and meanwhile she didn't want him to run. *Just be a little nervous.*

The mayor's eyes narrowed, but he hadn't been totally convinced. Then Amanda remembered the accidents.

"You had some accidents on the Jersey side of the river?"

"Yeah, but that's not so unusual in an evacuation."

"Planned," Amanda said. "To make it all worse. C'mon. It really doesn't matter if I'm right or wrong about that at the moment. The important thing is we've got people in the streets and a lot of them are going to die unless you get them off the streets."

The mayor chewed his lip and studied her. "You were right earlier."

"And I'm right now."

"OK, we'll get people inside." The mayor offered his hand to Amanda. "Thank you, and I'm sorry."

Amanda couldn't take his hand. Too many people were going to die anyway. She turned to leave.

"Where you going?" the mayor asked.

"Out."

"But I thought you said everybody should stay in."

"I've got some things to figure out. And I've got one more person to take care of."

CHAPTER 51

OUTSIDE SANTO DOMINGO,
DOMINICAN REPUBLIC
5:55 P.M.

Maximo had two distinct moods going when the phone rang. He was still fuming over Terese running off. He hadn't heard yet from his men, and that was a bad sign. Either they hadn't found her or they were doing things to her that he didn't want to imagine. But his latest stock market bet was already paying off as the general market turned lower before trading was halted mid-day because of the approaching storm.

"Nombre?"

"Octopus."

Hearing from the Octopus let the better of his two moods float to the surface. "Hello, my friend. I see on the television you are about to be, how do you say it? Pummeled?"

"Your bet is well covered, Maximo. But there's a little trouble on this end."

"Oh?"

"There's a woman from the Hurricane Center who's figured the scheme out. She knows it's you."

"Not a problem. It is done. No one can touch me here,"

Maximo said with more confidence than he felt. Terese scratched at the back of his mind.

"But she can touch *me,*" the Octopus said.

"She knows you are involved?"

"No, but she's close. I'm afraid she might figure it out."

"Then we must get you out of there quickly," Maximo said.

"That's a problem. I can't go anywhere until the storm is over. And I don't know if I'll be able to get a flight tomorrow. Airports could be down awhile."

"How close is she?"

"I think I have a day or two, at least," the Octopus said.

"Then stay until morning. Get out of the City any way you can tomorrow, but make sure nobody is looking for you. Catch a flight somewhere else. Of course, I will keep my promise. Once you get here you have no worries."

"Thank you, Maximo. I will see you soon, then."

CHAPTER 52

MANHATTAN
6:02 P.M.

Juan Rico huddled under a maze of metal pipes and two-inch-thick planks that made up a construction scaffolding against the north wall of the Holland Plaza Building. His camera, resting on the cast on his left arm and under his rain poncho, was already fitted with a 200 mm lens, chosen to perfectly frame the entrance to the Holland Tunnel, which was closed now and blocked by heavy orange construction cones.

Rico estimated he was a foot or so above the crest in the road, where the water would shoot down into the gaping black hole. The surge would come quickly and rise fast. But he wasn't sure exactly where from, as there was no way to gauge with his eye where the low spots were in the maze of intersecting roads and sidewalks. Rico wanted only to get the photo of the tunnel entrance turned into a river, one river flowing under another. That was *the shot*. Nobody else would have it. Then he would head back to his apartment to relative safety.

He acknowledged the risk. What else is there, he had asked himself. *I am a photojournalist. This shot will happen once in my lifetime. I'll get it. Maybe I'll die. I almost died in North Carolina, and for what? Didn't even get a picture out of it. This time, I at least get the fuckin' picture.*

A Port Authority guard was throwing sandbags into the roadway, more to stop cars than to stop the surge, Rico figured. He snapped a couple frames of the guard and the sandbags. He glanced at his watch.

The cab came from Canal Street. A long black gouge ran down the side. The guard stopped it. Rico couldn't hear, but by the gestures he could tell that there was an argument. Then the guard stepped back and bowed as he let the cab pass. Then he flipped the bird at the back of the cab and went back to his work. Rico snapped several frames of the cab as it disappeared into the tunnel. *Who is this fuckin' idiot?*

In the last shot, through a lens blurred by raindrops, he made sure he had the license plate.

Rico was wiping his lens and didn't see the water coming. When he looked up, the rising river lapped gently against the sandbags, as though it had been there before, then found its way around the partial wall and rolled down into the tunnel.

Click click click.

Fuckin' a. Shot of my life.

Rico ducked his head down into his poncho and opened his laptop. He plugged his digital camera into the computer and transferred the images to the computer's hard drive. Then he typed an email to the photo editor at the *Times:*

```
Holland Tunnel
5:38:  Unknown  Port  Authority  guard
sandbags  closed  entrance  to  Holland
Tunnel  after  orange  cones  had  blown
away.
5:40:  Unknown  cab  driver  enters  tunnel
after  argument  with  PA  guard—
5:41:  Surge  of  water  flows  into  tunnel.
River  under  the  river.
NOTE:  Pls  check,  but  I  think  Jersey  side
floods  first.  This  guy  won't  be  coming
out.  Note  license  plate  number  for
```

```
possible ID.
Rico
```

Rico closed the computer, stuck his head out of his poncho and found the water curling around his boots. He tried to send the email and the digital pictures to the newsroom, but the cellular modem in his computer got only a busy signal. He had the picture, but now he couldn't transmit it. He cursed the storm. The water rose. He needed to find a safer place and try again.

He left the relative protection of the north wall of the Holland Plaza building and waded out into the street and was immediately blown onto his back. His first thought was that his equipment would be ruined. His second thought was of being washed down into the tunnel.

Not again, you son of a bitch.

On his hands and knees he crawled against the rising surge toward his apartment. He glanced back. The scaffolding he'd been standing under was coming apart, board-by-board. A window blew out of the Holland Plaza building. Then another.

Sharp objects pelted his back. One embedded itself in the shoulder above his good arm, and he winced, folded his arm inward and pulled the projectile out, cutting his fingers. *Glass. It's raining glass.*

"Jesus fuck," he said aloud.

***

Once the hole in the bricks was wide enough for Jonathan to squirm into, Sleepy sent him through with a flashlight to check out the abandoned construction tunnel. There had to be a way out, or the whole plan would be destroyed, their lives in jeopardy. Hammer would come at six, give or take. The boy had piled several pails full of dirt onto a chunk of plywood next to the escape hole. Another mound was on the floor next to the plywood. PJ had scrounged a pulley that looked as though it might hold up. Sleepy had hung it from the ceiling and strung a length of rope from the plywood up to the pulley and down into the hole.

Sleepy himself was in the hole again, working the crowbar with what remained of his energy.

Sleepy felt the brick he was working on come loose; he gave the crowbar a mighty swing and the brick flew free. He tested the hole and was able to squeeze his shoulders through.

Sleepy hollered up to PJ, who handed down the first of the pails full of dirt from the second pile. Sleepy poured it through the hole and it fell six feet to the floor of the old construction tunnel. He passed the pail back up and PJ filled it again. They continued until the dirt was gone.

Sleepy threw the tools through the hole. He grabbed the rope that dangled from the pulley, strung it through the hole and said the first silent prayer of his life. The work was done.

He sent PJ up the ladder with instructions to do what he did best: hide. Then, when Hammer descended into the Block House, simply replace the metal plate, throw some nearby concrete blocks onto it so Hammer and his men could not get back out the way they came in.

His mind freed up, he began to worry about Jonathan. He stuck his head through the hole and hollered, heard nothing but his own echo. When Sleepy crawled up into the Block House PJ was coming down the ladder.

"Water," PJ said.

It took Sleepy a moment to jog his thoughts away from Hammer and comprehend what he'd heard. "What?"

"Water comin' in. Risin' fast. Old tracks are full, almost up to the platform. It comes in the street vent."

The street vent in the abandoned tunnel was a hundred yards to the north. The plan was unraveling. They had to go one way or the other, regardless of Hammer. He calculated how quickly they could make it up the ladder and out through the abandoned tunnel, into the main tunnel and out the exit from the Canal Street station. It would take nearly ten minutes, even though they knew the route well. There was no way to know if they had ten minutes. The Canal Street station might already be flooded. And then there was Jonathan. They couldn't leave without the boy anyway. Maybe they should go into the escape hole and look for him, he considered, but they still didn't know if there was a way out.

"Shit," Sleepy said. Then he heard Jonathan's voice, faintly. He jumped into the hole, crawled the two feet horizontally and stuck his head through the hole in the bricks.

"Jonathan?" he shouted.

"Father! I found the way out."

"Stay put," Sleepy said, and he hustled back up into the room. "Let's go," he cried. "Through the hole. Jonathan's found a way out."

The plan was ruined. They wouldn't get Hammer. Now they just had to try and get out alive. He sent PJ through first. It was a tight fit for his round body, and he groaned a little from the uncomfortable position, but finally Sleepy shoved him through.

He checked the rope where it was tied to the holes in two corners of the plywood, then he tugged on it to check the pulley. He suddenly heard the metal plate scrape against the concrete at the top of the ladder. A red, pockmarked face emerged below the ceiling, upside down from Sleepy's view. The flat nose, crowded by mean eyes, was breathing heavily.

It was Hammer. The sight frightened him. There would be other people with Hammer, and it would take them only a moment to get into the room. Hammer glared at Sleepy. His voice was evil, coarse with hatred, and familiar: "You're mine."

Sleepy could barely breathe with all the fear bundled in his chest. They would escape. Hammer would chase him relentlessly. That had been part of the plan. But now, for it to work, he needed...

Then Sleepy saw a slow trickle of water began to drip into the Block House from behind Hammer's head.

Images flashed quickly through Sleepy's mind: Jonathan's mother on the cold steps of the old warehouse the night he found her, drugged, raped and left to die; the small old man in the tunnel, writhing in utter agony and screaming as his leg spurted blood at the ankle while his foot lay on the other side of the tracks.

A grin came to Sleepy's face, not out of any feeling of self-satisfaction but out of justice and, yes, even revenge for the others, out of *victory*. It would be a grim victory, but one that was necessary. Time froze for a moment as the two stared each other down. *All week you've been threatening. All week I've been digging. I win.*

"Fuck you." Sleepy mouthed the words, but he could see Hammer understood.

The words would enrage him even further, and he would follow, and in effect Hammer would kill himself with his own rage. Sleepy ducked into the hole and spit himself through the other side as quickly as he could. He and PJ heaved on the rope until they lifted the plywood up and about a cubic yard of dirt fell into the hole. Then with the shovel Sleepy tossed the dirt they had put into the abandoned construction tunnel back into the escape hole. It would take Hammer and his men a half hour or more to clear the escape route, and Sleepy knew they would try.

Sleepy, PJ and Jonathan headed quickly to the way out. They rushed to the vent, following Jonathan and his feeble flashlight, moving through the cluttered former construction tunnel faster than was safe.

The vent was in the ceiling and led into the main subway tunnel north of the Canal Street Station. No water came through it. That was a good sign. It was a heavy metal grate. Sleepy was the only one tall enough to reach it. He pushed up. It was stuck. He pushed harder, but it wouldn't budge. He found a two-by-four and banged the vent loose. Tried again. It opened.

Sleepy got on his hands and knees so PJ could get on his back and climb through the vent. He lifted Jonathan. Then he climbed up himself.

Now they were in the main subway tunnel, well lit. It was 200 yards to the breach in the wall that led to the parallel but abandoned tunnel—the crawl hole that was part of the route to the Block House. If Hammer and his men had retreated, that's where they would come out.

They ran down the narrow walkway along the edge and reached the crawl hole. Water spewed from the hole and onto their feet. That meant, to Sleepy's delight, that the water that poured into their home had come from the street vent in the abandoned tunnel. If Hammer hadn't already gotten out, he wouldn't now. Sleepy was sure he had stayed and tried to dig his way through the escape route.

They continued on to the subway platform, where a dozen or so other people milled about. Sleepy hollered at them to leave. Only about half of them followed him. They went through the turnstiles and toward the stairs. The water had just started flooding the stairs. It ran down in a gentle cascade. But Sleepy could hear the howl of the wind above now. They climbed the stairs against the flow of the water and stepped out into the first hurricane any of them had ever witnessed.

CHAPTER 53

MCGUIRE AFB,
NEW JERSEY
6:14 P.M.

The wind pulled at Hugo's wings, tried to pry the WC-130 from the ground. Hugo was tied down as well as was possible. All the available hangar space had already been occupied, and the remaining planes at McGuire Air Force Base in southern New Jersey were flown to safer air bases hundreds of miles away.

Captain Glen Barnes and his crew were well aware that Hugo had little chance of surviving the storm. But there was no question of putting the crew at further risk by trying to fly the plane anywhere on only three engines. It was hair-raising enough just getting to McGuire on three, fingers crossed that they didn't lose another.

The only hope was that Hugo would ride out the winds without too much damage and it could be repaired and flown home later. It was bad luck that Hugo had lost an engine in a hurricane again, just like back in 1989. A coincidence. But the coincidences were stacking up. Mission control had made a rare move, keeping them on the ground for an hour and then switching their mission from Irene to Harvey at the last minute. He had a reporter on board with whom he had argued before takeoff, possibly diverting his attention from some detail he might otherwise have picked up on. Then a Hurricane Hunter plane had been lost in Irene. There was still no word on them. The 53rd had never lost a plane. Nothing had been routine about this day or this mission, and routine was the key to avoiding mishaps. His superstitions got the best of him. He pulled a stick of Doublemint gum from his shirt pocket, unwrapped it and stuffed it glumly into his mouth.

"Fucking Jack Corbin," Barnes said to his copilot as they peered out a window of the hangar, keeping an eye on their airplane a hundred yards away.

"What about him," Duggan said.

"It's his fucking fault."

"Oh, c'mon, Cap'n. He's just some hot-headed newsie."

"Who disrupted our routine. Bastard got me riled up before takeoff. That's not good. Maybe I missed something, who knows. Maybe we should have done the preflight over again after control held us on the ground."

"It's nobody's fault," Duggan said. "Hugo's just old and tired."

Just then the winds increased and one of the cables holding Hugo to the tarmac snapped and the left wing lifted into the air. The other cables let go and Hugo quickly flipped onto its back and skidded across the asphalt, then was lifted again and did a series of cartwheels before crashing into another hangar.

Barnes watched the scene with no visible emotion. Inside, he wanted to cry for the wonderful machine he'd flown for more than a decade.

"Fuckin' a," Duggan said. "Looks like we walk home."

Barnes thought again of the other crew, the one that had presumably gone down in Hurricane Irene over the Gulf of Mexico. "Maybe we're the lucky ones," he said.

CHAPTER 54

CONEY ISLAND
6:19 P.M.

Edward Cole listened to the sick whistle of the wind as it found every crack in the Seaside Nursing Home and forced its way in. He lay face down on the floor of his room, where he'd retreated after the lobby flooded. The wind blew mostly over him.

His mind found a clarity it hadn't experienced in a long while as he listened to every new sound. The shattering of windows. The slosh of waves outside, below.

The wind was blowing out of the south, directly into the ocean-facing window and out the door, into the hallway.

He had never seen wind like this. It picked a lamp up from his nightstand, hurled it into the hallway. Two oil paintings had been torn from the wall. Rainwater coursed through the room as though a showerhead were on.

He understood that it was a hurricane. Amanda had told him so. He'd gotten to a higher floor, like she'd said. He was safe.

In his mind, he tried to imagine what was going on out there. If the water was in the building, there must be no beach left. No boardwalk. The amusement park would be under water. He smiled.

He pushed himself up on his elbows, crawled infantry style to the east-facing window, put his hands on the ledge and pulled himself up. The first thing he noticed was the ocean, just four or five feet below the window, waves rolling by.

Half of south Brooklyn must be under water.

He looked out over the waves, over what had been boardwalk and streets, toward the Wonder Wheel. It was partially submerged and seemed to quiver in the mighty wind.

He grinned.

Next to it, the Cyclone's roller-coaster peaks rose above the waves, its valleys submerged.

He looked out to sea. A towering dark mass was rolling in, breaking from east to west. It crashed through the Cyclone, shredding it, then struck the Wonder Wheel, which keeled over in slow motion, a gentle acquiescence amid the fury of the storm.

Then Ed Cole had his most lucid thought of the afternoon: The wave was coming his way. It didn't frighten him the way he thought it would.

But his next thought terrified him: *Betty Dinsmore. I asked her to stay. Did she? No, please don't be here, Betty. I couldn't bear it.*

Her room was on the third floor. He crawled out his door, into the hallway. He heard the wave strike the building. The whole building shook. Water gushed out his door into the hallway and engulfed him. He rode the rushing water to the door of the stairs, grabbed the door handle to stop himself. Other peoples' doors up and down the hallway blew out, and the hallway filled with water.

The building groaned. He forced the door open, made it into the stairwell. Water rushed in from behind him, and the stairwell was filling from below, too. He groped in the gray for the stairs, his mind a confused jumble.

Third floor. Got to find...

Got to find — Sarah?

"Sarah! Grandpa is coming."

He made it to the stairs, climbed one, then another. The water chased him, rose to his chest. He hollered again for

Sarah. He heard a feeble reply from above, couldn't make the words out. The voice sounded too old to be Sarah's.

Distant cracking noises. The building lurched. Everything seemed to drop out from under him, and his body floated free for a moment, then settled onto the stairs again. He reached up for the next stair. More cracking noises. Plaster fell into the water.

Edward Cole put his hands over his head in the stairwell between the second and third floors of the Seaside Nursing Home. He was surprised at how calm he was. He really had only one worry on his mind: whether or not Sarah was safe.

The stairs dropped out from under him and he sank into the cool, black water. Something of immeasurable weight slowly crushed him from above. He could not hear it, but through his body he felt the vibrations of cracking bones and then he felt nothing.

~ ~ ~

EXCERPTED FROM
HURRICANE HARVEY: CHRONICLE
OF DEATH AND DESTRUCTION,
BY NICHOLAS K. GRAY (2000)

A thick black wall stretched across the horizon of lower New York Harbor and moved upriver. The left side of the wall engulfed the protruding lip of Governor's Island before washing over all but the highest patch. The right side of the wall slammed into the Statue of Liberty, washed the feet of the still-defiant lady.

The storm surge moved inexorably toward lower Manhattan, split at the confluence of the Hudson and East rivers, and continued as two parts. It moved onto the island and up the rivers, followed by even higher surges.

It picked up a sixty-foot yacht and a half-dozen small sailboats—all that were left at the Manhattan Yacht Club in a small marina notched into the concrete abutment—and tossed them into the glass front of a towering atrium that served as an entrance to the World Financial Center.

The water pushed up a wide marble staircase, plowed through a bank of revolving doors, and surged across the North Bridge, an enclosed walkway *over* the West Side

Highway. Soon, fed from side streets, the highway itself was a river. Water was running in every direction, through buildings, under overpasses, and even *over* streets.

CHAPTER 55

MANHATTAN
6:23 P.M.

The *Slow Times* usually rocked gently, its ropes making the sound of someone snoring or the gentle sawing of wood. The creak of the ropes struggling against the pull of the trawler had lulled Walter Beasley to sleep many times this summer. He tuned into the melodious sounds, let them drift into his head late at night after he'd taken his glasses off and laid down.

The gentle, rhythmic scrape and buckle of the dock provided the beat.

Now the ropes complained, moaning monstrously against the strain of the heaving trawler. The dock's *ker-chunk, ka-clink* was harsh, frantic.

Beasley's stomach was in his throat. It wasn't seasickness. It was fear. There was no one else at the marina. He could not see two feet in front of him. He called the Coast Guard on his marine radio and they requested he leave the frequency free for real emergencies. The *Slow Times* was in port. Get off the boat, he was told.

Walter wasn't sure if it was fear or desire that confined him to the rocking trawler.

He was afraid to negotiate the dock without his glasses. But he probably could have made it if he'd taken it slowly, carefully. He could have crawled.

Where to? Where would I go? Back to the newsroom? Continue the charade? The boat is everything now. It's my life. We'll ride it out together.

A firecracker. *Here? How?* He slid the cabin door open and the wind blew him back. He stumbled and fell, recovered, and crawled out of the cabin onto the rear deck. His mind had figured it out, but his emotions were hoping he was wrong. He felt along the port rail, found the cleat, reached out and felt the taut stern line. He ran his hand along the rail and found the other cleat, its knot still attached. The line was slack. The storm was beginning to tear the *Slow Times* from its mooring.

A wave crashed over the transom and rolled through the cabin door. The Hudson River had become part of the ocean.

Walter Beasley was on his hands and knees on the rear deck of his first love, nearly blind, soaking wet, while the greatest storm he'd ever seen threatened to sink him, and he'd exhausted all of his nautical knowledge. He had posed as a seafarer, much like he had posed as a newspaperman, and the gig was about up. Beasley had never felt much more than adequate in his whole life—successfully shrewd, maybe—nor had he ever felt defeated.

It felt like the *Slow Times* was rising. He held to the side rail and stood halfway up. He squinted into his unfocused circle of view. The dark shape of a piling was getting shorter. The whole dock was surging upward. Desperation turned to panic. Beasley crouched down out of the biting wind and crawled back into the cabin.

Couldn't stand up without holding onto something. Another loud snap and he felt the stern drift away from the dock. Everything was coming apart. He made his way forward to the wheelhouse, deciding that if he were to be cast free he ought to start the engine. He turned the key, pushed the starter and the reliable diesel fired up.

A wave lifted the boat up, pitching him to the hardwood floor. He scrambled to his feet and peered out the window toward the City for a reference point. He could make out the difference between the dark marina building and a lighter-colored area behind it. The two shapes moved in relation to each other. He glanced down at the dock. It was not moving. The whole dock had been lifted up off the pilings and was floating up the river with him.

The stern drifted away from the dock. A bowline snapped, then another. Only the crisscrossing spring lines tethered the boat. Then they snapped, too, and the *Slow Times* floated free, upriver and toward the shore.

Beasley was not an adept pilot even in the best conditions. The trawler had a top speed of eight knots. He watched the marina building slide in front of the bright spot and estimated that he was doing eight knots now.

Backward.

He put the gearshift into forward and applied full power, turned the wheel hard to starboard in an attempt to head out into the river. The bow rose as if on the high seas, plunged down the other side of a wave unlike anything ever seen on the Hudson. The dock, which had disappeared momentarily, reappeared and slammed into the fiberglass hull of the trawler. It was only a moment before the boat began to list.

Beasley shoved down again on the throttle, but it had no travel left. He felt warm urine run down the inside of his left leg. A wave crashed into the cabin, starboard side, and blew the windows out. The engine died.

He put his hands over his ears. *The sounds, the sounds.* A man who could not see was more in tune with the sounds of a storm, and Walter Beasley had never heard anything so evil. The rush of waves as though waist-deep in a crashing surf. The gurgle of remote space filling with water. Grind and tear of failing fiberglass. And the wind, the wind, *the goddamn wind.*

The trawler lurched backward. There was a loud crash and a sudden jerk as the boat changed direction and seemed to twirl around a pivot point at the stern. Beasley clung to the wheel and squinted out the window. The blurry circle of darkness framed a brick wall, not six feet away.

I'm on the goddamn streets of Manhattan.

A huge wave washed over the *Slow Times*. The boat flipped. He saw the bright wallpapered ceiling come toward him. Water rushed in and his blurry circle of vision faded out.

***

Amanda reached Rico's apartment from the south, carrying Sarah. The water was above her ankles and rising faster than even she could believe. She wanted to round the corner and check on Henri Mouchet at the restaurant, make sure he'd evacuated. But there wasn't time. She had saved as many people as she could today, and now it was time to worry only about Sarah. She had to get to a higher floor. Now.

She pulled the outer door open and the water followed her into the entryway and was at her knees in a second. She left the door open and sprinted up the stairs. The water rose. This was where they would stay.

She was close now. Rico would be here, at least. And maybe Jack. *God, let Jack be here.*

The overwhelming cacophony outside was replaced by an echoing mix of shrill whistles in the stairwell. At the second-floor landing Amanda glanced at the window. Rainwater spat through its corners. *They're not designed for a wind like this. Got to get inside.*

By the time Amanda got to the sixteenth floor, she hadn't an ounce of energy left.

It was the end of a horrific journey. Rico's apartment would be safely above the surge. It was time to rest. She tried the door and found it unlocked, pushed it open.

She walked into Rico's apartment, put Sarah down. Sarah instantly grabbed her mother's soaked shirt and followed her into the living room. The orange juice stain was still on the wall, the broken phone still on the floor. The room was otherwise empty. Amanda's heart sank. She closed the door behind her and headed for the hallway—the safest place—hanging on to one final shred of hope. She rounded the corner and saw three people. PJ was sitting against the wall. At the back of the hall she saw Jonathan and Sleepy. Tears welled up in Amanda's eyes. Jack wasn't there.

In her grief, she stared at the boy and his father, and the vague recognition she'd felt the first time she saw Sleepy crawled back into her consciousness. Then she understood: He looked like a normal-sized version of the wide Leonard Lassitor.

She wanted to make some sense of that. It meant something, her frazzled brain told her. She went to the end of the hall and shouted into his ear. "You're Leonard Lassitor's brother?"

Sleepy hesitated, then nodded. Amanda remembered Lassitor's bruises. "What did you do this morning?"

He stared at her, didn't answer.

"It's important," she shouted.

"I let him go."

As Amanda toyed with this new information, she saw from the corner of her eye a fourth figure emerging from Juan Rico's study and into the hallway. It was Jack.

She rushed to him and Jack dropped the portable radio in his hand and absorbed her wordlessly, with Sarah sandwiched between. Amanda closed her eyes, pushed Leonard Lassitor, Maximo Perez and the storm out of her mind and let herself feel Jack's body press against her own. It felt good to be the comforted one for a change.

Then Juan Rico popped into her mind. "Jeez! Where's Juan?"

"Don't know," Jack shouted over the whistling wind, holding Amanda's shoulders. "Any ideas?"

"He's shooting," Amanda said. "Only question is where."

"Who knows?" Jack shrugged. "Hope he gets *the shot.*"

"Oh, shit," Amanda said. "That's it!"

"What?"

"The shot. The tunnel. I told him earlier in the week how the Holland would flood. He said that would be *the shot.*"

Fear crossed Jack's face. He pushed Amanda aside and

headed for the door. Amanda grabbed him by the forearm. "No!"

"But he's probably at the goddamn restaurant."

"It's no use." She firmed her grip and shook her head. "It's flooded. You can't even get out of this building."

Jack's eyes watered, then he seemed to deflate. He looked at the floor, leaned against the wall, slid down into a squatting position and grabbed his knees. Amanda sat next to him and put her arm around his shoulder.

Then she heard something bang against the side of the building. The storm was still growing. Amanda picked the portable radio up from the floor and tuned it to WCBS.

"...report that the World Trade Center building is flooding. On the scene is reporter Mary Simms. Mary?"

Mary Simms sounded less like a professional reporter and more like a scared victim.

"I'm standing near the large bank of revolving doors that separate the World Trade Center Tower 1 from the large concourse that leads to the subway entrance." She spoke hurriedly, her voice cracking. "To my right is Tower 1 and the Marriott Hotel. Just moments ago water began flowing into the hotel and the tower lobby from West Street, then through the revolving doors here. I'm already in about six inches of water right now, and it seems to be rising still. The water then flows to my left, down the concourse, through a set of double-doors and down into the subway. I was just at the top of those stairs, and it's like a waterfall already. Now, hundreds of the roughly 20,000 people who work in the 110 stories of this building had earlier taken refuge in this main-floor lobby to escape the hurricane's fierce winds. There is considerable panic right now as people scramble for the stairs to escape this flooding. Also, an unknown number of people had been lingering down in the subway platform, even though the trains have not been running for hours. We're still seeing people scramble out of the subway entrance, but it looks like they're having difficulty making it up the stairs against the increasing flow of water..."

The radio cut out. Amanda turned the volume up, and

there was only static. She tried other stations, but found nothing.

She listened to the wind. The combination of screaming and moaning was frighteningly similar to a noise she had heard before—at Bill Leaderman's house. There was something about hurricane winds that sounded the same in a city or on a beach, in a wood-frame home or a solid brick structure. Maybe it was the way the wind seeped into every crack, whistled and pulled and pushed and tore.

From the sound and direction of the wind Amanda guessed the worst of the storm was upon them. Hurricane Harvey was racing with incredible speed, and as soon as it was no longer moving toward them the winds would diminish rapidly.

The wind barreled in from the south now, blowing in the same direction as the storm's movement. The right-side eyewall was upon them. The building had survived the surge. Now it had only to survive the wind, for a few moments, and the worst would be over.

The light went out in the hallway. Then there was a large crash, metal against brick.

Sixteenth floor. What the hell?

***

Rico was shivering and exhausted, bleeding from the shoulder and the fingers of his good hand when he got to the stairs. He thought of continuing around the corner to his apartment, but knew he didn't have the strength to fight the surging river much more. Not with one arm. So he crawled into the doorway of Chez Henri, turned and took one last look at the Hudson River two steps below. He closed the door solidly behind him. In the entryway, he lay prone and rested until his thoughts, which were telling him the worst was not over, forced him to stand up. The power was out, the sky ominously dark, the restaurant dim. He grabbed a small card from a table in the entryway. On the card was printed the restaurant's address and a small map showing directions.

Henri Mouchet seemed glad to see him and made a nervous joke. "How many in your party, Juan?"

"Gimme a pen."

"Here. What?"

Rico glanced around the room. The old drunk with the white hair and the purple nose sat at the bar. Six other heavy drinkers sat at various tables. Rico sat down at an empty table in the middle of the restaurant and oriented himself to the map. Watts ran east-west. The restaurant was on the south side of the street. *Blocked the wind.* He drew an arrow running north. *Wind's blowing north. Rotates counter-clockwise.* He made a dot on the left side of the card, west of the restaurant. *Eye has to be here.*

"We're in the right-side eyewall," he told Henri Mouchet.

"What does that mean?"

Means I owe Jack Corbin a hundred bucks. Rico turned over in his mind conversations with Jack and Amanda. To his chagrin, nothing they had said told him what would happen to this restaurant.

Whether it was fear, intuition or an educated guess didn't matter: It dawned on Juan Rico that he'd made a mistake. And it was too late to change his mind, with the street now a river.

"Don't know for sure," Rico finally said to Henri. "Jack and Amanda always talkin' about it. It's the worst part, right around the eye. And right now it means the worst is yet to come. Jesus fuck, Henri, we shouldn't be here."

Rico was overcome by a sense of dread. The warm and high-ceilinged restaurant seemed suddenly oppressive. The life had gone out of it. It felt like Bill Leaderman's house.

"Fucking fish in the window." It was the old drunk at the bar.

Rico ignored the man for a moment, as usual. Then his blood went cold. He looked over at the windows along Watts Street. The water was a foot above the bottom sill. He looked toward the door. Water was streaming in underneath. The same was happening under the door on Washington Street.

"Jesus fuck, Henri."

"What do we do?"

"No fuckin' clue." The water rose as they talked. *Can't open the door. Windows don't open. A tomb. A fuckin' tomb.* "There another way out?"

"Just the doors."

A window on Watts Street gave way to the weight of the water. A wave washed tables and chairs across the room, knocked Rico off his feet. Another window gave way, then another. He got up and found himself in waist-deep water that was rising quickly.

"Tables! Get on the tables," he shouted.

The water continued to rise, floating the tables. Rico clamored atop one and laid flat to keep it from tipping over. The inflow of water pushed everything that floated, including Rico and Henri and the six other men, to the back of the room.

Where's the drunk old man? Shit.

The water was above the windows now, gushing in from underneath. Only one window remained visible, a high one over the door along Washington Street. With his bleeding but usable arm, Rico paddled toward it, instructed the others to do the same. He saw the pool of blood, trailing behind him like chum. He thought briefly of the snakes Jack had told him about that hung in the trees of the Carolinas after Hugo.

When he got to the six-foot tall window, the water was halfway up. *Rico* found a chair, pounded at the window, but lost his balance and fell into the water. The weight of his camera equipment and computer pulled him down. He struggled to remove it all, swam one-armed back to the surface. Henri Mouchet was near the window. "Henri! Break it! Break the fuckin' window."

On the second swing, the chair went through the window. Water and wind came through the other way and broke glass out in panes, which sank like guillotines.

"Go," shouted Rico.

"You too," said Henri Mouchet.

"The old man," said Rico. "Go!"

He dove and tried to see under the water but there was

nothing but murk. *The fuckin sea again.* He felt a beer tap at the bar, dove deeper. Nothing.

Juan Rico was out of air. He struggled to the surface. Up, up, up. He hit his head on something. Frantically, he reached up with his good arm and felt around. It was solid. He moved to one side. Still solid. In the darkness, he heard Bill Leaderman's chimes, saw Amanda pulling him up onto a scrap of tattered floor on a piling. His mind filled with a vision of Terese. She was moving toward him, her arms open. Then the darkness turned inward. *At least I got the fuckin' shot.*

~ ~ ~

EXCERPTED FROM
HURRICANE HARVEY: CHRONICLE
OF DEATH AND DESTRUCTION,
BY NICHOLAS K. GRAY (2000)

Hurricane Harvey couldn't reach all of Manhattan with its storm surge, but no spot was safe from its vicious winds, which by late evening were peaking at 185 miles an hour with stronger gusts. Elements of the city's infrastructure that nobody had considered began to fail.

A wooden water tower in Chelsea pulled at the bolts that held it to a steel frame over a twelve-story apartment building. A gust that may have exceeded 200 miles an hour provided the final push and the tower toppled, crashed through the roof and through another floor. The roof began tearing away section by section until seven apartment dwellers were sucked up into the storm and tossed through the streets like rag dolls.

Construction sites throughout the region proved menacing. Supplies and tools flew from open floors. Hardly a scaffolding remained intact. Times Square was almost completely stripped of its famous billboards. Large images of men and women in stylish underwear flew through the square, knocked out windows and rendered the headline-scrolling Zipper useless.

CHAPTER 56

MANHATTAN
6:52 P.M.

There was another crash. Amanda's mind raced. *What could be hitting the sixteenth floor of a building?*
Something from a higher building.

The only higher building nearby was the construction site to the south, directly across the street. Amanda pushed herself up and ran out of the hallway to the south-facing window. It was streaked with rain, giving a blurry, surreal view of the naked building in progress across the street. Concrete floors and steel pillars. No exterior walls yet. The orange nylon netting, which had encircled each floor, had all been ripped away. She could see straight through the sixteenth floor into the skyscrapers of the financial district to the south.

On each floor were partially erected inner studs. And toolboxes, wheelbarrows, aluminum framing studs, plywood and other supplies. It was all lifting up, skidding across the floors, destroying the inner walls. And heading toward them.

The construction crane, a temporary tower of crisscrossed steel attached to the north wall of the naked building, was vibrating. Amanda craned her neck to look up. Lumber rained down. The top of the crane swayed. Teetered.

Coming down.

She bolted from the window, scurried into the hallway. It was a straight shot from the south-facing living room window. Sleepy was against the back wall of the hall.

Jonathan closer, just past the door to Rico's study. PJ, Jack and Sarah were on this side of the door.

Creak. Groan. Snap.

Amanda hollered, but nobody could hear her. She grabbed Sarah with one hand, then ran past Jack and grabbed Jonathan with the other. The others saw what she was doing and got up. Jack opened the door to Rico's study. He and PJ went in. Amanda shoved Sarah in and followed her with Jonathan in tow.

There was a horrendous crash, a whoosh of dust and glass.

The crane was inside the building and had destroyed much of the roof of Juan Rico's apartment. The back wall of the hall blew out. Jonathan was in Amanda's grip, but still in the hall.

Sleepy was sucked out, tangled momentarily in the crossbars of the temporary elevator still attached to the north side of Rico's building. Then Hurricane Harvey picked him up and tossed him beyond the roof of Chez Henri below and into the river that used to be Watts Street.

Amanda lost her grip. Jack lunged for Jonathan, landing face down in the hallway, but missed.

Jonathan slid down the hallway. On his stomach, pleading eyes wide, he reached out with both hands for Jack and Amanda. An instantaneous moment seemed to take forever, and Jonathan slid out the hole in the wall.

The vacuum settled, became an unbearable wind. Stronger than anything Amanda had ever experienced. But already it was changing direction as the storm raced north. Less of the wind funneled down the hall.

Would be coming out of the southwest now. Sixteen floors up.

"He's gone," Jack shouted.

"Maybe not," Amanda said.

Jonathan hadn't flown through the opening as Sleepy did. He'd just slid out. Amanda remembered what was out there. She put Sarah in a corner of the study, told her not to move, and crawled back into the hallway.

***

Jack watched as Amanda dropped flat to her stomach and crawled quickly but cautiously down the hall. He followed her, hoping. The wall was broken out, torn and twisted as though a monster had walked through it in some B movie. Amanda stayed to the left side of the hall, wary of the hole. She braced herself against the remaining portion of the end wall with one arm, looked out. Jack did the same on the opposite side, but his fear of heights gripped him and he was barely able to look.

Jonathan clung to a two-foot-wide steel catwalk, two feet beyond the hole in the wall and six feet down. He was alive, shivering, crying. The building offered just enough protection from the wind.

For now. Will be out of the west in a moment. Blow him right off—

"Jonathan!" Amanda shouted.

The boy couldn't hear her. Again, louder. Jonathan looked up. Amanda reached out a hand. Jonathan reached up. Not even close.

"Stand up!"

Jonathan braced himself, stood on shaky legs.

Amanda leaned out, but she couldn't reach his outstretched fingers. She ducked back into the hall.

"You have to do it," Amanda shouted.

"Can't. No way."

"Do it!"

***

Jack looked down. Fear seized him. The roof of Chez Henri, below, spun like a scene change in a Batman episode. Jack closed his eyes. Steeled his nerves. He searched for a way to free the boy. Faces zipped through his mind like a flipbook.

Bill Leaderman, Juan Rico, Sleepy.

No more. No more death.

He reached out but inches separated their fingers. "Don't move!" He retreated into the hallway, back to the study and got PJ, who followed him back to the hole. Amanda braced her body against the left side of the wall, PJ against the other.

Each took a hold of Jack's belt.

The wind had shifted, coming almost directly from the west and beginning to buffet the north side of the building where Jonathan was trapped.

Jack had to quell his fear. He kept his eyes on Jonathan, whose face glowed blue-white with each flash of lightning in the otherwise dusk-like conditions. Jack let the sounds of the storm fill his mind. Symphony of low roars, high whistles, drumming of rain, background bass of thunder. Riffs of creaking, tearing, twisting.

He leaned out into the storm.

Jonathan reached up.

Jonathan's fingers touched Jack's. Then a gust of wind nearly knocked the boy off the catwalk. He squatted, shifted his feet to regain his balance. Wrapped his arms around a vertical member of steel. Froze.

"Reach!" Jack shouted. The boy didn't move.

The wind was full force now and strafed the elevator shaft.

Jack looked down. Dizzy. He shook his head and reached out again. The shaft buckled. The catwalk lurched.

Jonathan jumped toward Jack's outstretched arm, gripped Jack's wrist. Jack did the same.

The elevator shaft screamed and peeled away from the side of the building. From the edge of his peripheral vision, Jack watched the tangle of steel disappear into the swirling wind and water below.

Jonathan smacked into the building. He dangled from Jack's arm. The wind tossed him side to side, a frantic pendulum of a human grandfather clock. Jack felt his legs going numb from the pressure of his belt.

Amanda and PJ heaved. Jonathan swung wildly away from the wind. Jack reached out and got the boy's other arm, pulled.

Amanda gave the final tug that pulled Jack inside the

building. Jack braced a foot against the tattered wall and pulled Jonathan in.

The roof was open, and the rain fell in buckets. An inch had already accumulated on the hardwood floor.

Jack had forgotten that it was raining.

Jonathan still held Jack's wrist. He pulled himself into Jack, buried a small head in his chest. Amanda wrapped her arms around both of them for a second, then tugged at Jack to retreat into the study, which still had a roof over it. Sarah was curled up in the corner, shivering. Jack and Jonathan sat down next to Sarah. Amanda found a blanket in Juan Rico's closet, sat down, and pulled the blanket around all four of them.

~ ~ ~

SATURDAY, AUGUST 28

CHAPTER 57

BUILDING 7,
WORLD TRADE CENTER
7:18 A.M.

L ike most of the emergency officials, Leonard Lassitor had spent the night at the Emergency Operations Center. For him, it had been a grueling night of feigning interest in the ongoing effort to protect the City, and that had exhausted him. But it was nearly over. And now he had the excuse he needed to get out: The mayor had asked Lassitor to hit the streets and inspect damage.

Lassitor's personal driver was on his way to pick him up. The mayor didn't know, of course, that Lassitor would have the driver head north to the George Washington Bridge, the only route out of the City that was open. His driver would take him straight to Teterboro airport in North Jersey, the only airport in the region that was open. A commuter flight would get him to Washington. By the time anybody wondered where he was, he'd be on his way to the Dominican Republic.

Lassitor smiled outwardly at his victory. He had helped to destroy the City and make Maximo rich. But the smile faded as he thought about the drugs he had been unable to retrieve from Walter Beasley's boat. They were probably in the bottom of the Hudson now. Lassitor worried about how forgiving Maximo would be on that point, in light of all the money Lassitor had just helped him make. In truth, he knew that his contribution to the death and destruction was minor. Harvey had done most of the heavy lifting. And Maximo had probably done more to help himself by orchestrating the auto accidents on the outbound routes.

Lassitor could have done more, if not for his meddling brother and the bothersome Amanda Cole. She was the one who called landfall despite the LORAX being down, then got the evacuation going, then stopped it just in time to save thousands of lives. Lassitor had never liked Amanda Cole, and now he despised her. He tried to let the emotion go. It was nearly time to leave, and soon he'd be sipping piña coladas and enjoying Dominican women. Amanda Cole would be a distant memory.

He fidgeted, pretending to do paperwork that no longer mattered, while he waited for his driver. Leonard Lassitor smiled again, this time at the reason he had to wait: Getting around New York City was next to impossible for everyone this morning.

CHAPTER 58

TRIBECA
7:20 A.M.

The sun shone brilliantly through the construction crane, a sick modern sculpture of twisted steel. The roof looked as though it had been peeled away by giant fingers. The south-facing windows were all blown out and there was a gaping hole at the end of the hallway.

Jonathan wouldn't speak. Nobody had said much yet. Amanda convinced Jack that they had to go out and take a look around. The boy needed to see the ground below the building to know that his father wasn't waiting for him there. He had to have some evidence so he could understand what Amanda already knew.

Amanda, Sarah, Jack, Jonathan and PJ descended the stairs and walked out into Washington Street, littered by a foot of river silt and tangled debris. Amanda led the way over tree branches and downed signs, through broken glass and around cars, all of which had been pulled toward the river when the surge retreated. The City was quiet, the air heavy with silence. A lone siren wailed in the distance. No other sounds. No rush of traffic. The walls of the buildings were discolored with silt well above the second-floor windows. A few people wandered aimlessly, some crying, some appearing to search, some just standing in a daze.

Amanda led them around the corner to Watts Street. Jack wanted to look inside Chez Henri.

"Later," Amanda said. "The boy first."

The discoloration on the buildings became lower and lower as they walked uphill, away from the river and toward the Canal Street station. Cars lay on their sides, their tops, along the street and in it. A small blue car sat upside-down on top of a taxi.

Another stood on end, leaning against a building. There was, as Amanda expected, no sign of Sleepy's body. It was probably out to sea by now. They continued on toward the entrance to the subway station, familiar ground for Jonathan.

Ahead, a boat lay on its side. Next to the boat was a body bag. And four other smaller bags. And an FBI agent.

"Damn," Jack said, his head cocked to one side to read the red script letters on the back of the boat. "*Slow Times.* That's *Beasley's* boat."

"What's the FBI doing there?"

"I don't know," Jack said. "Hang here for a minute. I'll ask."

A familiar idea, unformed again, was tickling Amanda's brain. Jack returned after a couple of minutes with a confused look on his face.

"Drugs on the boat," he said. "And a weird coincidence: Turns out the FBI guy is the same one who called me earlier in the week asking about Perez. Anyway, he wouldn't tell me any more than that. But it makes no sense. Beasley was a heel, but I can't believe he was into drugs."

Amanda felt a rush of adrenaline as a mass of confusing data put itself together in the scientific part of her brain. It was only a rough understanding—not unlike what she was used to experiencing with hurricanes. But just like the partial understanding she had of Hurricane Harvey yesterday morning, it was enough to go on. "You said Beasley was a friend of Lassitor?"

"Yeah, so?"

"Jack, Lassitor's the one who was trying to stall the evacuation."

"He was what?"

"You heard me. I'm sure of it now. And guess who he was working for?" Jack didn't have to think long. "Maximo Perez."

"Yep. And you know what Perez does when he's not betting on hurricanes. "

"Drugs. But I don't get how Beasley figures in."

"Don't you see? You were the only reporter in the City who understood the hurricane threat. Lassitor knew that. He didn't want you stirring the waters up or putting anything useful in the paper. He had Beasley get you out of town."

"Holy sh—" Jack looked at Sarah and Jonathan and stopped himself. "But why the drugs on the boat?"

"Can't say. Haven't figured that far yet. But I bet it ties the two together. There's a lot that I don't quite get, but I'd bet my winnings from Harvey that it's Lassitor."

"So I guess I should tell the FBI guy."

"No," Amanda said firmly. "I want to get to the EOC first. Lassitor should still be there. His ass is mine."

"I'll go with you."

"No. Just me this time. They won't let you in, anyway."

"How will *you* get in?"

Amanda just grinned.

***

The guard near the elevator only smiled and nodded as Amanda breezed past him.

She rode the elevator alone to the twenty-third floor of Building 7.

At the entrance to the Emergency Operations Center she found two droopy security guards who looked like they'd been on duty all night. She moved purposely past them without incident, then once she was a safe distance inside the room she looked over her shoulder at them. "You might want to wake up," she said. "There's going to be a little trouble."

She headed straight for the mayor's office. She spotted him from a distance, talking to Leonard Lassitor. Lassitor was putting his coat on. The door was closed.

Amanda opened it and walked in.

Lassitor was buttoning his coat. He gave her a sharp look, and began moving toward the door. Amanda stepped in front of him, closed the door behind her.

She felt closer to physical violence than she'd ever been before. She hadn't prepared herself for this part of the confrontation. Up to now, Hurricane Harvey had dictated her actions, and she had just done what seemed scientifically necessary to make it through everything the storm had thrown her way. She stared at Lassitor with a hatred that welled up from deep within. It was a new feeling for Amanda Cole, and it made her feel dirty. But it also gave her strength. Leonard Lassitor had killed people, she was nearly certain. Her hatred was deserved.

"Well," the mayor said in a tired monotone. "I'm not surprised. What should I do now?"

Amanda let the hatred shoot through her, then she let it slip away, and the rational scientific part of her brain took over again. "Arrest him." She spoke with confidence and pointed at Lassitor.

"It's been a long night, Ms. Cole," Lassitor said impatiently. "Excuse me. I've got to go out and serve the City some more."

"Wait," the mayor said, standing.

Amanda spoke to the mayor. "Where'd he tell you he was yesterday morning?"

Lassitor answered: "This is New York. I got mugged, now I really must go."

"You were with your brother." She watched his face.

Lassitor's eyes narrowed. His jaw quivered for an instant. It was all she needed. "Beasley's dead. They found the drugs on his boat. FBI has it tied to you." The last part was a lie, but he wouldn't know that and it generated the desired response.

"Shit," Lassitor mumbled softly.

It was just loud enough for the mayor to hear. The security

guards were at the door. The mayor waved them in. Then he pointed at Lassitor.

In Leonard Lassitor's eyes, Amanda saw something like the death of a dream, one that had so consumed the man that he didn't even resist as his hands were cuffed.

~ ~ ~

EXCERPTED FROM
HURRICANE HARVEY: CHRONICLE
OF DEATH AND DESTRUCTION,
BY NICHOLAS K. GRAY (2000)

The death toll from Hurricane Harvey was remarkably low given the utter lack of preparedness throughout the Northeast, most notably in New York City. Though the totals are high in comparison to other modem-era hurricanes, they must be viewed under the light of circumstance: the highest winds at landfall of any storm since Camille in 1969 combined with a population largely ignorant to the dangers.

In all, nearly 7,000 people perished. An unknown, but presumably high percentage of those deaths were people who chose to ignore evacuation orders, or those who tried to evacuate when it was too late. The highest concentration of casualties was in New York (especially south-facing beaches of Brooklyn, Queens and Long Island) and along the Jersey Shore. Fewer than 200 deaths were reported in the rest of the Northeast, mostly in Connecticut.

The dollar cost of the storm is another story, one that will be adjusted for years to come as insurance companies battle resulting lawsuits and scholars argue over what to include.

Conservative estimates to date, however, put *property damage alone* at more than $200 billion. (Compare that to Hurricane Andrew, the 1992 Florida storm that caused, in today's dollars, less than $30 billion in damage.) Nobody has begun to calculate the overall costs of the storm (lawsuits, lost business, etc.) which will likely dwarf the property damage. Some examples:

Two weeks after the storm, there was still no rail service into or out of New York City, the lines hampered by flooded tunnels and destroyed tracks, especially in the New Jersey Meadowlands.

Intracity subway lines were functioning on a limited basis. Streets, many of which were torn up and have yet to be repaired, were overcrowded beyond anything New Yorkers ever imagined.

Dozens of basement-level parking garages, including the one beneath the World Trade Center, were still brimming with water and unusable.

Entire neighborhoods along the south-facing shores of Brooklyn are gone.

The area's major bridges all reopened within a week of the storm, but every single auto tunnel leading to and from Manhattan was still closed to traffic and there were no firm estimates on when they would re-open.

None of the area seaports were functional. Significant maritime shipping may never return to New York Harbor as the major shipping lines have been forced to contract with other Eastern ports.

Air traffic has suffered nearly as much. Parts of JFK International Airport were under more than eleven feet of water. Most of the resulting silt and debris has still not been cleared. The control tower was heavily damaged by wind and several hangars were destroyed. The first flights are not expected to begin for another four to six weeks. LaGuardia suffered similar damage and is closed indefinitely.

CHAPTER 59

IN THE SKIES WEST OF MANHATTAN
EARLY SEPTEMBER, 1999
8:42 A.M.

Amanda bent her head to peer out the window on the far side of the plane. The jet banked sharply and the New York City skyline disappeared from her view, leaving only the thin blue of a perfect late-summer sky.

The plane bound for Miami was the first flight to leave Newark airport in two weeks.

Sarah had her headphones on, listening to *Winnie the Pooh* on tape. Amanda draped her left arm around the girl and leaned over to Jack, who sat across the aisle.

"They picked up Maximo Perez," Jack said. "Lassitor buckled, told the Feds everything in exchange for partial immunity."

"I'm surprised," Amanda said. "Dominican officials aren't usually so cooperative, right?"

"No. But Perez kind of wrote his own sentence. Seems he tried to shut up the local official, some guy named Santino, by kidnapping his daughter. Didn't go over too well."

"I can imagine."

"Supposed to extradite him," Jack said. "What about

Terese?"

"I told the FBI about her. They found her in Miami. So I got two strange calls last night."

"From?"

"First was Terese. She was a little pissed that I'd had the FBI find her, but then when I explained everything she was OK with it. Then she wanted my advice. I told her to testify, of course. Took awhile, but she finally agreed."

Jack nodded. "Perez is done, then," Jack said, the pain returning to his eyes. "It won't bring Rico back, or your father, you know, but in a strange way it makes me feel a little better. Who's the other call?"

Amanda retreated again into the sorrow. She'd been fighting it for two weeks, weighing it against the good and the new. It was foolish to compare, she knew. Rico was gone, and her father would probably never be found. But life would go on after Harvey. It *was* going on. And there was good in it. But the tradeoff was as close to unbearable as life could get.

Amanda closed her eyes and squeezed the comparison into a corner of her mind until she couldn't feel it anymore.

"Guy named Nicholas Gray. He's a..."

"...forensic hurricanologist," Jack said. "I didn't know you knew him. He's done some of the best papers on the 1938 hurricane. What's he want?"

"He's already working on a book about Harvey. Historical account. He wants to interview me."

"Wise man."

"But I'm just a forecaster. What's he want with me?"

"You read my last article?"

"Sorry. I barely made it to the airport in time. Didn't even glance at the paper."

"I quoted Frank Delaney: 'The death toll would have been far worse but for the heroic forecasting effort and direct involvement in the evacuation by Amanda Cole.'"

"Frank always exaggerates."

"Frank *never* exaggerates. Come off it, Amanda. This was your storm, start to finish. Nick Gray knows that. Anyway, everybody and their brother is gonna write some crap about this storm. The first paperback hit the shelves yesterday. Did you see it? Pure garbage. At least Gray will do it well."

"I guess." Amanda thought for a moment. She reached across the aisle and laced her fingers through his. "Jack? You sure about what you're doing?"

"I've never been more sure of anything."

"I would have waited for you," she said. "You didn't have to quit."

"Yes I did. He needs me." Jack nodded his head toward Jonathan. "At least for a few months. Let him adjust to school and everything. I can take him and Sarah and pick them both up, try to cook a few dinners. Then maybe I'll go back to work. Maybe." He grinned. Amanda squeezed his hand.

Amanda looked at the seat next to Jack. The window seat. Jonathan was straining to see the last of the City disappear below. In the reflection from the window, Amanda witnessed the nearest thing she'd seen to a smile on the boy's face.

Jonathan had his own set of headphones on. He was nuts about listening to stories.

He'd already heard *Winnie the Pooh* about a hundred times in the past two weeks. Now he had Amanda's favorite tape in the Seuss collection. The one with *The Lorax* on it.

ABOUT THE AUTHOR

Robert Roy Britt is a science writer and author of the Eli Quinn Mystery Series: *Closure*, *Drone*, *First Kill* and the short prequel *Murder Mountain*. He lives in Arizona with his wife, their youngest son and two dogs. In the mid-1990s, Britt reported on hurricane potential for the *Asbury Park Press* in New Jersey, and later was an editor at *The Star-Ledger*, across the Hudson River from Manhattan. For sixteen years he was a science writer and editor at Space.com and its sister site, Live Science. You can visit his website at robertroybritt.com.

ACKNOWLEDGEMENTS

Too many people were involved in the creation of this book to adequately thank them all. I am grateful to the science community—at NASA and the Army Corps of Engineers, and in particular meteorologists at the National Hurricane Center—for giving their time and sharing their expertise over the years. Scientists are amazing.

Mike Patterson helped me understand what it's like to fly a rescue mission under unthinkable circumstances in a Coast Guard helicopter. Jennifer Toth's excellent 1995 book, *The Mole People: Life in the Tunnels Beneath New York City*, was an indispensible resource. I treasure my 1976 copy of *A Wind to Shake the World: The Story of the 1938 Hurricane*, by Everett S. Allen, who reported on said storm for the *Bedford Standard-Times* on his first day on the job. Queens College Professor Nicholas K. Coch, in interviews in the late 1990s, did more than any single person to enlighten me to the true risks presented in this book.

Without the editorial direction of Allison Wolcott, this book would not exist. Russell Galen, quietly and professionally, provided more motivation than any writer could expect. Peter Miller, wherever you are, thanks for a great ride. Lauren Craft, as always, found a sea of things to change, all for the better.

And to my family, who encouraged me to cross the finish line, to sprint those final yards after a marathon: Thank you. There it is, then.

51017378R00211

Made in the USA
San Bernardino, CA
10 July 2017